PRAISE FOR ALLISON BETTES AND RED FLAG WARNING

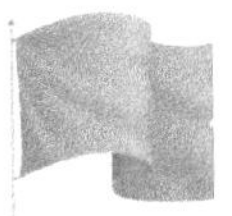

"If you're into suspenseful romance with heart, heat, and high stakes, this one's for you!"
Literary Stitch Society

"Allison's books are the perfect cozy, spicy read. Whether you're in a slump and need a pick me up, or just a good book with a happy ending, her books are always a great read."
@She.reads2escape (Instagram)

"The perfect ratio between love, spice and everything true crime!" —*Midoris Bookshelf*

"This book sucked me in immediately and I could not put it down until I finished."
The Bookery with Leslie

ALSO BY ALLISON BETTES

Cupid Meets Crime Scene Series

HEAT ADVISORY

ROGUE WAVE

ZERO VISIBILITY

* * *

The Ranger Shield Security Series

BETRAYAL & NEW BEGINNINGS

INSTINCT & NEW IDENTITY

DECEPTION & NEW DIRECTION

RESTART & NEW REVENGE

* * *

The Raising the Bar Series

A Ranger Shield Security Spin-Off Series

NEW ROOTS

NEW RULES

* * *

For more information visit www.AllisonBettes.com.

RED FLAG WARNING

CUPID MEETS CRIME SCENE BOOK ONE

ALLISON BETTES

DEDICATED TO:

Every National Weather Service employee—
You work an often-thankless job with shitty hours, and nowhere near the credit you deserve for saving countless lives and keeping people informed with critical information.

The real Christine—
Thank you for answering my 4.5 million texts about the NWS and still choosing to be my friend afterward. This entire book is dedicated to you, except for one page which I will dedicate to Kyle.

And to U.S. park rangers—
Many of whom are unpaid volunteers, who do the job because they want to ensure our parks stay clean and accessible for all to enjoy.

RED FLAG WARNING

1

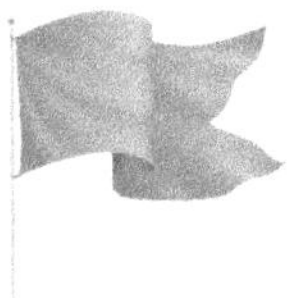

"The probability of storms ruining your photo shoot is directly proportional to how much you paid your photographer."
—*It's science*

Iris

If eye rolls burned calories, I would be so skinny.

I've been told I have one of those faces that can't hide my emotions—terrible poker face. People saw exactly what I was thinking without me saying a word.

Today was no different.

Part of me thought I should just say "yes, sir" and be the better person. But where was the fun in that?

I was on the phone with a man who was trying to convince me—poorly, I might add—that climate change was actually caused by government-triggered volcanoes and secret Russian nuclear submarines. Thankfully, he couldn't see my annoyed face right now.

I had only picked up the phone in the first place because I was waiting on two of my coworkers, who were set to accompany me on a field trip.

"Sir," I tried to politely interrupt the man ranting in my ear.

"No, you listen here, young lady," he snapped right back, causing my eyes to roll yet again. "If you're gonna be responsible for telling people about the weather, you gotta understand how it works."

While most people got their weather forecast from an app or website, the weather service had always offered people the ability to call a number and have the forecast read to them. This was really important for people who were blind, but we also had a few elderly people who liked to call for the forecast simply because that was what they were used to. However, having the phone line also meant the crazies could call. Like this guy.

"Your forecasting sucks because you aren't taking into account that the Russian subs are warming our oceans," the man continued to rant.

"Ooooh," I said loudly into the phone as though I was shocked. "So that's why I've been wrong all these years. Thank you so much for letting me know. Have a great day!"

My last words were said in a high-pitched, overly chipper tone before I hung up the phone.

I was the Warning Coordination Meteorologist for the National Weather Service office in Las Vegas. It was my dream job, and I loved it.

I still got to forecast the weather like I had at my previous job, but now I also got to head up our public awareness programs.

That was my main job for today. Doing a photo shoot and taping some PSA videos on weather safety that we could post on our website and social media channels for our partners and community to watch. Ben and Christine —two of my co-workers—were going with me to help record these segments.

Our main goal was to shoot a video about pop-up thunderstorms on Lake Echo during monsoon season. Many people didn't realize those storms could pop up with little notice, leaving people in a sticky situation of being on the lake in a lightning storm. See…lightning and water don't mix. You are at a much bigger risk of being struck by lightning if you are out on the water.

What I *didn't* normally do for my job was answer the phone, but since I was waiting for Christine and Ben to grab our equipment, I decided to help Calvin, one of our other meteorologists, who was off assisting with a weather balloon launch. Normally it was a one-person job, but today was very windy, so our lead meteorologist, Leah, needed help. That meant I got stuck answering the phone.

"Didn't your mom ever tell you that if you roll your eyes too much, they'll get stuck in the back of your head?" Calvin said, walking back over to the desk with a smile on his face.

"No," I responded as I leaned against his desk.

"Mine either, but I feel like if it *were* true, *you* would be the one it would happen to," he chuckled as he grabbed his drink and took a swig.

I snorted as I shook my head and started to walk away. "Let me go see if Ben and Christine are ready. Good luck if that man calls back," I said as I walked down the hallway in search of the pair so we could all go on our field trip.

"If that man calls back while you're gone, I'm giving him your personal email address!" Calvin yelled in warning.

I chuckled because I knew he wouldn't actually do that...hopefully.

By noon, we were hauling our gear out to the lake, and it was already hotter than Satan's armpit outside.

I lived in the desert, so I was used to heat, but it was only the first week of May, so it was entirely unfair to be this hot already.

I literally had sweat on my eyebrows. Super classy.

The good news was that we were finally out at Lake Echo. Hopefully, I could stick my feet in the water to cool off for a bit in between taping the videos.

Lake Echo was a large reservoir on the outskirts of Las Vegas. The shoreline of the lake stretched for more than five hundred miles and was filled with beaches, coves, and steep cliffs, with beautiful desert mountains as the backdrop. Granted, these mountains were mostly bare rock with some Joshua trees, yucca, cacti, and vast amounts of sagebrush. Because this was situated in the middle of the desert, it was a popular place for people to go boating, hiking, camping, and even swimming.

The water levels at the lake were really low because we'd had a bad water year so far. By that I meant we'd had very few storms to help fill our reservoirs up, so when the winter passed without many storms, we ended up with a very low lake. In the desert, we relied on all the rain and snow that came through in the winter to replenish our lakes and reservoirs. We also relied on neighboring states to have a good winter too, because when all their snow melted, it flowed down through the Colorado River and helped fill up the lake.

Still, low levels or not, I was thrilled to get in the water and cool off, even if it was only for a few minutes.

Christine was setting up our camera since she would be our photographer for this task, and we were just waiting for a park ranger and a member from the U.S. Coast Guard to join us.

While we waited, I dipped my toes in the water to cool off a bit. The water in the shallow area was already getting warm thanks to the ongoing heat wave, but it was still cooler than the air temperature, so it felt very nice on my feet. I looked up to take in the beauty around me. The muted red, orange, and brown colors of the Anvil

Mountains in the background provided a beautiful backdrop.

Alas, I only got to enjoy the refreshing feeling for a few moments before two new vehicles pulled into the parking lot, indicating our guests had likely arrived.

A few moments later, two men started walking up to the pier where we were set up to record. Slipping back into my socks and shoes, I made my way over to Ben and Christine, who were making introductions.

The newcomers had their backs to me as I walked up. Christine handed them wireless microphones to put on and asked them to say their full names and titles into the camera so we could credit them properly.

"Lieutenant Patrick Michaels with the U.S. Coast Guard," the man on the left said.

Then the other man spoke and rocked my world.

"Chief Ranger Hector Madeira, U.S. Park Service," he said in a gruff voice.

Hector? The same Hector Madeira that saved my sister's life? The same one I flirted shamelessly with at her wedding, only for him to stare at me silently and then walk away? I'd only met the man twice, but he was not a man you forgot. Could it be the same person? I thought he was a cop...

"Hector?" I said, wondering if this was another man with the same name.

At my questioning voice, he turned around to face me. I swore I saw recognition dawn in his eyes just like mine when I noticed his gorgeously chiseled face staring back at me.

He looked similar to the first time I had met him. Short beard, gorgeous black hair, and deep-brown eyes, and yet somehow hotter, though I couldn't quite put my finger on what made him hotter. Maybe I was just delirious from the heat.

But seriously...What were the odds he would be here today?

He just stared at me, and I realized that maybe he didn't actually recognize me back.

"Iris," I said like a total dork. "You met me at—"

"I know who you are," he said, seemingly angry about it, if his irritable tone was anything to go by.

Well, okay, then. Clearly, he was not happy to see me. Wait...The park ranger who was supposed to join us today was a woman. Her name was Josie Jones, and she had helped with these videos several times in the past few years.

"Where's Josie?" I asked, since she was who I had been told would be coming today.

"Ranger Jones broke her foot," he answered gruffly, as if I was supposed to have known that fact.

I didn't know what it was about this man, but the few times I had been around him he seemed so displeased to have me talk to him or even stand nearby.

Attempting to save myself any further embarrassment, I turned to the other man to introduce myself just as Christine and Ben introduced themselves as well.

"Hi, I'm Iris O'Hara," I said, holding my hand out to him. "I'm the Warning Coordination Meteorologist at the Las Vegas Weather Service office. Thank you so much for coming."

This man had a totally different demeanor and even seemed excited to meet me. "Lieutenant Patrick Michaels, but please call me Patrick," he responded with a smile on his face.

It was a good-looking face, too. He was very fit—something I was sure his job required. He was also tall like Hector, but with blond hair and light-blue eyes, and had a sharp jawline and dimples that I was sure women fawned over. But not this woman. Nope, I preferred my men to look more like Grumpy McThunderbolt, who was standing to my side glaring at me with the hatred of a hundred blazing suns.

Hector may be a curmudgeon, but he was a sexy one. He was muscular, with broad shoulders and a stocky build. He was also taller than I was, though that wasn't saying much since most people were taller than me. But still, he had to be well over six feet.

I was five foot three and a half, but I rounded up—as any normal person would do—and told people I was five foot four. Usually I wore glasses, but knowing I was going to be in front of the camera today, I'd opted for wearing my contacts. I'd also worn my long, curly hair in a nice braid to keep it from sticking to my sweaty face in the heat.

Not only was it already hot outside, but I could feel

extra heat coming off the man's gaze in front of me, as well as the man beside him—though one appeared to be from lust and the other from anger.

Feeling the need to move this into safer territory, I decided to push this along.

"If you don't mind, we'd like to shoot this with the lake behind us. Perhaps down there by one of those coves," I suggested by pointing to the area about a hundred yards beyond where we had parked our cars.

"Not a problem. That sounds like a perfect place," Patrick said, again with that dimpled smile, while Hector McGrouchy-pants just nodded in response. "Ladies first." He held his arm out in front of him to let Christine and me pass.

We set the two men up with the lake and mountains behind them to highlight the surrounding beauty. After we did a sound check and confirmed we were recording, I began to ask questions.

"Patrick, we'll start with you," I said, knowing I wasn't going to get this interview going on the wrong foot by starting with broody Hector. "Many people visit the lake from out of town. What would you say to tourists visiting the lake for the first time?"

"Our desert environment can lead to extreme heat and intense sun exposure, so visitors should take extra precautions against dehydration and sunburn."

I turned to the broodier half of the interview to ask my next question. "Hector, what about the people who *do* live nearby and come to this lake frequently? What advice would you give them?"

"Water levels here are at historic lows," he responded, sounding oddly more pleasant in his professional mode. Clearly, he had a game face that he could turn on when he needed to. "Coves and even traditionally deep-water areas are now very shallow, and if you aren't paying attention, you can damage your boats by running aground or hitting rocks."

Despite both men giving wonderful interviews, I was drawn to Hector. His voice was deep and sexy, albeit not the warm growl I usually preferred. But for whatever reason, he was not a fan of *me*, so I focused on the mission at hand and continued on with our interview. Ben and I took turns asking a few more questions about swimming and lightning safety before we wrapped up.

We thanked Hector and Patrick for their time, and they made their way back to their cars. Christine and I trailed them slowly so we could grab some props from the car that we needed for our separate piece on lightning safety.

After we grabbed the items we needed, we headed toward one of the nearby coves so that Ben and I could stand ankle deep in the water—a perfect excuse to cool off. Ben and I both had made sure to pack water shoes since neither of us wanted to accidentally step on broken glass from bottles people had thrown overboard from their boats.

I noticed that Hector and Patrick were talking

together by their cars as we walked by, Hector's eyes meeting briefly with mine. I felt his gaze follow me the entire way as we walked to the cove. I suspected it was because to get there, we needed to walk around a roped-off area, though we had permission to be there. Because the water levels were so low, some of these areas had a steeper drop-off compared to normal.

Ben and I had on our standard uniforms of khaki pants and government-issued polo shirts with the National Weather Service logo. I rolled the pants up to my knees and began to wade into the cool, shallow water.

I let out a deep sigh. "Oh, my goodness, this feels so good."

"Yeah, it does," Ben confirmed as he stepped into the water behind me.

"Okay, where exactly do you two want to stand for this?" Christine asked.

We were in the water up to our calves and only about fifteen feet from shore. I looked around and noticed that if we stepped to my left a little and went a tad bit deeper, we could angle it so the larger Anvil Mountains were nicely centered in the background.

"What if we try over here so we can..." I began to move backward until my foot caught on something in the water. I flailed my arms, trying to reach for something to grab onto, but Ben was too far from me, and I fell backward with a big splash into the water. I landed hard on what felt like jagged rocks, and I yelped as shooting pain coursed through my butt, tailbone, and lower back.

Ben quickly walked over to me, pinching his lips as though he was trying hard not to laugh.

"Are you okay?" he asked, extending his hand out for me to grab. "Are you hurt?"

"My tailbone and my pride are sufficiently bruised, but I'm otherwise fine," I responded as I reached for his hand.

"What happened?" Ben asked as I rubbed my lower back to soothe the growing pain.

"Are you okay?" Christine yelled from her perch behind the camera on dry land.

"You know, girlie, if you wanted a proper swim, you should have brought a suit," Ben teased as I stared down at my clothes, which were now soaking wet.

Good thing I'd brought an extra set of clothes—though I'd thought I would need them in case I sweated through my first pair, not from falling into the water.

"I was taking a step back and tripped over a rock or something right there," I said, pointing to the spot behind me.

"Well, let me nudge it back a little so you don't trip over it again," he said, leaning over to push the rock back a little with his foot.

Just then, Ben's face shifted from teasing to a look of confusion, and then he went pale as a ghost.

I looked down to see what he was looking at and noticed a large, oval-shaped rock. It had a yellow-brown tint to it with a greenish hue, likely from algae that had accumulated on it. The image was distorted as the lake water rippled over it, but there was no hiding one very obvious feature—the two dark circles on the top that looked exactly like eye sockets on a skull.

"Holy shit," Ben murmured next to me. "Is that a skull?" His question ended on a partial shriek.

Before I could answer him, though, a loud scream sounded nearby. It took a moment for me to realize that scream actually came from me.

2

HECTOR

The man in front of me was pissing me off. I wasn't sure why I was even talking to him, honestly.

I was supposed to be heading back to my post for the rest of the day, but I'd hesitated once I'd gotten to my car. The weather service folks didn't need me anymore, but I just felt this pull to stay nearby. Years of working in both the military and as a police officer had taught me to trust that instinct. It also didn't hurt that the most drop-dead gorgeous woman I had ever seen, Iris, was close by.

That woman screamed red flag. Not because she was a bad person—quite the opposite, actually. She was flirtatious, sexy, and smart as hell—a deadly combination, especially for someone like me. I, too, was a red flag, but for a whole other set of reasons—bad ones. I watched as she and her co-worker grabbed items from their white

SUV, but that was my fatal error. By pausing at my vehicle to watch them, I gave the lieutenant time to strike up a conversation.

"Hey, man, nice to finally meet you," he said to me, holding his hand out to shake mine. "Heard a lot about you."

"Don't believe everything you hear," I told him, not sure what kind of stories this man had been told.

He laughed and then spoke again, though his gaze moved to the weather service crew as they walked back down to the water. "So, I couldn't help but overhear that you know the woman from the weather service we just interviewed with."

I wasn't sure where he was going with this, so I just nodded in return.

"You happen to know if she's single? She's not my usual type, but I'm thinkin' maybe I need to open my selection up a little more."

This was when my agitation picked up. Partly because the man was essentially asking me to help set him up with Iris, and also, I didn't like the vibes this man was giving off.

First of all, if she's not your type, then don't ask her out.

Second...*Open my selection up*? The hell did that mean? The woman wasn't a restaurant choice.

Third, I didn't know if she was single or not, but I sure as hell didn't want her hooking up with this asshole.

"Yeah, I'm pretty sure she's taken," I told him, not caring one bit that I might be lying through my teeth.

I had two sisters, and if I thought for one second that some prick was making a move on them, I would do whatever I could to steer that dickwad in the other direction and feel not a single ounce of regret about it.

"Ah, crap. Alright," he said, though he didn't seem that torn up about it. "Figures. All the good ones are taken."

Before I could respond one way or another to his comment, a high-pitched shriek came from the water. My head shot up to see Iris in the water, soaking wet, standing next to her completely dry coworker, Ben. My legs were moving before I knew it, and I was jogging down to the water.

The photographer, Christine, had moved to the water's edge and was shouting at them, obviously trying to figure out what was going on. As I made it to the edge of the water, I noticed Patrick arrive at my side, clearly having followed the commotion as well. Ben was assisting Iris back to the dry ground when I arrived.

"Everyone okay?" I yelled to them.

"I don't know," Christine responded next to me. "Iris tripped on something and hurt herself, and then they both looked into the water and freaked out."

I moved the few steps to where Ben had deposited Iris, and then he turned to me. "There's...There's a dead body in there." His face was pale, and his words were slightly panicked as he pointed out to the water.

What did he just say?

"She tripped over the skull," he added. "We thought it was a rock until we looked down."

Not wasting any time, I slipped my socks and shoes off quickly, rolled my pants up a bit, and walked a few steps into the water. Sure enough, about a dozen steps in, I saw what appeared to be a muddy, partially algae-covered skull.

I reached for my cell in my back pocket before turning to Patrick, yelling to him, "Will you call and see if the Coast Guard can send a boat over here to block this area off? I'm going to call in a dive team and the coroner."

He nodded and jogged back in the direction of his truck. Christine had managed to walk over to where Ben and Iris were.

I knew I needed to call this in right away, but the urge to check on Iris felt more vital.

I walked back out of the water and made my way to Iris. "You alright?"

"She fell pretty hard and complained her back hurt," Ben mentioned to me. "She also looks really pale—like she might vomit."

"*She* isn't dead and can answer for herself, thank you very much," Iris responded, wiping a wet, curly strand of hair from her forehead.

I crouched down to get to her level since she was still sitting on the ground. "You need me to call an ambulance?"

"Yes," Christine answered behind me. "We're required to if someone gets injured on the job."

"I'm not at the office, Christine," Iris shot back before turning to face me. "I'm okay. I think I just landed funny on my back and tailbone when I hit the...the s-skull."

She stuttered saying that last word, and I wasn't sure if it was because she was chilly from being wet or if the thought of seeing the skull itself freaked her out.

"You landed *on* the skull?" I asked.

"I'm not sure if I tripped over it and landed on a rock or tripped over a rock and landed on the skull."

I mentally catalogued that possibility to mention to the coroner since it could affect the autopsy.

"A boat's on the way," Patrick said to me as he walked back up to our area.

Then he glanced down at Iris. "Are you okay? I'm a trained EMT. I can help look you over if you need someone to."

I knew he was offering to help, but I did *not* want that man touching her, especially knowing he'd already asked if she was single. I had no claim on her, and I knew I never would, but that didn't mean I had to help another man out.

"Why don't you call in an ambulance just in case it's bad and she needs transported," I told him but turned immediately to Iris, knowing she'd heard me and would fight me on it.

"Hector," she said, but I held up my hand and spoke quickly.

"If he doesn't, it appears Christine will," I told her, which Christine confirmed. "But if *we* call, it'll get here faster since we know this area and can direct them to exactly where we are."

She sighed in exasperation. I knew she wasn't happy, but I would take the win.

I began walking back to my vehicle, making the necessary calls on the way.

Lake Echo technically fell under National Park Service jurisdiction. We handled law enforcement, search and rescue, and body recovery. Many people didn't know, but rangers were fully commissioned federal law enforcement officers. We had boats, dive teams, and recovery training, but in instances like these, we still needed to go through the proper channels. This skull could be from an accidental death, but it could also be from a murder.

Lake Echo was so large that it spanned nearly two full counties. This made it a bit more complicated because you had to know which county to call for the medical examiner's office to assist.

I was the head of the visitor and resource protection division for the park, but also, my background in law enforcement and the Army Rangers made it hard for me to back away from these kinds of situations entirely.

After making the proper calls, I moved my vehicle closer to the water's edge so that it would block access on the footpath to the area where Iris and her team were. Once the sheriff and our team arrived, any tourists nearby would surely take notice, so I wanted to prevent any additional attention if at all possible.

Patrick walked up as I stepped out of my vehicle. "Our crew is here," he said, nodding behind me to the water.

Damn, that was fast.

"You call the Feds or just the ISB?" he asked.

ISB—or Investigative Services Branch—was a specialized unit of investigators within the National Park Service. The ISB usually focused on investigations into crimes of violence, property crimes, and homicides. However, because national parks were federal land, we often had to involve the FBI, especially if the crime somehow crossed state lines.

"Just the ISB for now since I don't want too many cooks in the kitchen," I told him honestly.

He lifted his chin in understanding. "I'm gonna walk down to the pier and hop on our boat to give them the heads-up."

I nodded back and gave him my cell in case they had any questions. I was grabbing some gear from my trunk when the sirens sounded behind me.

The ambulance had arrived, and the cavalry was not far behind, based on the three NPS standard-issued white SUVs pulling in right behind.

I knew I needed to meet with the other rangers to get a perimeter set and secure for when the ISB and coroner arrived, but there was also an overwhelming urge to go check on Iris.

I kept telling myself it was because I knew her—sort of.

Iris's sister, Anna, was married to a man who'd worked at LVPD with my brother. Last year, I was working an undercover case when the man I was after began targeting Anna and her husband, Archer.

Iris first crossed my line of sight at the hotel where Anna was staying—the same hotel where I was on a stakeout. I had no idea she was Anna's sister at the time. I only knew that she was gorgeous and that, if I hadn't been working at the time, I would've asked for her number.

Once I realized who she was, I backed off, not needing that kind of complication in my life.

Fast forward a few days later when her sister and brother-in-law found themselves in a dangerous situation, I was fortunate enough to be able to assist.

This was me just assisting again—at least that was how I was justifying it in my head.

The EMT crew hopped out of the bus and headed my way.

"How many patients?" the male EMT asked me.

I pointed toward the water and began to explain. "Just one. Female. I'll walk with you. She's lucid, no issues with vitals. She fell in the water and tripped over part of a corpse. She may have injured her tailbone or lower back. Coworkers are with her and say she is mandated to get checked out since she was on the clock."

"Got it," the female EMT replied.

I took in Iris's face as we got closer, and I was happy to see she had her full color back.

"Miss, do you mind walking us through how you landed and what areas are uncomfortable?" the female EMT asked her.

I wanted to stay—keep an eye on her—but I knew I needed to do my job. I walked back up to where the other NPS vehicles had parked. I gave the full story to the three rangers who'd shown up—Jennings, Lewis, and Diden. I told them we would need to secure the area so that we could preserve the scene for when the ISB and coroner—or medical examiner—showed up.

"She just fell and landed on the bones?" Diden asked me, the shock and confusion made clear in her voice.

"Yeah," I confirmed, and she just shook her head in disbelief.

"Just a skull, though?" Jennings asked. "Seems weird. There were no other parts or identifying things like clothes?"

"I'm guessing there will likely be other bones nearby, but not sure," I told him. "Coast Guard just pulled up and will block off water access so we can get our dive team in there for recovery once the medical examiner arrives."

"Diden, I'll have you get Iris's statement, and Jennings, why don't you get her colleagues' statements," I directed and then had Lewis go and secure the area.

Jennings was a hell of a good ranger, but he didn't have the best bedside manner. Plus, I felt Iris would do better with a female.

The next hour was only one level slightly below chaos as an epic number of people descended upon the scene—both people who were supposed to be there and ones who were not.

Sure enough, the dive team had, in fact, found additional remains scattered within roughly a hundred feet of where the skull was found. It might not have been that far away from the original skull, but the bottom of the lake dropped off quite quickly, so I was glad we had the dive team to assist.

Assistant Special Agent in Charge Heather Andrews was the agent assigned from the ISB on this case. I'd worked with her before when we had a car theft ring, but nothing this serious. She was intelligent, paid attention to small details, and didn't beat around the bush, so I was happy she was the one leading this case.

She had just finished interviewing the weather service employees—Ben and Christine—and was now walking in Iris's direction, which brought my thoughts back to Iris.

Despite my initial reaction upon seeing her today, I knew who she was. I'd been keeping an eye on her from a distance for nearly a year now.

When I'd first met Iris, she'd had a riot of curly hair on top of her head and was wearing glasses. She reminded me of old-school Mariah Carey with her tanned skin, brown hair, and natural curls. Her hair was on the longer side, and it looked soft as hell. And I couldn't forget that body of hers. She was short, but that body was full of curves. She had more than a handful up top and bottom, and her hips were nice and full—my dream woman.

Yes, Iris was gorgeous. She was also sweet, kind, and insanely smart—all the things I wasn't. I was morally gray at best, thanks to my stints in the Army and undercover work at the LVPD. I was also grumpy as hell and had the patience of a gnat.

I was all wrong for her, but that didn't mean I didn't enjoy staring at her and checking up on her frequently. But it ultimately meant that was all I would ever be to her —someone who watched over her from afar.

3

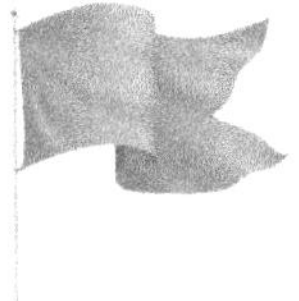

Iris

After Hector and Christine insisted I get checked out by the EMTs—both of whom said I had a swollen tailbone and recommended X-rays—I began what felt like ninety-five hours of interviews. Both Ranger Ann Diden and Agent Heather Andrews, as they introduced themselves, had offered to send someone to the hospital to do the interviews if I'd wanted to go, but nothing felt broken—just sore. I'd just wanted to get the interviews over with and go back to work. Work was always a good distraction, and that was what I needed most.

When Christine, Ben, and I finally all returned to work, it was to find two other coworkers, Calvin and Leah, all deep in a very intense conversation. That stopped abruptly as we walked in, and I realized everyone already knew what had happened.

"Holy shit. So you, like, really touched a dead body?" Calvin asked with shock and awe written all over his face.

I sighed, not really wanting to talk about it since it had been all I'd talked about and thought about the last few hours. But I also knew that in situations like this, it was better to answer the questions than let their imaginations run wild and start coming up with rumors.

"It was very decomposed, so it wasn't really a body per se," I replied.

"I already told him that in a text, but clearly he didn't believe me," Christine answered.

"You tend to embellish the truth sometimes, so I needed to hear it from Iris," Calvin shot back.

"I don't embellish stuff, and I told you the same thing," Leah said with a grin on her face, meaning someone had filled everyone in.

Calvin sighed, throwing up his hands dramatically. "Ugh. Okay, fine. I just wanted to hear Iris say it so she could give me more details since you two were too damn vague. Plus, Christine said there were two *very* hot men there to help you with what happened, and I'd like to know if either of them are single and might be willing to help me through my emotional trauma too."

I snorted. Calvin was a shameless flirt and didn't care who knew it.

"I'm not a hundred percent, but I'm pretty sure they're both single," I said, but quickly held up my hand to stop him from saying anything else. "But I'm also pretty sure neither of them bat for your team."

Calvin let out a deep, defeated exhale. "Ugh. All the good ones are taken or prefer girl parts."

"Even if they were interested, why would you have emotional trauma from Iris finding the skull?" Christine asked.

"I don't, but I would pretend to if I thought one of them would help me through it," he replied with a mischievous grin.

Ben and Leah laughed, and Christine and I just rolled our eyes.

"In all seriousness, how are you holding up?" Leah asked. "You don't have to talk about it if you don't want to, but I'm available if you need to."

I appreciated her offer and told her as much. Christine had already offered on the car ride back to the office for me to sleep over at her place in case being alone freaked me out. I was definitely freaked out, and sleep would not come easy that night, but I needed to work through this on my own. Just like I always had.

You'd think after you'd discovered a dead body that dating would be the furthest thing from your mind. Instead, it just made me more aware of how short life really was, and I wanted to experience life, travel the world, get married, and have kids.

After I got home last night, I'd reached out to a guy I had been chatting with to see if he wanted to grab some drinks the next day. His response was short but simple, saying he was "no longer interested." This was my third strike in just as many weeks.

Welp, I guess this was the last straw.

I was officially done with men.

Period. Forever. Full stop.

I didn't think I could hack it as a lesbian since I would always be comparing my body to any romantic partner, so I guess that meant I was destined to be an old maid.

So be it.

At least I wouldn't be with a creepy man-child or sleazy bastard. And that's what all the men I had found lately were. At least the ones who were in my dating pool.

With that thought, I walked into work the next morning, and was quickly met with greetings and hellos, though I could hear Leah shouting from the hallway.

"Why does the printer in the hallway *never effing work?*"

"I never use that one," Ben commented.

"Normally I don't either, but it's the big color printer, and I'm trying to print these flyers for our booth at the Boy Scouts event next week," Leah explained, pouting.

"You have to treat that printer a little differently," Calvin told her. "It only works when you push the blue button on top three times, shake it delicately, and then pray to the demon witch who lives inside."

I chuckled.

"Hey, how did the conversation go with that guy last night?" Christine said to me as she walked into the room. "You guys going out tonight?"

Now I regretted telling her my plan.

My grumbled sigh and overly dramatic eye roll must have been clear enough.

"That bad, huh?" she said, grimacing.

"Why can't the guys in romance books be real?" Leah questioned, practically swooning in her desk chair, likely thinking about her latest romance novel.

"Hey, finding a good gay man isn't any easier than a straight man, so I get it," Calvin chimed in, shaking his head. "Plus, our pool to pick from is much smaller than yours."

"I don't feel like I'm asking for much," I pointed out. "Just a man who likes me as I am, can carry on a witty conversation, makes me laugh, and isn't an asshole."

"I know romance novels aren't really high on many straight men's book lists, but they really should be," Leah said. "You can learn a lot from them about what women like and how to win a girl over."

"You are so right," Christine agreed.

"I know," Leah said back. "I get all my relationship advice from the queen—Taylor Swift."

"Amen, sister," Calvin added, putting his hand up in the air as an affirmation. "Though I'm always here for any advice you may need, too."

Calvin and Leah were the best. They were the most supportive coworkers and always there to lift our spirits.

Calvin was the first one to swap shifts with anyone who needed it. Leah would drop everything to help mentor any new team member so they transitioned smoothly and felt supported. And both of them were always trying to organize team-building activities or potluck meals at work.

I chuckled at their back-and-forth banter. "I think I'm just going to get a dog."

I'd always wanted one, but the hours at my previous job hadn't really been conducive to owning a pet. Now that my hours here were more stable, I really didn't have an excuse.

"We could do playdates with Oscar," Calvin said, referring to his Corgi.

Oscar, whose full name was Oscar de la Renta after the famous designer, would occasionally come to work with Calvin.

We didn't get thunderstorms very often, but when we did, Oscar panicked, so Calvin brought him to work. I loved those days and realized maybe that was my sign to just get a dog.

"I'll go with you to pick one out from the shelter," Christine offered. "I think we both have a Wednesday off in two weeks. I'll look some places up, and we can go."

I nodded in return. Yeah, that was what I needed. A companion. One that didn't care what I looked like or complained that I resembled a starfish when I slept and took up the whole bed.

Did I want a man? Sure. But not just any man. I had standards—clearly low ones, but standards, nonetheless.

What I wanted was a man like Hector. When I'd first met him last year, I remember thinking he was one of the most attractive men I had ever seen.

A few months later, he had been at my sister's wedding since he knew her and her now husband, Archer. I had tried to approach him—because who wouldn't if there was a hot man in front of you—but he shot me down quicker than your Wi-Fi drops out in a storm.

It was more than that, though. I also knew he had helped my sister and Archer out, and he was big on family and protecting the people he knew and loved. That was the kind of man I wanted.

Oh well. I guess I'd just have to settle for a dog named Hector instead.

4

"Tears are mostly water, which means the more you cry, the more you are hydrating your skin."
—*It's science*

Iris

It was amazing how quickly twenty-four hours went by when you were having fun. It was equally amazing how pathetically slow twenty-four hours went by when all you could think of was dead body parts.

I tried. I tried really hard the next two days to fill my time with busywork instead of worrying and crying. I was off work and tried to distract myself as best I could but ultimately failed to have as normal of a day as I could, especially when every time I sat down, I was reminded of my sore tailbone and what had caused that injury.

Now I was back at work, just four days after the lake mishap—which was what I was referring to it as so I didn't get stuck fixating on a dead body.

Our building was a single story with a few admin

offices, a supply closet, and break room up front and the operations floor in the back. This was where all our meteorologists worked. It was a huge open space with a few small cubicles, but the walls were low so that you could communicate with each other easily. This setup was really important during big weather events, but it also made it easy to just chatter back and forth on normal days.

Today I didn't want to chatter—at least not yet.

I knew my friends wanted to ask questions and find out about any updates, especially Christine and Ben since they had been there with me, but I chose to hide out in one of the media offices we utilized for TV interviews.

I told everyone I needed a quiet space to work so I could get those videos we shot edited. It was true, but I could have just as easily edited them in the main office with everyone else around while I wore headphones.

I was a social creature by nature, though. So after a few hours of working in the private room, I chose to go eat my lunch with everyone else, even knowing there might be some hard questions.

"Ooooh, good, you're here," Christine said upon my arrival. "We're trying to decide what to get delivered for lunch. Do you want yummy, super delicious pizza, or a boring, healthy salad?"

I chuckled, but before I could answer, my phone rang. Agent Heather Andrews' name showed up on the screen.

"Sorry. I gotta take this," I told them, holding up the phone and then walked out of the room and down the hall back to a more private space.

"Hello, this is Iris," I answered, though I realized she probably already knew that.

"Hi Iris, this is Agent Andrews from the ISB. Is this a good time to talk?"

"Yes of course," I told her as I slipped back into the media office, though I hoped she wasn't calling with bad news.

"I wanted to let you know that we identified the remains you encountered at the lake."

Encountered. As though I just happened to walk right by them casually.

"You did? I didn't know you could figure it out that quickly."

"Usually, we can't. This victim, however, had a plate in her leg from a knee ligament surgery that we found with the other remains we were able to collect that day."

"I'm not sure I understand," I told her.

"Things like that have serial numbers on them, so we were able to contact the manufacturer and find out who that plate belonged to."

Holy crap. I had no idea you could do that. That was insane.

"The reason I'm telling you this is because we contacted the family, and they have requested to meet you. In no way are you obligated to say yes, but I told them I would ask, and that's what I'm doing."

I wasn't sure what to say to that.

"Why would they want to meet me?" I asked her.

"They claim they want to thank you personally for

finding her body and giving them closure," she responded. "Their daughter, Chantal Simpleton, was in college when she went missing, and while not the ending they were hoping for, at least they now have some answers."

I understood that, but it still felt weird.

"Is this normal?" I asked. "I mean, have you done this before?"

"No, it's not very common, but even if it were, you are under no obligation to say yes."

My silence must have been an indicator of my hesitation, because she spoke again before I had the chance.

"Why don't you think about it for a few days and let me know? The family can't come out 'til the weekend anyway, so take your time. You have my cell phone now. Just text me one way or another, and I can arrange it if I need to."

"Okay," I responded. "Thank you for telling me. I'm happy you were able to figure out who she was."

"Same. It will make the investigation a little easier."

I hadn't thought of that, but she was probably right. I thanked her for calling and hung up. I was feeling all the emotions as I walked back into the common area. Happiness that they identified the body. Sorrow that such a young woman had died. Anger that she didn't get to live a very long life. Shock and amazement that they could use a surgical implant to identify bodies. Grief for her family.

I was so deep in my emotional roller coaster that I hadn't realized everyone was staring at me when I walked in.

"Everything okay?" Christine asked, clearly worried.

I don't know why, but I wasn't ready to share the news I had just received, so I just brushed it off. "Yeah, it was the agent calling to just follow up on some questions. No big deal."

They all either believed me or decided to cut me some slack, because they moved on.

"So," Leah said, clapping her hands conspiratorially. "Who is this Hector guy you interviewed? Christine and Ben said you guys knew each other and that he was super-hot."

"I did *not* say he was hot," Ben protested.

"No, but you didn't disagree with Christine when she said it, which is basically guy code for *he's hot*," Leah rebutted.

Ben just rolled his eyes as Christine chuckled.

"Describe him to me, and *I* will decide if he's hot," Calvin directed.

I did my best to explain not only Hector's good looks, but also his broody demeanor and standoffish nature.

"Ooooh. We should call him Hector the Convector," Christine yelled out and then laughed at her own joke. "You know, because he's all stormy like a convective thunderstorm."

"He can't have that name because Australia already owns the rights to it," Ben countered. "Hector the Convector is literally the most famous storm in all of Australia."

"I don't think Australia would mind sharing it with a hunky guy," Christine refuted.

"Maybe you should call Hector and see if he likes the nickname," Leah added and smirked at me.

"All of you are nuts," Ben said, rolling his eyes. "My shift is over, so I'm taking my leftover food from earlier and heading home. See you weirdos tomorrow."

He waved goodbye as he left. Calvin departed shortly after, as his shift had just ended too.

Leah and Christine came over to the desk I was sitting at, clearly ready to have more girl talk now that the guys had left.

"Christine said the other guy at the lake seemed to take an interest in you. What about him?" Leah asked.

"Who?" I asked, trying to remember who she was referring to.

"*Who?*" Christine looked at me like I was crazy. "Lieutenant Patrick Michaels. You know, the hottie Coast Guard guy you interviewed?"

Oh yeah. I'd kind of forgotten all about him.

"I guess when you see dead body parts, it kind of distracts your brain," I told them, but Christine clearly didn't believe it.

"That, or you were so focused on Hector that you didn't notice the other man. The one who spent a good portion of the interview sneaking looks at your butt."

"Shut up! Did he really?" Leah asked Christine.

The two of them went back and forth discussing the man from the Coast Guard, but my mind wandered to

Hector, then Patrick, and then any other potential prospect for a date.

I was in my thirties now. I needed a man who was mature. A man who had his shit together. Not a man-child.

Sure, I'd had fun in my twenties, dated guys who were a good time but not keepers, but now I was too old for that. I wanted someone I could come home to at the end of a long shift and just relax and talk about my day with—and maybe give me a good snuggle-fuck when I needed it.

I wanted that to be with a man who looked like Hector, but Hector clearly wasn't interested in filling that role.

But what if he was? Finding a dead body wasn't exactly the most romantic time to ask a girl out. Maybe I needed to take the first step.

I know! I'll text him about what Agent Andrews had told me. Maybe try to strike up a conversation and see if he seems interested. I knew it might be a bit weird starting the conversation around the case, but it was the only excuse I had at the moment.

He had given me his number the day at the lake in case I thought of anything else about the case. I stood there for a few moments, debating the merits of randomly texting him about the case. *You never know if you don't try, right?* I decided to go for it and pulled my cell out.

Iris: Hey Hector, it's Iris. Agent Andrews just called me to tell me they identified the body. I'm glad they were able to get closure for her family.

A few minutes later, my phone buzzed.

HECTOR:

I'm glad Andrews told you.

ME:

She said the family wants to meet me.
I'm not sure if I want to. Do you know if
that's normal?

HECTOR:

Let me know if you decide you want to
do it. You shouldn't be alone for
something like that.

Gasp! Was he offering to go with me? It would actually
be very nice to have him go with me, since something like
this could be very awkward for everyone involved.

Shoot. Okay. Breathe. Be cool. Be smooth.

I was in the middle of typing out my response when a
new text came in.

HECTOR:

I'll have Ranger Diden join you if you
choose to meet with them.

I instantly deflated.

Yep, Hector clearly didn't reciprocate my feelings.

5

"Newton's Third Law: for every action, there is an equal and opposite embarrassment."
—It's science

Iris

I was greeted by our administrative assistant, Dorothy's, sweet voice as I walked into the office the next day.

"You've got snail mail!"

She was eating what looked like a jelly donut in one hand as she used her other hand to give me a stack of letters. I took the bundle, assuming they were thank-you letters from a few recent school talks I had done, and thanked her as I walked through the door that led to our offices.

I walked over to my desk and dumped them out to read them. Kids' letters were great for uplifting your soul because they were always nice, included colorful drawings, and sometimes had very funny things written in them.

A few of them had already been opened by our boss, mostly because people would address mail to whatever the first name was they found on our websites or social media pages, even if the subject really belonged to another person or department. It was pretty common for things to get rerouted before they made it to the right hands.

In this case, I'm guessing after the fifth letter she opened, she assumed that most of these were for me.

Thank you for teaching me about the weather. My favorite thing was learning about boobs.
—From Lucas in Miss Shirley's class.

I rolled my eyes. Of course, boys would hear anything with the word boobs in it and gravitate toward that. The correct word was *haboob*, which was a type of dust storm, but boys would hear what they wanted to.

Thanks for visiting our school. I liked your presentation because we didn't have to take any tests or sit in boring classes.
–From Andie in Miss Frizzle's class.

Oh, and kids were also usually brutally honest.

"Any good ones in there?" Leah asked over my shoulder.

"A couple, yeah," I told her, handing her some so she could help me read through them.

We chuckled at a few and shared them with each other and everyone else sitting nearby.

The next one I opened was different from the others. First, it was stuck to the bottom of the other letters thanks to jelly—the kind that came from a jelly donut. Second, it actually had a stamp and everything on the outside. Usually, the school letters came in a large mailer envelope sent by the teacher if there were a bunch of them together. Other times the teacher would put a dozen of the best ones in one single envelope and mail it. Every once in a while, you had one single letter that the teacher wrote but had all the kids sign the back of it. This one felt like that last option.

I opened it and began reading, noting very quickly that this was not from a teacher or a school.

Hello Iris,

My name is Steve, and I'm a crime podcaster. I read in a news article that someone from the weather service found the body in Lake Echo, and then I saw you on TV at the crime scene. I tried to search for an email address for you but was only able to find your name, so I hope this letter makes it to you. I am hoping you would be interested in letting me interview you for my podcast about what you saw that day. Even better, maybe you would be willing to meet me at the lake to show me where exactly the body was found and if you could re-enact the scene for my listeners. Did you happen to take any bones or even some of the dirt that was around it that day? If so, I can help you analyze it. Or maybe you could get some from the police and bring it to me. I'm an amateur sleuth, so I would be able to help you in that matter.

—Steve Stanton

"The hell?" I mumbled the question to myself, but Leah must have heard me.

"What?" she asked, grabbing the letter from my hand and reading it. "This dude is nuts!"

I muttered my agreement while pulling out my phone to text Agent Andrews and let her know about the letter and that if she hasn't blocked off the area already, she may need to since some crazy person wanted to re-enact it. Oh, and that this guy wanted me to grab some of the evidence from the police so he could "borrow" it for his crime podcast.

She called me almost instantly, wanting details. "Are you okay?" she asked me, and I appreciated the concern, though it felt a bit like an overreaction.

"I'm good," I responded. "It's mostly just weird that someone would even ask this."

"You'd be surprised at some of the crazy things these podcasters home in on."

"How did they even know it was me who found the

body?" I asked her, knowing my name wasn't publicly released.

"As much as we tried to hide it, the TV crew that showed up was clearly able to get some of your faces on camera," she explained. "These people may be amateurs, but some of them do have some basic hacking skills and ways to get information. As long as there is even one picture of you on the internet with your name next to it, they can find it and go from there."

That made sense, especially because I knew there were photos of me with my name out there from other public service events I had done in the past. But it was still creepy as hell how easy it was for people to get information about you.

"I'm headed out of town for a few days, but if something comes up, please feel free to reach out to me I just may not be quick to respond," she told me. "I'd like to send someone from our team over to your office to pick up the letter if you don't mind."

She let me know to put it back in the envelope and prevent anyone else from touching it before they arrived.

"*Do* you mind if I send someone over to collect it?" she asked. "Just in case he does show up at the crime scene, I'd like to have this as evidence to use if we need to arrest him."

"Yeah, sure. I have absolutely no desire to save it, so it's all yours," I told her.

She let me know someone would be by within the hour, and then I thanked her and hung up the phone.

Leah was still leaning against my desk, as if she had been waiting to pounce. "People are crazy," she remarked.

"I just hope this guy doesn't keep sending letters," I told her.

"My mom always told me that you never let bad people take up your time or brain space just because they think they're entitled to it."

Her words hit closer to home than she knew. My mom had also taught me something similar too—before she left.

My father had already walked out when I was five, causing my mother to turn to whatever bottle of alcohol she could find. When my mother finally spiraled, I ended up in the foster system. It wasn't much, but it stuck with me.

I never knew much about my parents beyond scraps of memory and what people had told me. Supposedly, I was a good mix of both of them. My father was Haitian, my mother Portuguese. From him I inherited my terrible eyesight—hence the glasses or contacts I wore daily just to see more than three feet in front of me—and a love of Caribbean food. From my mother I got my super curly brown hair, short stature, my curves—complete with big hips and big boobs—and a complexion that settled somewhere between her fair skin and his darker tone, leaving me with a bronzed look that was all my own.

After entering the foster system, I was placed with the O'Hara family, and they were great. I honestly couldn't have asked for a better family to end up with.

Winnie and Tia O'Hara were sisters who had also been through the foster system, constantly bumping around because no one wanted two older sisters.

They had dedicated their adult lives to opening their doors to as many foster girls as they could, determined to give them stability instead of endless moves. Some girls hadn't stayed long, usually because a parent or relative eventually stepped in to care for them. But for the ones whose families either couldn't—or simply wouldn't—take them back, the O'Haras made sure we always had a place to belong. I was one of those lucky ones.

Winnie—who we just called Mom—and Tia—which was Spanish for aunt, so we'd always called her Auntie—lived on a small property in Stratus Cove, a coastal town in Northern California. The place was beautiful—lush green landscape, salty ocean air, and friendly people who waved at you on the street. Being a small town, everybody knew everybody's business, but that also meant they knew what the O'Hara women did. Nobody batted an eyelash when another foster kid appeared at their house. It was just accepted.

Most people couldn't imagine what it felt like to wonder if anyone would remember your birthday or whether you'd have a seat saved for you at Thanksgiving dinner. For kids growing up with their own families, that kind of security blanket was a given. For foster kids like me, it wasn't.

In total, there were more than fifteen girls the O'Hara

women had fostered, but only five of us had stayed permanently—Gale, Cora, Anna, Hazel, and me.

I was closest with Anna because she and I had arrived around the same time, when I was eleven and Anna was ten.

Anna and I had shared a room and instantly bonded. Not just because we arrived at the same time, but also because we realized over time that we shared a lot in common. We had never had pets growing up but always wanted them. The O'Haras had them. We had two dogs, three barn cats, two llamas, and an ostrich. We all had chore duty on the small farm, helping out, but I loved it. Animals didn't judge you like people did. You could just be yourself around them, and they didn't care.

As if I had conjured them up with just my thoughts, my phone buzzed with several incoming texts.

HAZEL:

Ladies! The storm last night was epic and washed up hella awesome shells for my collection! I got a fully-intact conch shell, four sand dollars, an iridescent pāua abalone, and perfectly symmetrical chambered nautilus!!!

CORA:

Nerd alert.

I giggled at the emoji with glasses she's included.

GALE:

I have no idea what half of that stuff is, but I'm happy for you.

ANNA:

Are you allowed to just steal all this stuff from the beach on a regular basis?

HAZEL:

It's not stealing if it's for research!

ANNA:

Famous last words.

ME:

Speaking of stealing…

I had been avoiding telling my sisters about the skull because I didn't want them to panic. Mostly, my sisters had big mouths and I didn't want them to tell Mom and Auntie and have them panic. And they would. But knowing that my face had been blasted on the local news, it was very possible word would somehow get back to them anyway. Mostly Cora, since she often heard what went on at Lake Echo for her job. Plus, Anna worked in TV news, and while she worked in Georgia, I was pretty sure a dead body in a lake still made for an interesting headline in other states. Especially one that had been a cold case for so long.

Time to rip off the Band-Aid.

ME:

So…I may or may not have accidentally tripped over a skull in Lake Echo, opening up a statewide investigation, which prompted some weirdo to write a letter to our office asking me if I would show him where the skull was located and help re-enact the crime scene. Oh, and steal some of the evidence for his crime podcast. NBD.

CORA:

Iris! What the hell?

HAZEL:

When did this happen?

Before I could respond, my phone was vibrating.

"Hello, dear sister. What's new?" I teased as I answered the phone, even though I knew exactly why Anna was calling me.

"Cut the crap, Sissy. What happened?" Anna barked into the phone, her voice only soft when she used my nickname. "Give me all the details. Don't leave anything out."

That was Anna. She had the investigative reporter slash cop brain always working. But I knew she would keep pestering until she had the answers, especially since her husband was a former Las Vegas cop and now private investigator. So rather than fight it, I gave in and told her everything.

Then, I spent the next twenty minutes talking her down from flying out to see me ASAP.

The phone at my desk rang, displaying an internal call from the front desk.

"Hey, Dorothy," I answered.

"Iris, you've got someone here to pick up a letter, he says," Dorothy explained. "He's not much of a talker, but he's very handsome, so even if you don't know who he is, I'm still inclined to let him stay up here for a little bit so I can just look at him. Oh, and he brought a friend, too!"

I chuckled at Dorothy's assessment of whichever fellow agents that Agent Andrews had sent. Dorothy was in her sixties and didn't take crap from anyone. She was also very organized and loved to bake and use us as her guinea pigs, which we loved.

"It's okay," I told her. "I knew someone was coming. I can come up there to your office."

"Oh no," she interrupted quickly. "I'll bring them back to you. Maybe give them a tour along the way."

I laughed some more, knowing this would likely be the highlight of her day.

I turned to let everyone else in the room know that some ISB agents would be coming in here anywhere from thirty seconds from now to thirty minutes from now, depending on how long Dorothy took to bring them back. Leah and Calvin chuckled when I explained why.

Dorothy definitely took her time, because it was nearly

ten minutes later before I heard her voice coming from down the hallway.

"And this is where our meteorologists work at saving lives," she said excitedly.

I turned to greet whichever ISB agent had been sent—only to freeze.

"Hector?" My voice squeaked like I'd inhaled helium. *Smooth. Real smooth.*

"What are you doing here?" I asked.

For reasons unknown to science, this man short-circuited my brain's ability to behave like a normal functioning adult.

"This is Hector?" Calvin chimed in. "As in, the park ranger from Lake Echo, Hector?"

He said it innocently enough, but I knew that tone. He was fishing, and he smelled blood. This was about to get humiliating.

"Yes," Hector responded to Calvin and then turned to Dorothy. "Thank you, Ms. Hollingsworth."

"Oh, please, call me Dorothy," she gushed, flapping her hand at him.

The woman was blushing. *Blushing.* She read some of the spiciest romance novels I'd ever seen, and *this* was making her blush?

"I'll be back at my desk if you gentlemen need anything," she told him.

That was when I noticed the other person who had been standing behind Dorothy. I recognized him from the lake.

"Hector, I'm Calvin, Iris's best friend." He stepped up to offer his hand for a shake, but I also saw his eyes gleaming at the fact that he knew who this man was.

Leah gasped so hard I thought that she might pass out. "Ummm, excuse me, no. That would be Christine and me," she disputed, whipping her head to face Hector. "Hi. I'm Leah. One of the lead meteorologists on staff here and one of Iris's *real* best friends."

Hector's lip twitched, which for him I assumed was the equivalent of rolling on the floor laughing. At this very moment, though, I wished he were more like me—a totally readable face so I knew exactly what he was thinking.

"Nice to meet you. I'm Hector, and this is Jordan Jennings, one of our other rangers," Hector said politely to Leah and then turned to me. "Agent Andrews called. All her agents were tied up, but she said that you had a piece of evidence she needed collected right away."

Well, that explained it. Half of me was thrilled he was here because he made me all giddy inside. On the other hand, he clearly didn't like me, so I wasn't sure I liked having him here, making things more awkward.

"Oh, umm...yeah," I stuttered. "Here's the...uh...letter thing."

Brilliant. Truly poetic delivery, Iris. You won't be winning any Oscars for that performance.

I practically shoved the letter at him as he held open a large plastic zippered bag for me to put it in, and then he sealed it up.

"I'd rather not get even more fingerprints on it, but do you mind telling me what was written?" Hector asked me while looking down at the envelope and letter inside the bag.

I filled him in on everything the letter had said, noticing his jaw tighten slightly—but otherwise, there was zero reaction. The man was practically a vault.

"Seriously?" Jennings said, shock written all over his face. "He literally asked you to steal evidence?"

"Personally, I think it's weirder that he asked her to re-enact the crime scene," Calvin chimed in.

"Do you guys have security cameras or night guards in case this guy shows up?" Jennings asked, then mumbled under his breath. "This dude seems unhinged."

I hadn't thought about that.

"Do you think he would?" Leah asked, eyes wide.

"It's not likely," Hector said calmly, his gaze directed at Jennings as if to tell him to tone it down. "The letter was stamped in Utah. Not the same state, but also not that far."

I hadn't even noticed the stamp.

"Do you happen to offer bodyguard services?" Calvin interrupted.

I glared at him, hoping to signal him to shut up.

Clearly unfazed, he just kept going. "Or maybe friends who are bodyguards? I mean, any one of us will gladly walk out to the car with Iris, but we don't exactly look as intimidating as you."

Liar. He just wanted a handsome guy to stare at while he worked.

"I know a couple of guys I used to work with at LVPD who do private security," Hector replied, eyes still pinned on me. It was so intense that it felt as if he were boring a hole straight through me. Or maybe he was just wondering why I was such a disaster.

"Thank you so much," Leah said to him. "And also, thank you so much for helping Iris at the lake. She couldn't stop raving about you and how wonderful it was to have your help."

What. The. Hell? That was definitely not how I worded it at all. Unless "he grunted at me a lot and glared daggers at me" somehow translated into "he was so wonderful" in Leah's brain.

"Yes, you should let her take you out to lunch as a thank-you," Calvin added.

Seriously? I was surrounded by traitors.

"We have security cameras scattered all around the building," I cut in, desperate to change the subject. "It's required since we're a federal building."

"Why don't we take a look at where they are to see if there are any blind spots," Hector offered.

I opened my mouth to pawn him off on Dorothy, but then—

"Iris will show you!" Leah and Calvin shouted at the same time.

"Jinx," Calvin said with a smirk.

Great. Beavis and Butthead were now taking the matchmaking to another level.

"It's a great idea," Jennings added.

"Yes, I'll take you. Let's go," I practically shouted, trying to grab Hector's elbow and steer him quickly out of the room before my *friends* said anything else embarrassing.

The instant my fingers brushed his skin, a warm tingle shot up my arm. I also noticed he smelled like spearmint and mountain air—a combination I found that I loved.

"Nice to meet you both," I heard Hector say behind me as I continued to walk forward, hoping he would take the hint to quickly follow.

"Nice meeting you too. Don't forget to take Iris up on that lunch date!" Leah yelled, with Calvin snorting.

God, they were the worst.

I knew they were just trying to help, in their own weird way, but it was actually making it way worse. Oh, and about a thousand percent more embarrassing.

His stride was much longer than mine, so he caught up to me rather quickly. I seized the opportunity to apologize without having to look him in the eye, nor would he have to see my face—which was likely bright red.

"I'm sorry for them. They mean well, but they're...a lot. I do appreciate everything you did for me that date...I mean day...but you don't need to feel obligated about a lunch date."

Oh my God. Why couldn't I stop saying date?

"They care about you," he replied. Neutral and noncommittal about lunch.

"Leaving so soon?" Dorothy said as we entered back into the front lobby area. "I have cookies and coffee."

"They want to see some of our security cameras," I told her.

"I wouldn't turn down a cookie," Jennings said.

"Oh, that's a wonderful idea," she replied. "Iris, why don't you take Chief Madeira, and I'll get this handsome man some cookies and coffee while you two are scoping out the cameras."

Before I could even add my opinion to the matter, both gentlemen chimed in.

"That sounds good," Jennings replied.

"That's fine," Hector said.

I turned to walk out the front door, hoping Hector followed.

Then, finally, we escaped. Free and clear of match-makers, meddlers, and embarrassing coworkers. Now, I just hoped I didn't humiliate myself. Again.

6

"Ladies, if he's older than 30 and dropping red flags, leave. His frontal lobe is fully developed and he's not changing."
—*It's science*

Hector

Iris was too damn cute.

I wasn't sure why I enjoyed watching her friends embarrass her. Likely it was because they were all awkwardly bad at trying to set us up on a date.

She seemed a bit more relaxed once we came outside, but not by much.

We had just looked over the camera setup for the front and left sides of their building, which also covered their parking lot.

"Around back, we have two extra cameras because we often come out this door to do weather balloon launches," Iris added, pointing to a small shed out back, which I assumed was where they had their balloon equipment.

"How often do you come out to do those?" I asked her.

"Oh, I don't usually do balloon launches unless we are short-staffed for the day or it's a very windy day and they need an extra set of hands to control the balloon," she explained. "But we typically do two balloon launches a day. Unless there's bad weather, and then we do more."

"You said two extras, but I see three cameras," I told her after spotting one on the far-left side.

"That one is broken, but they left it there to make people think it still works," she answered. "If you look under the gutter, you can see the back part snapped off."

She walked closer to lean in, pointing at some cords in the back. As I took a few steps closer to get a closer look, she screamed.

"Snake! Holy crap! Big snake! Oh, my God!"

She tried to take a step away from the supposed snake but tripped and fell backward into me. My arm circled around her waist, holding her upright so she didn't fall on the ground. That just made it worse, because now her plush ass was nestled right up against my upper thighs.

She squirmed, trying to back both of us up, so I turned to my right side and pulled her with me. I was about to release my arm from her to go see if there was, indeed, a snake. However, she pulled away first. She whipped around, stared at me with a frightened look on her face, and began to apologize.

"Sorry...umm, jeez. I'm sorry," she said, looking to the ground and shaking her head.

I wasn't sure if she was still nervous about the snake or if it was me she was nervous about.

I hadn't seen anything at first, but after looking closer, I found the snake coiled up against the building. The camera she had pointed at was positioned above three small sagebrush bushes—making a nice spot for the snake to hide.

"It's all good," I told her after seeing it. "It's a Great Basin Gopher Snake. They're nonvenomous."

"Umm...no. That thing definitely hissed and rattled," she argued back.

"Gopher snakes can mimic the sounds rattlesnakes make, but unlike rattles, these guys are harmless," I informed her.

"I'll just take your word for it and stay back here, *away* from the snake," she said as she did a whole-body shiver.

I smirked. I had two sisters and a mother who were all petrified of snakes, so I knew when to let it go.

"Well, that completes our tour of embarrassment today," she muttered, but I still heard her.

"Thanks for showing me around," I told her. "Again, the odds of someone nefarious coming onto the property are extremely low, but I'd just like to be sure."

She nodded at me as we walked back around to the front of the building.

"I'll get this letter over to the ISB," I said. "Reach out if you get anything else."

"Okay," she said, not really making eye contact with me. "Have a good day, Hector."

I told her to do the same, though I wasn't sure if she heard me, since she practically bolted into the building.

I spent most of the car ride back to the office thinking about the case and the letter since Jennings brought it up as soon as we drove off.

That was a lie.

I only spent about ten percent thinking about that. The other ninety percent was spent thinking about Iris's ass up against me when she found the snake. My arm wrapped around her waist as she wiggled up and down against me. Goddamn, it had taken everything in me not to get a hard-on standing there. Being a bigger guy myself, I preferred women who had some meat on their bones and weren't going to snap if I touched them—and this woman did it for me.

It was her reaction to me that had my near-hard-on retreating. Once I had moved her to the side, she had practically jumped away from me as though I was on fire. I had noticed several times now that she was nervous around me. What I *wasn't* sure about was whether it was something I said or just my general size and demeanor. It could be either.

My large frame and not exactly friendly demeanor often made people keep a distance. I wasn't a dick on purpose, but I just gave off a vibe that told people to stay away. It was thanks to years of being special ops in the

Army as well as an undercover cop. You learned to channel the *don't mess with me* vibe quite well in those roles specifically.

It was that intimidation factor that made me perfect for undercover work at LVPD. After coming home and retiring from the Army, I'd struggled to settle back into civilian life. I hadn't known exactly what I'd wanted to do, but my brother Manny had been a cop. It was all he'd ever wanted to do—get justice for the good guys and lock up the bad guys.

I was proud of my Army career, but it had kept me away from my family, and I'd missed many important events. It was part of the job, and I'd known what I'd signed up for, but missing my brother's funeral had been my breaking point.

When Manny died, I had been knee-deep in a top-secret special ops mission, and by the time I had been located and informed of my brother's death, the funeral was the next day. Thanks to bureaucratic red tape and a few weather-related flight delays, I'd ended up missing the funeral by seven hours.

I still got to see the rest of my family and had been given two weeks of bereavement leave, but I hadn't been the same person after that. Hearing how Manny had died, and knowing he would never get to have kids of his own —one of his biggest dreams in life—had officially flipped a switch in me, turning me into my infant stages of curmudgeon.

After he died, I made the decision not to re-enlist, but I'd struggled with what to do when I came home. Ultimately, I'd decided to follow in his footsteps. His captain had been more than willing to hire me and had welcomed me onto the force and told me my background and intimidating appearance made me ideal for special operations. After my last case, though, I'd known I needed to get out, which was why I'd transitioned to the Park Service.

While it may have worked for my jobs, apparently being a large, intimidating guy was not so great for meeting women. Especially gorgeous women like Iris. In an ideal world, I would attempt to pursue her anyway since she was everything I wanted in a woman. But the vibes she gave off were full of uncomfortableness, not to mention I really should keep my distance because of this active case.

Speaking of the case, I shot off a text to Agent Andrews as I pulled into our parking lot, and she let me know someone would be by to collect the letter by the end of the day.

I walked back into our main visitor center and headed back to our break room which connected to our offices in the back.

I walked in to find a few of my colleagues there eating their lunch when I spotted something on the middle table.

"Oh, what in the fresh hell is this," I grumbled, looking at the large display of dinosaur cupcakes surrounding the table.

"Good afternoon to you too, boss," Lewis said with a grin on his face. That asshole was enjoying this because he knew I hated this sort of thing.

"Yeah, yeah," I grumbled. "Where did these come from?"

"Your mom brought them by," Diden mentioned, smiling with her mouth half full of a chocolate cupcake. "She said you told her you'd never forgive her if she brought you cake to the office for your birthday, so she decided to bring cupcakes by—which she emphasized are not cake—several days *before* your birthday, so it doesn't count."

The muffled chuckles told me they were all getting a kick out of this. My meddling mother just couldn't help herself.

"However, she did apologize because she said your sister Rita ordered them, so your mom didn't realize they had dinosaurs on them until she picked them up," Jones added.

"She said your sister told her you had quite the excavation dig at the lake, so it reminded her of dinosaur archeologists," Lewis noted, and I heard the sarcasm in his voice. "I'm guessing you didn't tell them what exactly was dug up at the lake?"

"I told my sister since her husband is a cop, but not my mother." I noted to myself that Rita had likely done this on purpose to needle me for not telling Mom the whole story.

Trying to control my inner aggression, I just shook my head and started to walk toward my office.

"Where'd you go, by the way?" Diden asked. "You bolted out of here real fast."

I turned and held up the letter, filling them in on what it said and that Andrews had asked me to pick it up.

"Wait, so he thinks she took some kind of evidence from the crime scene and kept it at her house?" Jones asked, looking shocked.

"I don't know what this guy thinks," I responded vaguely, not wanting to get into it.

"And he really asked her to take something from police evidence to give it to him?" Diden questioned.

"Yes. The guy is a loose cannon in my opinion," Jennings added.

"Someone from the ISB is gonna swing by in a bit to collect this, so let me know when they get here," I said, hoping to redirect the conversation.

"Will do," Lewis replied.

Diden had been here several years now—longer than I had. Jennings was relatively new, having transferred from several other parks. He'd even done a brief stint in Canada through our Peace Parks program. All rangers were trained the same, so I never doubted his skills, but Diden, having been here in this particular park longer, held a bit more of my trust in her judgment for dealing with our local officials.

"You really think this weirdo is gonna try to go to the crime scene?" Jennings asked.

"No clue, so I'll have whoever's on duty on that side of the park put some extra cones and barriers up, not that those would stop them entirely," I told them.

"Shit," Jennings muttered.

My sentiment exactly.

7

"Calories don't count when you're on your period. You're losing enough blood throughout the day to make up for the cake, pie, and cookies you just ate for breakfast."
—It's science

Iris

After thoroughly embarrassing myself in front of Hector a few days ago—with extra help from my coworkers and the evil snake—I was thankful for a busy day at work to help distract my mind.

All I had thought about the last few days was Hector. Mostly my awkward moments, but also how good it had felt when he'd wrapped his arm around me when I'd stumbled near the snake. I'd felt his hard body up against my back, his muscular arm wrapped around me—tight, but not too tight—and my whole body had shivered as his scent also surrounded me.

My body had reacted not only with the shivers racing through me but also my nipples hardening—thankfully with him behind me, he couldn't see them. But then he'd practically lifted me away and shoved me to the side as if merely holding me made him uncomfortable. I wasn't a skinny woman, so I'd had that reaction from a few other men before, but having Hector jerk away from me bothered me more.

Today was a prep day at work for the big event in two weeks with the Boy Scouts and Girl Scouts, so that had helped to keep my mind off Hector—mostly.

Hours later, I had finally made it home. I had just pulled up to my apartment complex building and saw my elderly neighbor, Nancy, with her dog, Cocoa, walking down the sidewalk.

"Hi, Nancy. Hi, Cocoa," I greeted as I got out of my car.

Cocoa immediately started barking at me and raced over on her tiny little Papillon legs to greet me.

"Oh, hello dear," Nancy responded with a smile. "How has work been lately?"

I knew it was a simple question, but the truth was, I didn't have an answer I felt like sharing. I didn't want to tell her all the details, though. Partly because she was a sweet old lady and I didn't want to worry her, and partly because I had just spent the past few days dealing with a crazy podcaster, embarrassing myself in front of the sexiest man I had ever met—multiple times—and also dealing with my mom and aunt calling to get the scoop about the incident at the lake.

"Busier than usual," I told her, sticking with *a truth,*

but not the whole truth kind of answer. "Got anything exciting planned for tonight?"

"Oh, not tonight," she said, continuing at her slow but steady pace next to me while we walked over to our first-floor units. "Tomorrow is bingo with the ladies, and this weekend my son and his family are coming to pick me up and take me to lunch."

"That'll be fun," I told her.

She had three sons, but only one lived nearby, so she mostly lived by herself, though she never seemed bothered by that. She had a revolving door of friends and family who always came to visit.

"If you're not too tired, why don't you come over tonight and crochet with me on the patio?" she offered. "I've got cookies. They're fresh, homemade, and double-chocolate chip."

I chuckled at her use of food to entice me to come over. "You had me at cookies, Nancy."

Her unit was across the hall from mine, so I turned to my door before responding. "Give me about thirty minutes to wash up and grab a real bite to eat, and..." I said as I put my key in the door, only to notice it was unlocked.

As I pushed the key to turn it, it was enough to nudge the door open, meaning it hadn't been closed all the way. The Type A personality in me always checked twice when I left, so I knew this wasn't a mistake on my part. Pushing the door open but staying rooted where I was, I noticed my throw pillows were on the wrong side of my couch.

My blanket, which I had always neatly folded over the arm of my L-shaped couch—as feng shui dictated—was now askew on top of the throw pillows.

A small gasp left my mouth as I took a look around the space.

"Iris, dear," I vaguely heard someone behind me say, but I was frozen in shock.

My place wasn't tossed, but someone had definitely been in here. By the looks of it, they were searching for something.

"Iris, what's wrong?" I heard Nancy ask next to me.

"I think someone's been in my apartment."

"Come, deary, into my place. Quickly. We'll call the police from there."

I watched her close my door and pull at my arm, leading us into her unit.

Once in, she closed and locked her door. "Do you want me to call the cops, dear, or do you want to do it?"

"I've got it, but thanks, Nancy."

I reached for my phone, realizing my hands were shaking. I called and gave the dispatcher the details, and she assured me someone would be there as soon as they could. There wouldn't be full-blown lights and sirens since most likely no one was still in the apartment, but an officer would be here soon nonetheless, and they knew I would be waiting in Nancy's apartment.

After hanging up with the dispatcher, I sat on Nancy's couch, staring off into space, thinking how weird my life had become in just the last week.

I was startled out of my thoughts when Cocoa jumped up onto the couch and into my lap. Cocoa didn't much like strangers, but once she added you to her circle, she was loyal to you for life.

"Here, honey," Nancy said, sitting down next to me as she handed me a small cup of tea.

"Thank you."

Nancy was like the grandmother I never had. She was sweet, cooked a mean lasagna, and always invited me over to hang out with her and her friends. In the last year since I'd moved in here, she'd taught me to play Mah Jong, to finger crochet, the intricacies of making homemade jam, and how to cheat at rummy. She also sprinkled in some life advice, which I loved.

A knock at the door startled me out of my thoughts.

"How about you restrain Cocoa, and I'll get the door," I told her, knowing her dog would not take too kindly to the new strangers in her home.

"Sounds good, dear."

Even though I knew it was likely the cops, I still checked the peephole since I was feeling a bit on edge. Confirming two officers—one female and one male—on the other side, I opened the door.

"Are you Iris?" the female officer asked me.

"Yes, ma'am," I confirmed for her, speaking louder so she could hear me over Cocoa's barking.

"I'm Officer Kelly Swift," she said. "This is my partner, Officer Taylor Clarkson. We already walked through your apartment to make sure it was clear, but we'd like to have you come over now and take a look and see if anything looks stolen or out of place."

"Yes, of course," I responded, thankful Cocoa had switched to a more muted growl.

I followed the officers over to my apartment. It was a bit unsettling knowing someone else had been in my space, but I also knew this needed to be done, so I put on my big girl panties and braved through it.

I showed the officers what I'd noticed when I first opened the door. As I moved through the rest of my apartment, a few other things felt off—though I couldn't tell if they truly were, or if my mind was playing tricks on me after everything that had happened.

"Is anything missing?" Officer Clarkson asked as we made our way from the bathroom to the laundry room.

"I'm not sure," I told them honestly. "If there is, it isn't anything big."

"What about family heirloom jewelry or even some expensive handbags or shoes?" Clarkson added. "Those are items that you may not notice at first but are popular to steal because they can resell them easily on the internet."

Wow. I hadn't thought of that, but I guess it made sense.

"I don't have anything like that," I told them and then noticed something odd on my floor.

I had bright-white tiles on my laundry room floor, so it didn't stand out very much, but there was a cotton ball on the floor underneath where I hung up my clothes after washing them.

"Do you see something?" Officer Clarkson asked.

I pointed down to the floor. "I don't own any cotton balls. They're not great for the environment because they are usually bleached or mixed with synthetic fibers, so they can't break down safely."

My laundry room wasn't big—maybe five feet wide by seven feet long—so when Officer Swift came into the room, it felt extra crowded with the three of us in there. He opened what looked like a Ziploc bag and picked up the cotton ball.

"When did you wash these clothes?" Officer Clarkson asked, pointing to the clothes above where the cotton ball had been.

"Two days ago. I just haven't gotten around to putting them away."

The two officers exchanged looks before Officer Swift asked me a question as she exited the room. "Is there anyone you can think of who might want to cause you harm or even play a prank on you? Have you had any disagreements with a coworker or recently broken up with a boyfriend?"

"No...I mean yes," I answered and then sighed. "No, I don't have any angry coworkers, and yes, I broke up with someone recently, but I don't think he would break into my house."

"We ask because this doesn't look like a regular robbery where people break in and take the biggest ticket items like laptops or jewelry," she explained. "If something was stolen, it appears it's because they were looking for something specifically."

It occurred to me this could be related to the letter I'd received from Steve the podcaster. He'd asked me if I had taken anything from the crime scene. Even though I would never do that, maybe he didn't know that and came looking for it here.

"Actually, there may be someone," I said to both of them.

I gave them all the details of what had happened at Lake Echo as well as the specifics regarding Steve Stanton. I let them know that the ISB had the letter now and gave them the contact info for Agent Andrews.

"We're going to take some photos and make some calls," Officer Swift said. "If you want to go back over to your neighbor's unit, we will swing by and let you know when we're all done here."

I nodded in return, feeling an urgent need to get out of my apartment.

When I knocked on Nancy's door, she was quick to let me back in and engulfed me in a hug the moment I was inside her apartment. I hadn't known I had needed that, but I was grateful for it.

"Here, dear," Nancy said as she released me from the hug. "I warmed up your tea. Have a seat and relax for a few minutes."

I wasn't sure I could relax, but I would take a seat, anyway.

"Do you have someone you want me to call?" she asked me from the kitchen.

I knew she meant a family member or a friend, but the first name that came to mind was Hector.

"You're welcome to stay here with me tonight, Iris, but if you'd like someone else, I can call them for you."

At her comment, it occurred to me that the police may not let me sleep at my place tonight, nor would I want to, even if they said it was okay.

I didn't know why I didn't text Leah or Christine. Instead, I grabbed my phone, and my fingers went to Hector's name in my contacts list. My finger hovered over his name for several seconds, as if internally I was trying to decide what to do.

"Go ahead and make your call," Nancy said, placing her hand on top of my leg. "I'll get your tea and some cookies."

I looked back down at the name on my screen, but before I could change my mind, I pressed the button.

8

Hector

I walked into my living room after heating up my leftovers and sat on my couch.

Sarge, my chocolate lab, followed me, hopping up onto the couch next to me, his face mere inches from my food.

"Don't even think about it, buddy," I told him.

He listened and backed off, but his surrender was also accompanied by mildly pathetic whining.

It was later than I usually got home, but I had stayed at work tonight trying to read over some extra files Agent Andrews had sent me. It wasn't that the files were complicated. It was that the woman *mentioned* in the files was.

Every time I read Iris's name in the report, my brain deviated to thinking about her instead of the case. Her spooked face after retelling the story of tripping over the skull. Her gorgeous body and what it might look like naked and underneath me. Yeah, it was the latter one that was the issue and what had gotten me in trouble at work. Every time my mind wandered, I got further and further behind on my work.

This is not about Iris. It's about the body. Not her *body, but the dead body.* Just as I repeated that thought again, my phone rang. I glanced down to see Iris's name on my screen.

We'd exchanged numbers the day of the incident in case I needed to ask her about the case. I hadn't expected her to use it, though she had texted me twice now, but this was a phone call—something she had never done before. My Spidey-senses were peaked. Something felt off.

I grabbed the phone and swiped to answer the call after the second ring.

"Madeira," I answered, trying to remain cool and calm.

"Hector?" Iris's quiet voice came through the line, but her tone was laced with a bit of fear.

"Iris?" I asked, though I wasn't sure why, since I knew it was her.

"Umm...I don't know if it's related or not, but someone broke into my apartment," she said, her voice still quiet, but I could hear her breath hitch at the end of her sentence.

"Where are you?" I asked as I jumped up from my seat and headed toward the door, grabbing my keys on the way.

"I'm across the hall in my neighbor's apartment. The cops came and checked everything out, but one of the officers said it didn't look like a *regular* robbery—or something like that." She mumbled the last part as if frustrated. "They started to ask if I had any enemies or something. I'm sorry to bug you, but I wasn't sure if it was related—"

I cut her off before she could continue. "I'm glad you called. Given the letter you got, it's always better to take precautions. Stay at your neighbor's. Share your location with me—I'll be right there."

I threw that last sentence out as a desperate attempt to hide the fact that I had memorized her address from the paperwork I had been staring at all day, but I didn't need her to know that.

I hustled to my car, trying to settle the mild rage coursing through my body at the thought of someone breaking into Iris's apartment. Knowing she was upset irritated me, even though I had no claim to her.

Agent Andrews had called me earlier, letting me know they had dug into the self-proclaimed "crime expert" podcaster a little more. Some podcasters were great, and what they did could work in tandem with police investigators, but others were just weirdos and were more of a hassle than anything.

It sounded like our letter guy fell into the latter category.

When I arrived thirty minutes later, I went straight to her apartment instead of to her neighbor's. I wanted to talk to the cops and see what they knew and also give them what I knew from our case to see if it was connected.

I knocked on the half-open door, seeing a male cop I didn't know, who instantly went alert at my presence.

"Sir, you can't come in here," he said to me, walking toward the door, ready to block my entry.

I knew procedure, so I stayed in the doorway as I reached for my badge. "Name's Hector Madeira. I'm the chief ranger over at Lake Echo National Park."

"Madeira?" a familiar female voice said. "Holy crap. Long time no see."

"Hey, Swift," I greeted her with a head nod.

"You know him?" the other officer asked.

"Yeah, we were rookies together. He used to work at LVPD before he bailed and got the cushy job for softies," she said, smirking at me. "Clarkson, this is Hector Madeira. Hector, this is my partner, Taylor Clarkson."

"I don't mean to interrupt, but Iris called me because this break-in may be related to a case we're investigating," I told them and then filled them in on the details I had.

They nodded and asked some questions as I explained, and then they gave me what they knew about her break-in.

"So far, we just have her word that things are out of place and moved," Swift said. "We have a crime scene analyst on the way to grab some fingerprints just in case. Otherwise, the only other thing we have is the cotton ball."

"Cotton ball?" I asked.

"There was a cotton ball on the floor of her laundry room, which she swears she never uses because they aren't environmentally friendly or some shit," Clarkson said. "Thing is, it was still wet. Even if it had accidentally gotten stuck on her clothes or something, it would have been washed with her clothes and dried during the hours she was at work. The fact that it was still wet means it was *newly* wet. Possibly by the person who broke in."

"Shit," I muttered.

"Exactly," Swift said back to me.

"Alright. I'm gonna go next door and check in with her. Keep me posted on anything you find so I can let Agent Andrews know," I told them.

"I'll be over in a few," Swift said. "I need to find out if she's planning to stay here tonight or if she's going to a friend's or something."

I hadn't talked to her yet, but I wasn't letting her stay at her own apartment tonight. Not until we got some more information.

Walking across the hall to where Swift told me the neighbor lived, I knocked on the door.

"Iris," a female voice called from the other side of the door. "Come look at the peephole, dear. There is a very handsome but slightly scary man on the other side of the door. Do you know him?"

I heard shuffling feet and muttered voices, and then the door opened.

I wasn't sure what I expected her neighbor to look like, but it certainly wasn't an elderly woman, barely five feet tall, wearing bunny slippers. A yappy dog started barking incessantly as the door swung open even wider, and I saw Iris.

"Hey, Hector," she said to me amid the loud barking.

She looked defeated and wrung out. Her eyes were dry, with no signs of having cried, but they also looked tired.

"Hello, I'm Nancy," the old woman said to me as she ushered me into her place, holding a tiny dog in her arms. "And this is Cocoa. Her bark is worse than her bite."

Hopefully, I wouldn't have to find out if that was the truth or not.

"I'm Hector. Thank you for watching out for Iris," I told her.

I was glad Iris had this woman to go to for support and comfort. She deserved it, though a part of me found I also wanted to give her some of that support.

"Thanks for coming," Iris said to me. "I can take you over to meet the cops if you want."

"I went there first, actually," I told her, filling her in on the fact that I knew Officer Swift. I chose not to tell her what they said about the cotton ball just yet.

"Here. Come have a seat, young man," Nancy said, pointing at her couch.

I took her up on that offer and sat down next to Iris, facing her and Nancy, who was sitting in the chair with her dog in her lap.

"I highly recommend you stay somewhere else tonight other than your own place," I told Iris, and I was about to suggest a friend or family member when Nancy chimed in.

"She can stay with me. I have a pull-out sofa, and Cocoa and I will take good care of her."

While I had no doubt this woman meant what she said, I wasn't sure she was any safer here than at her own place. Not to mention, her dog wasn't exactly ideal protection material. I just needed a delicate way to tell her that.

"That's very kind of you, but it might make her relax a little more to be away from this apartment complex for a night," I informed her.

She looked at me and nodded as though she understood where I was coming from.

I hated where my next thought went, but it needed to be asked.

"You got a man, Iris?" Because if she did, and he was a good man, he would want to know about the break-in. "One you can go stay with?"

"Not anymore," she said, grumbling.

I was happy about that for reasons I chose not to think too deeply about. I was not, however, thrilled with how she muttered it.

"Why?" I asked before I thought better of it.

"Because men suck," she murmured, looking down at her cup of tea.

I knew I shouldn't ask. Shouldn't get involved. But I wanted to know what happened. If someone had hurt her, even if they'd just disappointed her, I needed to know.

Before I could say anything else, Nancy took that

moment to fill me in on some of the losers Iris had dated —including one who wanted her to lose weight. That one pissed me off the most because Iris had an incredible body and didn't need to change a damn thing. Any guy would be lucky to have her at his side—or underneath him.

Shit. I needed to bring my thoughts back to the here and now.

"You can stay with me," I blurted out, suddenly unsure if it sounded too forward.

"I don't want to inconvenience you," Iris replied.

"I've got a spare bedroom you can crash in until you figure something else out," I offered, hoping she didn't fight me on it and just accepted.

"I think that's a wonderful idea," Nancy chimed in, clapping her hands.

"Okay, thank you," Iris said, twisting her hands as though nervous. "It'll just be for one night. I just hate texting some of my friends so late, but I can make arrangements for the weekend."

"I'll go next door and ask Swift if it's okay for you to grab some things and pack a bag," I told her as I stood and made my way to the door.

I was just about through the door when I heard Iris mutter quietly, causing me to pause and listen.

"This could be a disaster," she said.

"Yes, but with that man along for the ride, it could also be a fun and spicy disaster," Nancy muttered back excitedly. "You could use a little fun right now, dear. Just promise to tell me all about it later."

On that note, I walked next door, but I couldn't help but grin a little. Being with Iris would definitely be a disaster. Not on my part, but on hers. I was a giant red flag—one that she needed to stay far, far away from. But damn if Nancy wasn't also right that it would be a fun and spicy disaster.

The car ride back to my place so far had been a quiet one. I knew Iris was processing a lot, so I let her have that space, but I also didn't want her to worry too much about it since there wasn't much else she could do at this point.

I knew she could have driven herself, but driving when you were emotional was never a good thing, so I offered to take her and would bring her back in the morning.

Not wanting her to feel any more uncomfortable than she already was tonight, I decided to ask her some questions to distract her.

"Iris, I know you have one sister—Anna—but you have another one if I remember correctly, right?"

She turned to face me but just stared for a beat before answering. "I actually have four sisters."

"For real?"

At her sister's wedding, Archer had mentioned her whole family was there, but I hadn't bothered to talk to anyone if I didn't have to. I was the exact opposite of a social butterfly. Plus, seeing Iris at the wedding in a skintight gown showing off all her assets made it hard for me to focus on anyone else in the room.

"Yes," she said, pulling me from my thoughts of her in a tight dress. "I assumed you already knew that. I'm adopted, so I have four sisters that Mom and Auntie adopted."

I knew Anna lived with her husband in Georgia, but I wasn't sure about the rest.

"Other than Anna, do they all live here?"

"No," she replied, shaking her head. "Mom and Auntie live on a working farm in a small coastal town in Northern California, and my sisters are all scattered about."

"Are you all close in age?" I asked, not knowing anything about how fostering and adoption worked.

"We're all within ten years of each other," she said. "Gale is the oldest of the sisters, in her mid-thirties, and lives in the converted guest house on the farm. She's a forensic scientist but can do most of her work remotely, which is good since she is extremely introverted."

Her face lit up while she talked about her family, and I loved seeing her ease out of her anxiety.

"Cora is the next oldest, and she's the Nevada State Hydrologist up in Reno. Then comes me, followed by Anna—who you already know. Finally, there's Hazel, who just turned twenty-six. She's a marine biologist and lives in a different coastal town not far from Mom and Auntie. Cora and Hazel are biological sisters."

"All girls," I noted.

She nodded before explaining. "In the beginning, they took in both boys and girls, but after Gale arrived, that changed. I wasn't there at that time, but I was told she had a really hard time with any male presence," she said softly.

There was clearly more to the story there, but I was trying to keep the conversation light, so I wasn't going to pry.

"Umm...what about you?" she asked me. "Do you have family here?"

I knew this was on me because I was the one to originally ask, but I also knew that by answering her, I was about to open a can of worms.

"My parents still live in the house I grew up in on the southwest side of Vegas," I told her. "I'm the oldest of four siblings. My sister Dani is next. She lives over by the UNLV campus where she works—she's an ASL instructor."

"ASL instructor?"

"Sorry. It stands for American Sign Language. Dani is deaf and teaches ASL classes at the university."

"Oh wow. Does that mean you know sign language?" she asked.

"Yeah, I grew up learning it, though now we stay in touch pretty regularly via texting."

"That's awesome. I've always wanted to learn sign language—well, really *any* language," she said, pausing for a moment as if to regain her thoughts. "Wait, you said you're the oldest of four siblings. What about the other two?"

Now for the hard part. "Manny was next in line, but he passed away a few years ago."

"Oh God, Hector, I'm so sorry," she said, reaching her hand out to put it on top of mine.

I knew it was just meant to be a kind gesture, but damn if it didn't feel nice having her soft hand on top of mine, even briefly.

"I vaguely remember Anna mentioning something about your brother working with her husband years ago as a cop and being killed on the job, but I forgot. I'm so sorry."

There was a lot to unpack there, but I didn't want to bring the mood back down again, so I continued on.

"No need to apologize. After Manny is my youngest sister, Rita. She's an elementary school teacher on the north side of town."

"That's great that you all live so close," she said wistfully. "I love my job so much, but I do miss my family. I get to see Cora quite a bit because our jobs intertwine a lot, even though she's based in Reno. She spends a lot of time down here in Vegas, especially during monsoon season."

We pulled up to my carport and parked. I looked over to see her face all lit up talking about her sister.

"That's great," I told her.

"It is," she replied, smiling. "I love having her semi-close by."

God, this woman was gorgeous and tempting at any given time, but when she smiled, she was a whole other level of temptation and beauty.

I stared down at her lips, wondering how perfect they would feel as I slid my tongue between them and tasted her—a thought I'd had nearly a million times since I'd first met her...and a thought I needed to shut down this very instant.

"Thanks for letting me stay with you tonight," she said softly. "I've got a few friends I can reach out to tomorrow to stay with."

"It's not a big deal, Iris. I've got a spare bedroom that no one uses. You're welcome to it as long as you need it."

The bedroom that was right next to mine.

This may not be the best idea.

9

**"The unique smell before a rainstorm is really a thing.
It's called petrichor."**
—It's science

Iris

Hector's property was idyllic.

He lived on the west side of Lake Echo in the town of Thunder Cove. To get to his house, we had driven through the Arroyo Wash, which was one of my favorite spots. It was a little oasis in the desert—literally. It was a wetland area filled with greenery and foliage that you didn't often see in arid regions. And on the few times it did rain, this place became full of color.

Thunder Cove was a great area, but since a lot of it was actually under the jurisdiction of Lake Echo National Park, there were very few houses allowed there.

"I don't see any other houses nearby," I mentioned as we got out of the car and began walking up to his house. "How much property does it sit on?"

"Several dozen acres, though I'm not entirely sure," he responded. "It actually belongs to the Park Service and sits on their property. It was built about three decades ago for whoever was chief ranger so they could get to our home base quickly if needed but also provide some privacy if they had a family."

That made sense and also explained why it was so remote yet had beautiful views.

I gasped as I looked around the side of the house. "You have a view of the lake!"

It was dark out now, but I could see the lights from the boats on the lake. I could only imagine how stunning the views were during the day, even though the lake appeared quite a ways away from the property.

I turned back to Hector and noticed he had my overnight bag in his hand—which I had forgotten to take out of the car in my excitement to explore his property.

"I can get that," I told him, reaching out for the bag.

He pulled it away and walked toward the door. "I got it. Just brace yourself for my dog."

Hector had a dog?

Before I could really even ponder that thought, the door swung open, and out burst a very energetic chocolate lab.

He sniffed Hector very quickly before realizing there was someone else—me. He took off at a sprint, even though I was only about thirty feet behind Hector, and crashed into my legs with his likely seventy-to-eighty-pound body.

Since I wasn't fully prepared, I fell back onto my butt —thank God it was fully padded—and was immediately gifted copious amounts of dog licks and slobber kisses.

"Sarge, *aus! Heir! Sitz!*" Hector shouted in what sounded like a different language, or maybe I just had too much dog slobber in my ears and the words were muddled.

"Sarge, you're a pain in my ass," Hector grumbled at the same time he pulled the dog off me by his collar. "Sorry. He sucks at commands."

Dog now restrained with his right hand—though barely since he was pulling to get back to me—Hector dropped my bag and stuck out his left hand to me to help me up.

"It's okay. He's very friendly," I told him as I grabbed his hand.

His rough, calloused hand engulfed mine and sent shivers up through my entire arm. Though it was temporary, since, once I was up on my feet, he let me go in order to more fully restrain his dog.

"His name is Sarge?" I asked as I followed him to the front door.

"Yes, he's a retired police K-9, which is where he got his name," Hector answered as he parked Sarge by the front door and gave another command. "*Sitz. Bleib.*"

"What are you saying?"

"His training was in Germany, so that's what most of his commands are in. I told him to sit and stay."

Ahh, got it. Sarge whined as he stared at me, voicing

how upset he was that he was not allowed to continue his kissing attack on me.

"Can I pet him?"

"Yes, but let me get your bag and we can head inside first."

We all walked into Hector's cabin, which was basic but beautiful from the outside but even more impressive when you walked inside.

It was a single-story ranch with high ceilings and large wooden beams. The cozy cabin featured a rustic but clean interior. It wasn't huge, but it had an open-concept kitchen, dining, and living room.

The first thing I noticed about the living room was the amazing stone fireplace and large leather couches and recliner that looked like you could just sink right into them.

"Sarge, *bleib*," Hector commanded, causing the dog to whine some more, but he stayed put. "Follow me, and I'll give you the ten-second tour."

We walked down the hallway, where we passed a small laundry room, a guest bath, and two smaller bedrooms, one of which was being used as a workout room.

"This is my guest room," he said, indicating the other small bedroom as he set my bag down just inside the doorway.

I guess this was where I was going for the night.

"Thank you," I told him.

"My bedroom and bath are down the hall if you need

anything," he said, and then he started to walk back in the direction from which we'd come.

I guess that was it for the tour. It was okay, though, because this was just for one night. I couldn't stay here longer in this close proximity to Hector, or I might do something stupid—like jump his bones.

After putting my toiletry bag in the guest bath and freshening up a bit—since I hadn't been able to do that at my place—I wandered back out into the living room. Hector was in the kitchen heating something up in the microwave.

"Did you have dinner yet?" he asked me.

My stomach chose that exact moment to give away all my secrets by gurgling. "No, not yet, but I'll be okay."

I didn't want to feel like a mooch since he was already letting me stay here. Maybe I could get food delivered here.

"I have leftover chili I can heat up for you. Would you eat it?"

I nodded in response and then glanced over the kitchen counter to see Sarge sitting perfectly in the kitchen.

"He seems to be doing well with the commands now," I noted.

"Only because he wants whatever I'm cooking," Hector replied.

I smiled because I understood that. I would probably be the same if I were a dog.

"He seems awfully young to be a retired dog," I pointed out.

"He's young because he was forced into retirement early because he's considered defective."

"How is he considered defective? He looks fine to me."

"He's defective because he gets distracted by food. Case in point," he said, nodding in Sarge's direction. "Anytime we would attempt to have him chase a criminal or focus on a mission and someone would offer him a piece of cheese, he would get distracted and not complete his mission."

"Same, Sarge. I feel your pain, buddy," I said to him, not that he could understand me.

"Yeah, well, unfortunately in police work, that's enough to get you fired from the canine program."

"Really? That's insane to me. Dorothy distracts us with snacks all the time at work, and they haven't fired her or me," I chuckled.

"Sarge," I said, and his ears perked up at the sound of his name. "Maybe you need to come to work with me. You would be loved there, and we *all* get distracted by food."

Hector just shook his head at me as if I was a little crazy, but I also didn't miss the lip twitch as he grabbed the food out of the microwave and handed it to me.

"Here," he said, handing me the bowl and nodding to the barstool next to me. "Have a seat."

We ate in relative silence, at his counter while Sarge sat at our feet, hoping and praying something would fall down to him.

Uncomfortable with the silence I decided to ask him a question that had been burning in my mind since the day I interviewed him at Lake Echo.

"You don't have to answer, but...at my sister's wedding, you were still working for the LVPD. Now you're a park ranger. Why the big change?"

He paused in eating his meal, and his jaw tightened before he finally stuck the spoonful of chili into his mouth.

I guess that nonanswer was my answer. Back to silence it was.

"After everything that went down on my last mission, I realized I wanted out," he said quietly but still loud enough for me to hear him.

"Can I ask what happened?" I asked, not necessarily because I was nosy, but because I just wanted to get to know him better.

"While undercover I watched one of the guys we were targeting sell drugs to a teenager," he shared. "I knew I couldn't intervene without blowing my cover but I could have found a way to call it in later, but I didn't. I got distracted by my target and didn't get a chance to call it in for almost twenty-four hours."

He paused again and then sighed. "The drugs were apparently laced with fentanyl, and he didn't make it. I still think about that kid often and how my slow response killed him."

He wasn't hiding the fact that this wasn't easy to talk about, so I said nothing in response, letting him choose whether he wanted to keep talking about it or change the subject.

"So, I left. It's actually not a hard transition because I was already a federal worker, had security clearance, and emergency response training and such. A buddy of mine was already working for the Park Service and told me about the chief ranger job, so I applied."

"I'm happy for you," I told him, and I was. If this job made him feel more at ease while still fulfilled, then I was glad he had it.

"What made you decide to become a meteorologist?" he asked.

"Honestly, it wasn't some big epiphany. I was watching this documentary, and they explained how clouds aren't actually fluffy—like they weigh tons. Literal tons. And I thought, how does the sky even hold them all up? And I was like, oh my God, that is so cool. And I started telling everyone I knew about it because I thought everyone should know this awesome fact."

He didn't say anything in return and simply stared at me, making me more nervous, so I just continued on, babbling about my nerdy weather obsession.

"I started telling people more random facts about how raindrops aren't actually tear-shaped—they're spherical until air resistance flattens them—or that a lightning bolt is five times hotter than the surface of the sun," I continued, noting that his face had turned into an amused smirk.

"Eventually I realized you could get paid to like these nerdy things and decided to make a career out of it," I added, noticing his smirk had turned into a full-blown smile.

He clearly found my random tangent entertaining. Time to end this.

"I'll stop talking now," I said, turning back to my bowl in slight embarrassment.

Hoping to change the subject to safer, less embarrassing, territory, I opted to convey my gratitude for his help. "Thanks again for letting me stay here."

I still wasn't sure coming here was the greatest idea, but after Hector's comment about safety, I realized it was the best option I had at the time.

"It's not a big deal," he replied, but he was wrong.

"Yes, it is. I could have stayed with Nancy, but I didn't want to put her in harm's way if this person came back," I told him.

Also, if someone did follow me, I already knew Hector was a great guy since he had helped protect my sister, and I told him as much.

"Plus, I find it comforting and safe around you," I told him honestly.

"Most people are scared of me because of my size," he added. "I'm told it's rather intimidating. Hell, even some of the kids who come to get their junior ranger badges look intimidated by me."

"I'm pretty sure that has more to do with your grumpy demeanor than your size," I told him. "Besides, I happen to like your larger frame."

He snorted. "Right."

"I mean it. I'm a bigger girl myself, so I've always been drawn to larger men because I figure they would be the only ones comfortable with...umm..." I quickly stopped talking, knowing I likely shouldn't share the rest of that thought.

"Comfortable with what?"

Crap. I guess he wasn't just going to ignore that slip.

"Umm...never mind." I tried to brush it off, waving my hand dismissively.

"Comfortable with what, Iris?" His question was a bit more demanding this time.

I stared right at him and blurted my inner thoughts right out. "Sex. Umm...like having me be on top."

He closed his eyes, and I wasn't sure if it was because he was still feeling weird about his size or because what I said had crossed the line.

"Sorry. I just..."

"Iris, stop talking," he said, running his hand over his face. "I'm gonna take the dog out really quick."

In a flash, he was gone. Once again, I had put my foot in my mouth and scared off the big hot guy.

Me and my stupid mouth.

10

Hector

I had to take Sarge for a walk. Not because he needed to go out, but because I needed to get away from Iris before I did something stupid, like kiss her or fuck her senseless.

When she said she was drawn to larger men like me because she wouldn't feel self-conscious being on top during sex, I instantly felt all the blood in my body rush to my dick.

Listening to her talk about her career and all her nerdy facts was damn adorable—all I wanted to do was kiss that super-smart mouth of hers.

If I dreamed up my perfect woman, Iris would be it. Yes, because she had the most amazingly sexy curves, but also because she was smart, kind, and loyal. She was everything you would ever want in a partner.

As much as I would love to be the man at her side, I couldn't be. She deserved so much better than what I could give her.

After giving myself fifteen minutes to level my thoughts—especially the inappropriate ones—Sarge and I went back inside. I found Iris sitting on my couch with a bag next to her, some kind of fabric circle thing in her lap, and a bunch of string.

"I'm sorry if I made things uncomfortable," she said, tucking a strand of her hair behind her ear and avoiding any eye contact with me, indicating she was nervous.

I didn't want her to feel bad, and even more than that, I did not want to discuss this topic further or risk getting another hard-on.

"Don't apologize," I told her. "I'm gonna go grab him a snack. Do you mind if I watch the game?"

"Oh sure," she said, starting to grab the items in her lap. "I can move all my needlepointing stuff over so you can sit here on the couch."

"I'll take the recliner. Don't worry about it," I told her, needing to keep my distance from her.

I had no idea what needlepointing was, but I guess I was about to find out.

As soon as Sarge got his treat, he bolted into the living room and jumped up on the couch to sit next to her.

"Watch out, buddy. I don't want to stab you," she said to Sarge, moving some items around on her lap.

I was just about to sit down in the chair and relax when I heard a car door slam shut outside. Sarge barked and hopped off the couch, heading for the tall, narrow window by the front door. I followed him there since I wasn't expecting any company.

I got there just in time to see Jennings and Diden walk up to my front door. I opened it since I knew they wouldn't come here without a good reason.

"Hey," I greeted them, opening the door.

"Hey, Chief. You mind if we come in?" Jennings asked.

Yes, I minded, because if they came in, it would take longer to get rid of them. Nevertheless, I opened the door wider and signaled for them to come in.

"Hey, Sarge," Jennings said, leaning down to pet him, and then he turned the corner.

"Oh, sorry, man. I didn't know you had company," he said to me, looking half shocked that I had someone in my house, and even more shocked that it was a female.

"You two remember Iris O'Hara," I said and then turned to Iris.

"Uh, yeah. I'm Jordan Jennings, but most people just call me Jennings," he said to her, the shocked look still on his face.

"Good to see you again," Iris said to him politely.

"I didn't know you guys knew each other that well," he said, and I heard the unspoken part about how weird he found this since I was one of the people originally assigned to the case.

Technically, it was pretty much fully handed over to

the ISB now, but the optics were strange, and I knew it, and so did he.

"I worked briefly with her brother-in-law and sister, so we've met before," I said, giving him just enough to answer his question, and then I tried to move on.

"What's up?" I asked him, hoping to make whatever this was quick.

"Uhh, some prick from the ISB called to let us know Ms. O'Hara's apartment was broken into and they think it might be from the podcaster, Steve Stanton," Diden chimed in, having just come fully into my living room after petting Sarge.

Both she and Jennings looked back and forth between the two of us, likely feeling uncomfortable talking about this in front of Iris.

"That's why she's here," I told them. "I met with the officers at her apartment and walked through what we had on our end so they had everything they needed to see if it is, in fact, the same guy. They suggested she not stay there tonight, so she came here."

Jennings nodded and then turned to Iris. "Uh, both of us have cabins nearby, so if this lug gives you any trouble, you're more than welcome to stay with either of us."

This motherfucker was not seriously asking her to leave my place and go hop to his...

"I'm okay. Thank you though," she responded politely. "It's just for one night until I can get myself set up at a friend's house. And Hector has helped my family out before, so I know he'll keep me safe."

I felt a sense of pride in her words and also enjoyed that she had essentially shot him down.

"Well, it appears that you already knew about the break-in," Diden said. "Sorry to bother you, Chief. You weren't answering your phone, so we figured we'd stop by."

I looked over at my phone, picking it up from the side table and noting the black screen. "It looks like it died. Sorry."

"No big deal," Jennings said. "Keep us posted on what you hear, especially if you need us to start making more patrols around the crime scene if this loser really does show up."

"I will," I told them.

"Thanks for taking the time to come by anyway," Iris said to him politely while I internally rolled my eyes.

I walked them back to the door and locked up before returning to my chair to finally relax.

"That was nice of them to stop by," she said to me.

Of course, she would think that. "Super nice," I said, and even I could hear my voice dripping with sarcasm and disdain.

"Do you not like Jennings and Diden?" she asked me.

I sighed. "I do. I just don't like people from work coming to my house," I explained, also not liking how he flirted with her but choosing to keep that part to myself. "I see these people all day, so of course I would be thrilled to see them after hours as well."

She smiled a weird smile at me.

"What's that look for?" I asked her, my curiosity getting the better of me.

"I just never pictured you as the sarcastic type—mostly just broody," she said with a grin.

"Yeah, well, punching people in the face is frowned upon by management, so I use sarcasm to get through the day," I grumbled.

"That's why I crochet and do needlepoint," she said, nodding to the stuff in her lap. "Murder is wrong. Needlepoint is safer. I stab fabric so I don't have to stab people."

For the first time in a long time, I burst out laughing.

I slept terribly last night. Tossing and turning to thoughts of Iris. Thoughts of her being kidnapped. Thoughts of her being harmed. And also, thoughts of her amazing body, naked and underneath me.

I had never really let a bystander from a case get to me like this.

Realizing sleep was never going to come, I finally got up and started to make some coffee just as the sun was coming up. After letting Sarge out to do his business, I came back inside to hear the shower kick on down the hallway.

I powered through while she showered. She already consumed my thoughts hourly. I didn't need a further reminder of how her body would look. It was excruciating knowing she was just on the other side of the wall—naked, wet, and touching her body.

Stop. Do not go there.

That would not be happening between us. It couldn't. She not only deserved better than a flawed grump, but also—as observed last night with Jennings—the optics were bad.

I busied myself with making breakfast, which, since I didn't cook very often, meant I was having a simple bagel.

I heard the bathroom door open and her bedroom door close, and images of her in just a towel filled my mind.

Focus.

With my mind distracted, I grabbed the bagel to spread the cream cheese but forgot I had just pulled it out of the toaster. I dropped not only the bagel slice on the floor, but the knife with the cream cheese spread already on it as well—directly onto my favorite flannel shirt.

I pulled it off and tried wiping the spread off, but I just ended up making a bigger mess. Giving up on the shirt, I threw it onto the far kitchen counter for now. I turned to put another bagel in the toaster just as Iris came into the kitchen.

"Do you want a bagel?" I asked her, looking up to see her eyes on my now bare chest.

She didn't respond, either because she hadn't heard me, or because she was too focused on my shirtless body. I watched in real time as the heat in her eyes grew darker, which caused my own lust to grow too, knowing she was enjoying what she saw.

If she kept looking at me like that, whatever morals I still had would be gone.

"Iris," I said a little louder, hoping to get her attention.

"What? Uh...sorry. Did you say something?" she asked, her eyes now on mine, but her cheeks started to turn pink.

"I asked if you wanted a bagel."

"Oh, umm, sure," she said, looking down at the counter now and avoiding eye contact with me.

Seconds later, a phone buzzed on the counter, followed by Iris's voice.

"Hello, this is Iris," she said and then paused. "Oh, hi, Officer Clarkson."

I turned to look at her to make sure what Clarkson was telling her wasn't going to upset her, but she mostly just responded with "uh-huhs" and "okays" and a few "thank yous."

"Okay, well, thank you for calling," she said and hung up the phone as I put a plate in front of her.

"I don't know what you like on your bagel, but I have cream cheese or butter," I told her as I set both options down on the counter.

"Thanks," she said, seemingly deflated.

"Everything okay?" I asked.

"Yeah," she answered, nodding as though she was trying to shake the worry out. "Umm, he said I can go back to my place today, that they're all done for now, but they may need to come back if they missed something."

"That's good," I told her, assuming she'd be happy about this news.

"Yeah, totally. Definitely. Yes," she said, nodding again as if saying it out loud multiple times would make her believe it.

"Do you work today?" I asked, something I probably should have asked her last night.

"No," she said. "Unless there's some kind of special event or we're short-staffed, I usually just work Monday through Friday.

"Okay, well, even though it's a Saturday, I have to run into the office for a few minutes this morning to sign some paperwork," I said, deciding not to give her the specific details that the papers I would be signing were to have more patrols and barricades put up around where the body had been found now that someone was escalating things. "If you don't mind, I'll just swing by and take care of that, and then I can take you over to your place."

"That's fine," she said. "My leasing office emailed and offered to change the locks and add a few more security features for me. I'm guessing because he doesn't want word spreading that we'd had a break-in at our complex. This should give him enough time to do that."

If not, I would offer to add some security features as well.

"Good. I can take a look at all of it for you when we get there," I told her.

"Thank you," she said, smiling up at me. "Can we bring Sarge with us?"

Did I want to? Not really.

Would I do it? Yes.

Why? Because she asked, and I was quickly learning that saying no to this woman was incredibly difficult.

11

"It's okay to eat junk food in the car on road trips because calories don't count at highway speeds. I don't have time to explain the science behind this, but it's sound."
—*It's science*

Hector

After my own quick shower—a cold one, I might add, thanks to Iris—we were finally on our way out the door.

"I'm actually really excited to see your office," Iris said from the passenger seat of my SUV while Sarge leaned over her shoulder from the back seat. "Despite living here for nearly two years, I haven't actually been to the visitors center."

"Let's take Sarge into my office when we first get there so he stays out of trouble, and then I can give you a tour after I get all this paperwork squared away."

"Oh, that would be awesome, thanks."

The minute we walked into the building, the few

rangers who were on staff all clocked me and the gorgeous woman at my side. She had on a simple red V-neck shirt with black shorts. Her hair was up in some kind of messy bun with a few loose strands framing her face and glasses. Simple yet so damn sexy.

Diden, having seen her the instant we cleared the door, took the opportunity and pounced.

"Hey, boss. What are you guys doing here?" she asked in all her nosy glory, hidden behind a sweet, saccharin voice.

I told her and the other three rangers in sight that I needed to fill out some paperwork and then give Iris a tour of the place.

Diden and Jennings looked at each other conspiratorially and then turned to us.

"I can give you a tour. It's the best part of my job," Diden said.

"I'll help you with the paperwork," Jennings said to me.

That must have been their plan. Diden interrogates—I mean, gives a tour to—Iris while Jennings gets the scoop from me, and then they would share all their gossip after we left. The only good news was that Jennings did, in fact, help fill out the paperwork with me, though he did it while asking me four-hundred questions about the case, including whether or not we should get a restraining order for the podcaster.

What I hadn't planned on was Ranger Diden giving

Iris the tour of a lifetime—a long one. So it had taken nearly two hours for us to get out of there.

At that point, I was already hungry since all I'd had was a measly bagel for breakfast. Given that I lived so far from the city, we still had roughly thirty more minutes to drive to her place, so we decided to grab some lunch on the way to her apartment.

Iris picked a spot that had a nice, covered patio with misting fans so we could have Sarge sit with us.

Knowing she was the weaker link, Sarge had set up shop directly next to Iris, setting his head on her thigh with the biggest pleading gaze I had ever seen.

"Hi, sweet boy," she said, leaning down to scratch his head. "I would feed you, but grumpy daddy over there is glaring at me with the heat of a thousand suns. I might get in trouble if I give you food."

"Yes, you would definitely be in trouble," I confirmed.

She looked at me and smirked. "But, like, how much trouble? And what kind? Might be worth it." She shrugged and popped a french fry into her mouth as she smiled wickedly at me.

"Dear Lord," I mumbled quietly. This feisty woman was certainly going to be the death of me. "Iris, do not feed him," I practically growled.

"Sir, yes, sir," she said, full of sass as she saluted me and winked.

Three words and a wink, and I felt myself getting hard under the table.

Fuck, this woman was definitely, one hundred percent going to be the death of me.

"I have dog treats at my place," she stage-whispered to Sarge. "They're really for Cocoa, my neighbor's dog, but you can have one when we get there."

Pretending I hadn't heard that, I intentionally broke my gaze from hers and chose to look down at my plate.

"Ann is really nice," she said.

Not following her line of thought, I lifted an eyebrow in question.

"Ranger Diden," she clarified, looking at me like I was supposed to have known that.

Yes, I knew her first name was Ann, but we all usually called each other by last names, especially since we had two Johns, two Amys, and two Davids.

"She taught me so much about the history of the park, and I love the topography maps you guys have on display," she said while taking her glasses off and wiping them with her shirt.

I stopped paying attention to what she was saying at that point. Pulling the hem of her T-shirt down from the bottom to wipe her glasses effectively caused the fabric to slide lower across her chest. As she leaned forward a bit, I suddenly had a clear shot of quite possibly the best pair of tits I had ever seen—and I was only seeing part of them.

"Don't you think so?" she asked, startling me out of my deep gaze.

Thankfully, Iris's gaze had been on her food when I looked up, so she hadn't noticed my staring.

Having no idea what she was talking about, I chose to reroute by not answering.

"I'm glad you had fun. Diden likes giving tours. It's her favorite part of the job."

"I could tell, and I'm happy to have benefitted from it," she said, now smiling up at me. "She asked me about the break-in. She seemed really concerned. She also asked me a bunch of questions about Steve's letter. She offered again for me to stay with her. Apparently, she was a big collegiate wrestler and won a state championship or something."

I hadn't known that, but then again, I didn't exactly try to get to know my colleagues outside of work. I knew Diden was probably just trying to be nice and offer protection for Iris, but if she needed to stay somewhere other than her own place, she would be staying with me. I didn't know why I had this overly acute sense of protection when it came to her, but I did.

Sarge whined loudly next to her, giving his best effort to con her into sliding him a fry.

Instead, she just leaned down to kiss him on the top of his head and scratch behind his ears. In return, he leaned up to lick her face, effectively getting slobber on her glasses.

"I just cleaned these, buddy," she sighed, taking them off to clean them again.

Not wanting to risk getting a hard-on—again—at lunch from watching her shirt slide down—also again—I chose to get up and dispose of my food tray and throw my trash out.

Fifteen minutes later, we were at her apartment complex. We swung by the front desk first to get the new key the apartment manager was supposed to leave for her.

She walked in to get it, but when she came out and slid into my car, she looked defeated.

"What's wrong?" I asked as she hopped back into my SUV, and Sarge immediately sniffed her from the back seat as if she had been on the most exciting adventure in the four minutes she was out of the car. "Sarge, leave her alone."

"Apparently, the maintenance supervisor had a family emergency, so he won't be able to change my door lock until tomorrow," she said, sighing.

Well, shit. There was no way I was letting her stay at her place until they replaced the lock. Was the same person likely to come back? No. But I also didn't want to take that chance, especially since she lived alone and didn't have any other form of backup security.

"You can go ahead and pull around," she said to me, looking down at her phone. "I need to pull up the schedule and see what shifts Leah and Christine are working, because I don't want to stay with one of them if they're on the overnight shift."

I should have nodded and let it go. That would be a better idea—a safer idea. But I found myself needing to be the one to make sure she was safe and covered.

"We'll go to your place and grab some more clothes,

and you can stay with me again tonight," I told her, even though I knew this definitely wouldn't be easy on me. But it would be easier on her, and that mattered more to me than my own discomfort.

"Hector, you've already let me stay with you one night. I don't want to be a burden or overstay my welcome."

"Iris, I wouldn't have offered in the first place if I wasn't okay with it."

She stared up at me, trying to gauge my sincerity or perhaps to decide whether she even wanted to stay with me another night. "Okay. Thank you. I know it's highly unlikely, but if this really was a targeted break-in, I don't want to take the chance they could break into Leah's or Christine's places too."

She turned to me, her hands twisting in her lap, and rushed to add, "Not that I want you to be a target either… It's just that…well, you can protect yourself better."

I knew what she meant, and she was right. I didn't want her to feel bad about her comments though.

"I get it, it's fine," I told her, reaching for her hands that she was twisting in her lap, but she pulled them away at the last second, causing my hand to land on her thigh.

Her skin was burning under my touch. The palm of my hand was on her shorts, but my fingers brushed against her incredibly soft skin, and I found myself wanting to run my hands over more of it.

I lifted my hand off her leg quickly, putting it back on the steering wheel.

"Let's go grab you some more stuff," I told her, driving the car over to her unit. "You can give Sarge a treat while we're there."

"Or two," she said, grinning. "Maybe three."

"Well, how else do I get to know you?" she asked while we were sitting in my living room after eating dinner that night.

We had been back at my place for two hours now after grabbing her stuff from her apartment and coming back to my place.

"You don't," I told her matter-of-factly.

She sighed loudly. "Why not? What's so wrong with me wanting to get to know you, Hector?"

"Because getting to know me complicates things," I grumbled.

If she got to know me, then I would get to know her, which would make me like her more and make her harder to walk away from. I needed her to keep a distance from me so I could keep this platonic.

She had tried asking me questions about myself at her apartment, on the drive home, and again at dinner—all of which I deftly avoided.

She threw her hands up in frustration and got up from her seat. "I'm gonna go pack and stay with a friend."

"You don't want to stay here?" I asked, now suddenly panicked that she wanted to leave.

I knew it was for the best, but it also didn't sit well with me.

"You don't *want* me to be here," she said, sounding exasperated. "I'm making things weird and *complicated*."

She was throwing my own words back at me, and I felt like even more of a dick than I already was.

Before she could fully retreat, she turned to face me. "Why?"

"Why, what?" I asked, a bit confused.

"Why does it make things complicated if we get to know each other?"

I paused, wondering how honest to be with her. But I realized that if I was going to get through to her—to where she really understood me—I needed to be completely honest. "Because a woman like you is impossible to walk away from. You're gorgeous, funny, smart, friendly, and you make the people around you better. I'm none of those things."

For a few moments she stared at me, her eyes wide with shock.

"You think I'm all those things?" she asked quietly.

I didn't respond but chose to stay where I was, silently staring at her.

"Hector, I've had the hots for you since the day I first saw you, but you were always grumpy and moody around me. I assumed you hated me for some reason. I had no idea you felt that way about me."

I did not need to hear her say she had the hots for me. *Focus on the latter points.*

"I was moody around you because you were off-limits," I explained, hoping she would understand. "You're the sister of someone we were investigating who also had a hit out on her."

"Okay, but that's over now," she shot back.

"You're off-limits now because of this investigation with Lake Echo."

"It's not like there's a rule against something like that," she argued.

"There is for me," I asserted, hoping she understood. "That's a line I don't cross. And you shouldn't want to be with me, anyway."

"Why?" She looked at me puzzled, sliding her glasses back up to the top of her nose.

"Because I'm not a good man."

Confusion was written all over her face. "Really? From what I know, you're a brave man who risked his life to save my sister and her husband. You also jumped in, no questions asked, to help protect me. So I call bullshit."

"I didn't save her life. I just helped stall until the good guys could get there."

"That's not how Anna tells the story," she said, putting her hands on her hips in defiance, which only made her more attractive.

"Iris, I'm about as morally gray as they come. I've killed people before—several people."

She stared at me as though she were taking in what I said. "These people you've killed…Were they bad people who did bad things?"

"Technically, yes."

"Did you get approval from the head of the police department or your military boss-person to kill them?"

Here we were talking about killing people, and all I could think about was how damn adorable she was using terms like boss-person.

"Technically, yes," I repeated.

"So, if you hadn't killed those people, would they likely have gone on to do more bad things to more good people?"

I sighed because she was coming to the same conclusion my parents and sisters had come to, but they didn't see the whole picture. Realizing she was waiting for me to respond, I went with a non-answer. "Maybe."

"Then I don't see a problem with it."

"Iris, it's not that simple."

I really didn't want to tell her the details, but I needed to give her something so that she would understand.

"I worked special ops for the Army, and one of our missions was to locate a known terrorist who was supposedly transporting some new drone technology that was stolen from the U.S. and our allies. We were told to retrieve it and kill him."

I took a deep breath and continued. "We found him, but we were far away, looking through scopes, and my commanding officer was having a hard time confirming the box in his hand looked like the one we had been shown. He told me to hold my fire for a few more seconds while he confirmed. Unfortunately, in those moments, the man must have been tipped off, because he turned quickly, grabbed a child from behind him, and pulled him in front to use the child as cover. My commanding officer gave me the call to fire at that exact moment. I ended up killing our target and the boy that day. All because I had waited to take the shot."

She said nothing, just placed her hand on my shoulder.

"I still think about that kid often and how my slow response killed him."

"We all have moments in life we regret, but many of them are not things that we had the power to change," she said, and I saw her eyes soften.

I didn't want that either. The sympathy card just made it worse. My parents had given me that when they heard about some of the stuff Manny and I had seen while on the force.

"Okay."

"Okay?" I asked at her sudden dismissiveness.

"Yeah, okay," she repeated as if that explained every-thing. "Hector, I don't know everything about you, and I likely never will. But what I *do* know, I like. You saved my sister. You saved her husband. You helped dismantle a mafia group, and you helped me when I found that body in the lake. I'm not worried about a couple bad guys you may have sent swimming with the fishies."

I snorted, and my lip twitched. "Did you just say swimming with the fishies?"

"Isn't that what bad guys say when they kill someone?"

"Only in the movies, sweetheart," I said, feeling myself smile for the first time today, thanks to the woman in front of me.

"Oh, well, whatever. You get my point." She shrugged as if it were so simple.

God, she was so damn cute.

She leaned in closer to me, staring right at me from only a foot away, and put her hands on her hips. "I know you think this would be a bad idea, but I disagree," she told me, full of attitude.

Most people were either intimidated by me or just avoided me. Not this woman. Her stubbornness and willingness to go head-to-head with me shouldn't be a turn-on, but it was. Likely because so few people ever challenged me.

"I not only find you incredibly handsome, but you also have integrity, loyalty, and you're protective of those who mean something to you," she asserted. "Oh, and you're a sucker for a cute dog like Sarge."

At the sound of his name, Sarge perked up and nudged his head over to Iris.

"I love you, buddy," she said, leaning down to rub his head.

Hearing she loved my dog too pinched at my chest in a good way.

"I don't want to force you to do anything you don't

want to, but just know that one of us is willing to take a chance on us."

She hesitated for a moment, and I was unsure if it was because she was waiting for me to respond, or if she was trying to think of what to say next.

"I'm headed to bed," she said and then gave a small smile. "Just know…when you're ready, come and get it."

She immediately turned and began to walk down the hallway toward the room she had been staying in. About halfway down, she stopped and turned to face me. "Oh, and Hector. Earlier you said you thought I was funny. If you ever meet them, can you tell my sisters that? They don't think I am, but if a guy like you told them you thought I was funny, it would carry a lot of weight."

Her smile reached from ear to ear, and then she walked back to her room.

God, she was so damn cute. Cute and dangerous, because I realized I was willing to do just about anything to put that large smile back on her face as often as possible. Even worse—the walls I'd built to keep her at arm's length were starting to crack and crumble.

12

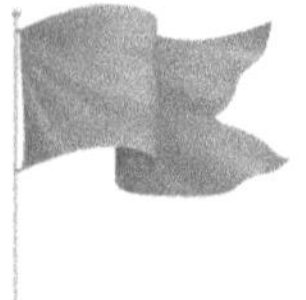

**"Fire is like a first kiss—hot, immediate,
and impossible to ignore."**
—*It's science*

Iris

After our awkward conversation last night, I decided that the best thing I could do was just give Hector time to work through his demons.

I appreciated his telling me why he thought he was morally gray and unworthy of love. I just happened to disagree. While I would be there to help in any way, I also knew he needed to come to terms with those demons himself. If it was meant to be for the two of us, then it would happen when the time was right.

What I wasn't going to do was mope around the house or work all day. I had decided to message Agent Andrews this morning and let her know I didn't feel comfortable meeting the family of the woman whose body I had found. As much as it might give them closure, it just felt awkward and uncomfortable to me. After I messaged her, I decided to redirect my energy toward having a good day.

Hector was right about me—I was a happy person. I loved finding things that made me happy and brought others joy. One of those things was cooking. So, I decided I was going to whip up a healthy breakfast. If Hector wanted some, I would share it with him. If he was still being a sourpuss, then I would take the extras over to Nancy and maybe play some cards with her today.

I also decided I might as well just go home. My landlord had finally texted first thing this morning that the maintenance guy was changing the locks.

I didn't want to bother my friends by staying with them—even though I knew they wouldn't mind. I think that was the reason I'd stayed with Hector for more than just the first night. Sure, it was also because he was gorgeous and I had a crush on him, but it was also because I secretly hadn't wanted to inconvenience any of my friends.

Hector didn't have a ton of things in his cabinets, but he did have an oddly large supply of canned pumpkin, so I decided to whip up some pumpkin pancakes. I know it was technically spring, but pumpkin spice pancakes sounded delicious.

Midway through mixing all the ingredients up, I heard the soft thuds of paws and the click-clack of nails racing down the hallway. I turned to see Sarge scurry up behind me, greeting me excitedly as if he hadn't seen me in weeks. My hands were coated in batter so I couldn't pet him, but I did at least acknowledge him.

"Hi, buddy. Good morning," I said softly, unsure if Hector was also awake or if Sarge had just escaped on his own.

Just then, Hector's voice called from down the hall. "I'm coming. Hold on, Sarge."

He turned to look at me when he came into view of the kitchen, stared at me for a second, smirked, and then turned to grab Sarge's leash and head out the door.

He'd smirked at me. Unprompted. Usually, he only did that when I said something stupid or funny. That smirk was hotter than a black car in the desert on a hot summer day. Living with this man for any longer might be the death of me—or the death of my vibrator from overuse.

He had been buttoning up his red flannel shirt when he walked out, giving me my second glimpse in a row of his gorgeous chest. He not only had amazing broad shoulders, fine-tuned to perfection, but he had chest hair—the perfect amount of chest hair.

I didn't know why I found that attractive, but I did. Hair on a man's back—no thank you. Hair on a man's chest—yes, please. I loved how a man's chest hair felt scratching up against me, and I just knew that Hector's wouldn't disappoint.

The batter was ready, so I slowly poured my mix onto the griddle. I'd honestly been surprised to find a griddle, but I assumed whoever lived here before had left it.

Five minutes later, I had my first batch of pancakes on

a plate and was pouring the next batch. I heard the door open and close and Sarge's claws scurry down the hallway. He started to whine as I finished setting the mixing bowl down.

"Whatever delicious thing you are making, do not give him any," Hector said, walking into the kitchen.

I turned to see Sarge looking up at me with big, pleading eyes. Hector was also looking at me. He leaned over to the side to see what I was making and then looked back at me again before a small grin broke out on his face.

"I think you're wearing some of your batter," he said.

I immediately looked down at the front of my shirt. Since I had a large chest, that was usually where stuff fell. I still had on my black cotton shorts and oversized, faded gray *Golden Girls* T-shirt that I had slept in, but I had managed to at least put on a bralette for support. However, bralettes weren't much, so they didn't leave much to the imagination.

Not seeing anything on my shirt, I looked back up to Hector, only to see his eyes had followed mine to my chest. His eyes were now full of heat and lust.

"I don't see anything," I told him, hating to take away that lustful look on his face, especially knowing I was the reason for it.

His eyes finally moved back up to my face, and he took two steps forward and used his thumb to wipe something from my forehead.

Crap. I must have wiped some on there when I pushed my hair back from my face.

"Do I have any in my hair?" I asked.

His eyes scanned the top of my head before looking back into my eyes.

"No, just your forehead," he responded and then curled his lip. "For now."

"I'm making pumpkin spice pancakes. The first batch is ready if you want some."

"Why did you make me pancakes?" he asked, looking at me very confused.

"I like cooking and thought it would be nice," I told him, because I wasn't sure what the issue was.

"Even after everything last night?" he asked.

I realized he probably assumed I was mad at him, so making a nice gesture clearly seemed weird.

"Hector, I'm not mad at you," I told him, hoping to clear the air. "I wish you would realize your broodiness and your past are not deterrents to me, but I'm also not going to be a jerk to you just because you don't want to be with me. I'm just not going to force myself on someone who simply doesn't want to be with me."

"Iris," he said, stepping closer to me. "Let me make something very clear. I want you. I want you more than I have wanted any other woman, but you deserve better than me, and if I let myself have you, I'll end up breaking you—ruining you."

"What if I want to be ruined?" I asked quietly, staring up into his eyes, clearly ignoring the red flag he was waving in my face.

He stared back at me for a long time. I could hear the

pancakes sizzling—likely burning—but I couldn't break away from his gaze. It was so intense, so powerful, I couldn't have broken away if I'd tried.

I could practically hear the wheels turning in his head, his mind warring over what was the right thing to do.

I knew he was never going to make the first move, so I decided to be the brave one.

I leaned forward and put my hands on his chest, continuing to stare right into his eyes.

"Iris." His deep voice made it clear that he was sending a warning not to cross that line.

Too late. I felt like being a line crosser today, because on the other side of that line was a sexy man who I knew would be worth it.

I leaned up on my tippy-toes and put my lips to his. He was stiff underneath me, as if frozen in time. He may not be reciprocating my kiss—yet—but he also wasn't pushing me away, so I sallied forth into the unknown.

I pressed my lips more firmly against his, my tongue sliding out to touch his mouth, one little lick of fire to tempt him. My hands slid up to his neck as my fingers weaved into the hair on the back of his head. It was so soft and just long enough to pull a little as I tugged his head down closer to mine to deepen the kiss.

That must've done the trick, because in that moment, Hector's body language changed. He was now an active participant, as his hands moved to my hips and pulled me closer to him while his mouth ravaged mine. One of his hands slid to my lower back, pressing me flush against him, my hard nipples brushing against his chest. His other hand moved to grab the side of my face and tilt my head exactly where he wanted it. He took control of the kiss and gave me the rough, deep kiss I had longed for. It was incredible.

I pressed my hips forward, feeling his cock rub against my stomach, wanting to feel more.

I moaned at the same time Sarge let out a loud bark and then another one, followed by a hard knock on the front door.

"Surprise! Happy birthday, big brother!" someone yelled from the other side of the door. "Open up!"

Hector released my mouth quickly. "Shit," he mumbled before leaning his forehead against mine as if to gather strength for what was about to come. "I'm apologizing now for what you are about to experience."

"It's your birthday?" I asked him.

He pulled back and stared down at me, his mouth a firm line, his eyes unblinking and serious. "Iris, do not, under any circumstances, leave me alone with them. If you're here, my family will limit their craziness. I will literally give you anything—any favor, any request—if you stay here."

I wasn't sure if I should be thrilled at what he just offered me or scared because of the underlying cause.

"Okay. Deal." I gave him a small smile in return as the wheels started turning in my head of the kind of favors I could ask for.

First, I had more important things to do. "But Hector, I need to go change first."

He looked down at me, his gaze still full of heat. "Okay, but make it fast. Do not leave me out here by myself."

"Super-fast. Promise," I said and then ran to change as fast as I possibly could.

I heard the door open, and Sarge barked a few more times as several voices filled the background. I felt this weird urge to make a good impression on his family. I didn't have enough time to fix my hair or add makeup, but I swapped my clothes, thankful I had packed my good pair of skinny jeans and a pink wrap blouse that tied around my waist and had cute flutter sleeves.

I took a deep breath and braced myself for whatever chaos Hector thought was about to happen. I was a little nervous, but Hector's eyes on me as he asked me to stay were so uneasy, I wanted to be there for him. I wanted to be the support that he needed, so I would do it. Plus, I was also secretly hoping that after they left, we could pick up where we left off in the kitchen.

Fingers crossed.

13

"A sunburn is like an ex—it leaves a mark and shows up at the worst possible time."

—It's science

Hector

"Open up, birthday boy," my sister Rita shouted again.

"Make sure you put clothes on first!" her husband yelled.

I groaned, turning to shut off the griddle so we didn't burn the house down.

Not that I hated birthdays, but my family didn't do *simple* for anything. So that meant my house was about to be invaded by my entire family, and with Iris here, there were bound to be a lot of uncomfortable looks and questions from all of them.

"Last chance," Rita yelled.

The door handle jiggled and then flew open. The family all rushed in one after another, practically tripping over each other. Sarge was already there, ready to greet everyone as they piled in. They were all talking loudly—everything from complaining that I took too long to answer the door, to why hadn't I answered my phone, to why my house smelled funny.

When you came in the front door, there was a narrow wall on the right-hand side, but it was open on the left, flowing into the living room. That small wall effectively blocked most of them from seeing me in the kitchen at first.

I noticed someone had left the door wide open, so my first task was to close and re-lock it while keeping an eye on the hallway, waiting for Iris to come back out. There was a small part of me that thought she might actually escape out the bedroom window. She would've been smart to do that, but God, I hoped she didn't.

"There he is," my dad said, followed by a round of cheers and people yelling happy birthday.

My mother and youngest sister, Dani, walked over to me and each gave me a hug.

"What is this?" Rita yelled from her spot over by the couch. "Did you pick up crochet and needlepoint as a new hobby now that you're old and in your forties?" she asked, pointing to the bag of supplies that Iris must've left on the couch.

"Those would be mine," Iris's voice sounded from the hallway. "Sorry. I can move them."

She walked into the living room to quietly collect her bag while my entire family silently stared at her, wide-eyed, as if she were an alien.

My mom, Dani, and brother-in-law JT all had giant grins on their faces, but it was my dad who spoke first.

"Hi, I'm Bruno, Hector's dad," my old man said, sticking his hand out to her as she put her bag of supplies on the side table.

"Umm, hi," Iris said nervously, shaking his hand. "I'm Iris."

"And I'm Elena, Hector's mother," she said, leaving my side to walk over to Iris and engulf her in a hug without giving her the chance to say no. "We're sorry. We didn't know he had company over."

"What she means is that we never thought you would be cool enough to have friends," Rita said to me, though loud enough for everyone to hear.

I rolled my eyes as Dani stepped up next to me and slapped me on the upper arm. I looked down at her to see she was signing to me.

Most of the time, we were good about signing while we talked so she was part of the conversation, but clearly the shock of Iris being here caught everyone off guard.

I turned to her and signed to her. *"This is Iris. She's staying with me until some repairs are made at her apartment."*

I hadn't wanted to tell everyone the whole story, so this was enough to fill them in without giving them everything.

"Is she your girlfriend?" she signed back.

Not yet, I thought.

I knew it was wrong. I had just spent the last few days

telling myself she was off-limits, that this would never work between us, and that I was no good for her. But this morning something had shifted. After seeing her this morning in her glasses and short shorts, with her amazing tits pressing against her T-shirt, messy hair, and batter on her face, something in me had snapped.

Then, she'd kissed me, and she'd tasted so damn good. Her body pressed up against me had felt so right. The control I had been reigning in just…snapped.

I decided that if she was still willing to take the risk after everything I had told her, who was I to stop her? Plus, after finally getting a taste of her this morning, I knew there was no way I could ever go back to not having her in my life.

My pause must have given my thoughts away, because Dani tapped my shoulder, bringing my attention back to her.

"Then you better introduce me if she's going to be in your life," she signed, and then her face softened. *"I'm happy for you."*

She gave me a big smile before I walked with her over to where everyone else was.

"Iris," I said, getting her attention as I walked right up next to her side. "This is my sister Dani, my other sister Rita, and her husband JT."

I pointed everyone out while also signing everyone's name so Dani could follow along.

I then introduced Iris and told them the same story about her staying with me while repairs were made to her apartment. Iris looked at me with a small smile, which I took to be appreciation for keeping it simple.

"Alright, all of you interrupted our breakfast, so make yourselves comfortable and let us finish making it," I told them, putting my hand at the small of Iris's back and guiding her back into the kitchen with me.

"We brought chilaquiles for your birthday, but I have to reheat them," my mom said, pointing to the bags on the coffee table.

"I'll put them in the fridge, and we can eat them later," I told her, knowing, like the last few birthdays, they would stay for several hours.

I grabbed the bags from the table and guided Iris back to the stove.

"You don't have to help," Iris said to me. "You can stay with your family, and I'll finish cooking. I have enough batter to feed everyone because I was going to take the extras over to Nancy later."

"I'd rather help you in the kitchen than be around them," I said, and it was the truth, because the moment they got me away from Iris, the new Spanish Inquisition would begin.

She smiled up at me. "They don't seem that bad, Hector."

"Just give it time. They're on their best behavior because you caught them off guard."

She continued smiling as she shook her head like she didn't believe me.

I turned the griddle back on as she moved to stir the

batter she had made and get ready for more pancakes. No one had ever been in this kitchen with me who wasn't related to me, but somehow it felt natural, comfortable cooking breakfast with her.

Ten minutes later, we had enough pancakes to start serving. I had a large dining room table that had come with the cabin when I moved in. It seated six, but we had seven people, so we grabbed one of my patio chairs from outside and added it to the table to make room for everyone.

Iris and I were the last to sit—by design, so I could avoid my obnoxious family as long as possible.

Don't get me wrong...I loved my family. I knew they had my back when I needed them, and I would do the same for them, but boundaries were just not something they understood.

"This is delicious," my mother said. "Where did you learn to cook, Iris?"

"My fairy godmother...Martha Stewart," Iris responded, and several people chuckled at her joke, including me.

"What was that weird noise that just came out of your mouth?" Rita asked me, looking puzzled. "Did you just attempt to laugh?"

I rolled my eyes at her as I continued to eat my pancakes.

"It's been a while since I've heard you laugh, *mijo*," my mom said to me and then turned to Iris. "You're good for him."

Jesus, I did not need these two making this more awkward and scaring Iris away.

"I'm glad you like them," Iris said to them. "Hector didn't have much in his cupboards, but he did have an oddly large supply of canned pumpkin, so I decided to wing it and go with pumpkin spice pancakes."

"Hector stocks up on those cans in the fall and keeps them around, hoping my mom will take the hint and make him pumpkin pie year-round since it's his favorite," Rita said.

Iris turned to me, a weird look on her face. "You like pumpkin pie?"

"It's my favorite," I told her.

Her face transformed into a small smile. "It's my favorite too," she said quietly.

Damn. The more I got to know this woman, the more I liked. And my mother was right—these pancakes were incredible.

A small knock on the table came from Dani, obviously trying to get our attention. She looked straight at Iris and signed, *"You've never made these pancakes before today?"*

I relayed the question to Iris and then signed back to Dani when Iris responded, "No, I will follow a recipe for a lot of things, but not usually for stuff like pancakes, soups, and omelets."

Clearly Dani—who loved to cook—was thoroughly impressed at Iris's ability to confidently create amazing tasting meals.

"They aren't always amazing," Iris shared. "I've had

some really bad ones before. I made a sriracha key lime pie that not only tasted awful, but ended up looking like soup."

There were several more chuckles from the table, along with other horror stories of things people had made or tasted over the years.

"Does anyone want any more?" Iris asked. "Otherwise, I'll wrap them up and save the rest."

"Go ahead, dear. We still have chilaquiles and birthday cake to eat," my mother replied.

I started to get up from the table to help Iris when my mom stopped me.

"Why don't you go help your father carry in the rest of the stuff from the car while I help Iris in the kitchen?"

I was about to tell her no because I knew she would just use that as an opportunity to corner Iris, but my sister interrupted.

"Oh, Dani and I can help in the kitchen too," Rita said and signed, prompting Dani to nod in response. "And JT can help you get the stuff out of the trunk."

"Let's go before it gets too hot outside," my dad said, getting up from the table.

Realizing that saying no was not an option, I decided my better alternative was to just get everything out of the car as fast as possible and be back before the women in my family scared Iris away.

Despite my best efforts to sprint to the car and gather everything in, it still wasn't fast enough. After setting all the games, presents, and items for Sarge on the table, I walked back over to the kitchen to hear my sister talking to Iris.

"I'm really glad you're not some super skinny chick with a thigh gap," Rita said to Iris.

"What the hell is that?" I asked, having never heard of a thigh gap before but not liking the fact that Rita would be nitpicking at Iris's body in any way.

Hearing my voice, Rita turned to look at me. "It was a compliment, bro, so calm down."

"Then what does it mean?" I repeated.

This time she pointed her finger in my face. "Are you a girl? No. So you wouldn't understand."

"It means she has thick thighs and big hips, both of which are *perfect* for birthing babies...and I *love* babies," my mom chimed in, emphasizing the last part.

"Mom," I warned.

"Don't *mom* me," she shot back. "Go do your thing, I've got her."

"I don't have a thing," I told her. "We already got everything out of the car."

"Okay, then go hang out with your father and JT in the living room," she countered.

She practically shooed me away, pushing me out of the kitchen.

"How old are you, dear?" I heard my mom ask Iris as I walked away very slowly.

My mother was trying to seem casual about it, but I knew damn well she was prying.

"I'm thirty," she replied.

"Oh perfect," Mom said. "Now that Hector is forty, he could use a friend who's younger to keep him on his toes."

"Mom," I all but growled.

"I'm ignoring you since you are no longer in the room and not part of this conversation," she yelled to me.

Thankfully, Iris seemed to just take it in jest by laughing.

"Do you like babies, Iris?" my mom asked next, and I just shook my head as I ran my hand up and down over my face, hoping to God Iris was still interested in me by the end of the day.

Dani waved at me from down the hallway and started to walk my way, signing, *"She'll be fine. They like her, so they won't say anything too over the top."*

I highly doubted that.

"How long have you two been seeing each other?" she signed.

"We're not," I signed back.

"So we didn't interrupt anything when we just showed up here this morning," she signed and grinned from ear to ear at me, winking.

"Possibly," I signed back, wondering how much to give away.

Dani was the sibling who would take your secrets to the grave if you asked her to, so I told her the full story about the break-in and why Iris was here.

"But you'd like there to be more?" Dani inquired, watching my face for any sign of emotion I didn't say in my words.

That was the thing about Dani—because she couldn't hear inflection in people's voices, she was incredible at reading faces, and she was one of the few people who could read me, even after all the training the military and police academy had given me on how to neutralize emotions.

Knowing she'd see right through me anyway, I simply nodded in return.

"I like her, and I hope it works out for you," she signed, smiling back at me before giving me a big hug.

Iris and Rita walked out from the kitchen, and I chose to take that as my opportunity.

"All done?" I asked Iris, and as soon as she nodded in response, I grabbed her hand. "Good. Let's go take Sarge out."

I heard Rita chuckle behind me, but I didn't care.

"I apologize on behalf of my entire family for anything that was said," I told her as we walked down the gravel drive to Sarge's favorite spot.

Iris snickered next to me. "Your family is really nice, Hector. Your mom told me that she's already picked out baby names for us and that you are prime dad material."

I stopped dead in my tracks and turned to her, shocked, my eyes as wide as they could possibly get. "She told you *what*?"

Iris full out laughed now. "Just kidding, but she did tell me that your sister Rita doesn't want kids, and Dani is too young, so the family lineage—and her hopes of multiple grandbabies—lies with you. No pressure," she said, smiling up at me.

"You do know that her telling you that means she hopes that *you* will be the one to give her those babies, yes?"

"Relax, Hector," she said, starting to walk forward again, and I followed. "I told her I don't sign contracts without reading the fine print first."

I said nothing in response, but internally I would have enjoyed seeing the look on my mom's face when Iris said that.

"Maybe she just sees something between us that you're too broody to admit," she said. "Guess it's a good thing I don't scare too easily when it comes to you."

God, this woman. I'd spent years building walls and keeping people out, and this woman was bulldozing them faster than a speeding bullet.

"Do you want kids…eventually, I mean?" she asked me, trying to sound nonchalant about it, but there was definitely genuine curiosity.

"I did when I was younger, and I can't say that I don't anymore, but I'm not getting any younger," I told her honestly. "You usually have to be married or at least in a relationship for that to happen, and I haven't had either of those."

I chose to deflect instead of allowing her to ask me more questions. "What about you?"

"I definitely want kids," she responded. "I'd like

several, but they don't have to be mine biologically. I'm open to adoption like my family did."

I was happy for her that she'd ended up with such a good adopted family, because not every child did. She deserved to have a family of her own, and I wanted that for her. I found myself wanting to be the one to give it to her—a thought I had never had with any other woman. Ever.

We walked to the side of the gravel driveway where it was a little flatter, and Iris started to throw the tennis ball for Sarge.

I just stood by and watched her, enjoying the view of her sexy body in front of me and her contagious laugh as she played with Sarge. I wouldn't mind having her around more to enjoy days like today—minus my crazy family.

We finally made our way back up to my house, only to find JT and Rita making out on my front porch.

"Dude, could you not feel up my sister right in front of me?" I asked my brother-in-law.

"Could I? Sure," he responded. "Am I gonna stop? Nope."

And he didn't.

"If you want, I can go tell your mom they're about to make her a grandbaby on the front porch," Iris suggested with an evil grin.

I laughed, genuinely laughed, at the thought of my mom coming out to chat about babies and essentially cock-blocking JT in the process.

Despite having just finished eating breakfast less than

thirty minutes ago, there was so much food back on the table. In the time we had walked Sarge, my mom had cooked up the chilaquiles and my father had whipped up some sangria.

My mother's side of the family was from Mexico, and my father's side was Portuguese and Spanish. They said all the time that food was their love language, especially when we had large family gatherings.

Two more meals, three games, and four pitchers of sangria later, my family was all finally packing up for the day and headed home.

Iris had been sitting next to me on the couch, leaned up against me, half asleep and hiccupping. She'd had three full glasses of the sangria—and my father usually made it strong.

Dani and JT were the designated drivers for the evening, so I helped them rally the rest of the troops into their respective car rides home.

When I walked back up to house, Iris was standing in the doorway with a goofy, semi-drunk smile on her face. God, I wanted to kiss her and take her to bed so damn bad, but I wasn't going to do that with her inebriated. I also didn't want her going back to her apartment like this either.

"It's late and you're not exactly sober, so just stay here again tonight, okay?"

"Okay," she said, still smiling, but she took a few steps closer to me and put her body flush up against the front of mine.

"I feel safe here with you," she said softly, mindlessly running her fingers over my beard at my jawline. "I know if anyone were to try to hurt me, you would stop them."

Damn, if that didn't make me feel good, knowing I gave that peace to her. One good thing about looking like a scary, dangerous asshole was that she took solace in that, knowing I could protect her.

"Your natural badassery skills are awesome," she said, moving her hand from my beard down to intertwine with my hand at my hip.

She pulled me inside toward the couch. We both sat, me sitting upright against the back of the couch, and Iris sitting facing my left side.

"Happy birthday, Hector," she said quietly to me. "Did you have a good birthday?"

I did, though I'd specifically told my mother I did not want a bunch of people over. I had told her earlier in the week that I would text her in the morning and meet them all for dinner somewhere. Somewhere that wasn't my house.

"Yes. That was the least awkward encounter with my family I think I've had in years, and it was all because of you, so thank you," I told her.

"I really want to make out with you like teenagers," she said, smiling, her glassy eyes and pink cheeks indicating she was still buzzed.

"I know at some point you'll regret being with me, Iris, because I'm a grumpy asshole who's done some bad things," I told her. "But I don't want to make that regret happen sooner by taking you to bed while you're tipsy and you wake up tomorrow morning wishing you hadn't let me take advantage of you."

She stared contemplatively at me for a few moments, or maybe she was struggling to get her thoughts together since she was still tipsy.

"You're a good man, Hector."

"I'm really not, Iris, but I'm glad you think so."

14

Iris

I woke up the next morning with a slight headache and my phone chirping like crazy.

I rolled over to grab the annoying device, realizing I was in Hector's guest bedroom. Memories from the night before started to flood back to me. I had practically thrown myself at him after having a few glasses of his dad's amazing sangria.

My heart melted a little more, knowing that he didn't take advantage because he didn't want me to think less of him. I didn't think that was possible, though. I'd watched this brute of a man almost throw down with Rita—his own sister— when he thought she was talking crap about my body. I'd also watched him sign back and forth to his other sister Dani and had seen her melt into him. The more I learned about Hector, the more I knew I wanted to be with him.

Opening up my phone, I pulled up the family group chat to see a whole bunch of messages.

AUNTIE:

Oooh, ladies, I got a new smut book from the book fair, and it is soooooo good! It's about a sexy Scottish highlander with a giant swizzle stick under his kilt.

HAZEL:

Did you seriously just say swizzle stick?

CORA:

She did, and now I think I'm going to puke.

GALE:

At least she didn't come and wake you up this morning and offer to read you one of her favorite scenes so far.

AUNTIE:

I'm just saying it's a good book and you girls should read it.

ANNA:

No, thanks. I'm good.

HAZEL:

Yeah, Anna has a husband now, so she prefers his swizzle stick.

MOM:

Now I'm the one who's going to puke.

I chuckled at the absurdity of their comments and then switched off that thread and went to my other unread texts. I saw a few from Cora only and pulled those up.

> CORA:
>
> Morning, sunshine! How are you feeling today? 😉

I rolled my eyes at the winking emoji she'd added.

> CORA:
>
> I think I'll swing by your office around 3p if that's okay?
>
> CORA:
>
> If you're still busy, I can occupy myself until you're done.
>
> CORA:
>
> Do you want to go out to eat, or just grab something and take it back to your place?

What was she talking about? She was coming here?

I scrolled back in the conversation to see that she and I had texted last night—after my multiple sangrias. Oh crap.

CORA:

Hey, I'm coming down to Vegas
tomorrow to set up some new testing
equipment at Lake Echo over by the new
bridge near the dam. I don't know how
long it's going to take, so I may just stay
the night and come back the next day.
Can I stay with you, or do you want me
to get a hotel?

ME:

Stay with me!

ME:

I haven't been back to my place in a
few days

ME:

I'm at Hector's house

ME:

But I have no more clothes

CORA:

What?! Who's Hector? Call me!

ME:

I can't

ME:

It's Hector's birthday

ME:

His family is here. They gave me sangria
and it is so yummy!

It was a little humiliating seeing the drooling emojis I
had put after that line. I definitely had too many sangrias.

CORA:

Lmao. How many sangrias have you had?

ME:

A few

ME:

I think I'm gonna make out with Hector again after his family leaf

ME:

Leafs

ME:

Shit

ME:

Leaves

CORA:

Go drink some water and go to sleep, but you better give me ALL the details tomorrow!

Welp. I guess I was going back to my apartment today, and Cora was staying the night with me. Apparently, in my drunken state, I had told her to bunk with me. Oh, and I guess I had a lot of explaining to do at dinner tonight.

I shot her back a quick text letting her know that three this afternoon worked fine and that we could just get food delivered to my place.

I didn't want to go back to my apartment. I knew I needed to, if for no other reason than to get my own sense of confidence back. I didn't want to let whoever broke into my place take over the space, and there was no time like the present. Plus, with Cora there, it would be a little easier.

But I didn't want to. I wanted to stay here with Hector.

He'd kissed me. Well, technically I'd kissed him first, but then he kissed me back. Part of me wanted to stay here to see if I could get him to open up to me more. But I also knew I needed to give him some time.

This wasn't about forcing him to be with me. He'd told me he'd wanted me—that he was interested in me—but he just didn't think himself worthy. I needed to show him that he was and that it was worth taking a chance on us.

There was just something about him that made me want to lay myself all out there. Lay myself bare—in more ways than one.

I knew I needed to talk with him about it, but I also needed to get ready for work, and so did he. But first... coffee. I needed one cup to get rid of my hangover, one cup to wake myself up, and probably one more cup to prepare myself for the intense conversation I would be having with my sister and co-workers today.

I set an alarm on my phone for twelve minutes. Long enough to brew a quick pot of coffee, enjoy the caffeine a little, and then get in the shower before Hector took me to get my car. It was a little chilly in Hector's house—I'd learned he liked to keep his air conditioning set for just barely above freezing—especially since the only other pajamas I'd brought were a pair of dark-gray cotton shorts and a lavender tank top with a built-in shelf bra. It was fine, though. This would be quick, and then I could take a nice hot shower.

I hadn't heard Sarge or Hector, so I assumed they were both still asleep. Trying to be quiet, I grabbed my glasses off the nightstand and made my way quietly out to the kitchen. As I turned the corner coming around to the kitchen, Sarge's cute face greeted me. He was sitting just outside the refrigerator. He seemed torn about whether to come to me or stay put, which meant Hector was awake and likely had food nearby that Sarge was hoping to benefit from.

Finally rounding the wall to the kitchen, I saw Hector leaning against the counter, eating one of the leftover pancakes with one hand and holding his coffee in the other.

There he was in that damn flannel again. This time it was a navy and green flannel shirt and some loose track shorts. The way his flannel shirt stretched around his arms like it was straining to break free made my ovaries swoon.

I smiled at him, even though that made my head hurt a little more, and made my way around the counter to get to some of that delicious-smelling coffee.

"Morning," I called out.

"Morning," his gravelly voice echoed through the space. "How're you feeling?"

"Slight headache, but otherwise good."

"I should have warned you that my dad makes the sangria strong."

"It's okay," I told him. "It tasted great. I'll be fine once I get some caffeine in me."

"Here, I'll get you a cup," he said, reaching up into the cabinet and grabbing me a mug. "What time do you need to be at work? I can drop you off before I head in for the day."

He worked at pouring the coffee while I grabbed the milk from the fridge.

"Actually, could you drop me off at my apartment? I need to get my car because my sister is in town today, and apparently in my semi-drunken state last night, I invited her to stay with me at my place," I explained. "And I'll need my car to drive us both home from work since she's meeting me there."

"Which sister is this?" he asked.

"Cora. She's the state hydrologist. She's based in Reno, but she does a bunch of work down here too, and she usually just bunks with me so she can save money."

"Doesn't the state pay for that?"

"They do," I told him. "But if she can save money on a hotel, then she can use that money for other research projects."

"Okay, give me ten minutes to shower and get dressed, and then I'll drive you to get your car," he said, taking another sip of his coffee. "I'd like to check your door anyway to see if your maintenance guy really did fix the locks."

God, he was so sweet.

"For what it's worth, Hector, I enjoyed staying here," I told him, walking closer to him. "Especially making pancakes."

I smiled at him, remembering what had happened while I made pancakes, and clearly, he did too, because he produced a large grin.

"You did, did you?" He set his coffee down on the counter and closed the gap even more between us. "What did you like about it?"

His hands went to my hips and pulled me closer as I tilted my head back to look right into his eyes.

"I liked how your beard felt against my face," I told him, running my hands over his flannel shirt, hoping I could sneak my fingers up to the top buttons and undo them so I could steal a glance at his chest hair. "I think I liked the kiss too, although it's been so long, I can't really remember."

I had no shame in flirting. If I were interested in a guy, I would go for it. Sometimes, it wasn't reciprocated, and that was fine. But I wasn't the type to sit back and wonder what-if about a scenario like this. Especially with Hector.

"Hmmm, then maybe I should kiss you again so you can see if you liked it," he said, his voice low and rough as he leaned down to do just that.

It was light at first, as his beard tickled my face. Then his hand sifted into my hair, and he pulled me in closer as he deepened the kiss. I felt shivers run through my whole body as I tasted his coffee on my lips and tongue.

I moaned, causing him to release my lips and pull back. I immediately felt gloomy and mourned his lips leaving.

Finally opening my eyes, I caught him staring. His expression was different—focused, almost speculative—and the weight of it made me squirm.

"What?" I asked. "Do I have something on my face again?"

I knew I wasn't much to look at in my ugly pajamas, glasses, and hair that would scare small children, but the way he looked at me felt like more than a casual notice.

"No," he said, though I wasn't sure I believed him. His gaze didn't falter, only grew sharper, and when I shifted uncomfortably, his arms tightened around me.

"Well, Hector, you're staring so hard, it's kind of difficult not to feel self-conscious," I pointed out.

His mouth curved, but his voice was rough. "Iris, you walked in here with totally fuckable hair and your nipples peeking through your shirt. You have no idea how much of a temptation you are right now."

I blinked, completely at a loss for words.

He leaned closer, voice low. "Ever since I was a teenage boy and discovered the joys of masturbation, I conjured images of my ideal woman. Every single one of those images looked exactly like the woman in front of me right now. I just need a moment to take this in. My dream woman is right in front of me."

Holy crap...Did he just say that?

"Tell me to stop, Iris," he said, and I could see the battle he was fighting internally with himself.

"I don't want you to stop," I told him, taking my hands and running them up over his chest, hoping to pull the top open a little more so I could see some chest hair. "I want you to kiss me, Hector. Kiss me again."

I slid my hands up higher, looping my arms around his neck and pulling his head down closer to mine. And that was the straw that broke the sexy camel's back.

His lips crashed onto mine, claiming them.

I opened my lips slightly, giving him my not-so-subtle permission to slide his tongue in...and he did. His tongue swirled in tandem with mine, letting me taste the coffee he'd just drunk while inhaling his natural scent of pine and clean laundry.

His hands slid down over my ass, and he squeezed tight as he pulled me impossibly closer. I felt his length harden against my stomach.

Brrrrrring. Brrrrrring. Brrrrrring.

My alarm startled me out of the kissing haze Hector had put me in.

"Sorry!" I scrambled to grab my phone off the counter and turn the alarm off. "I set that so I didn't run late getting into the shower before we had to leave."

I turned back to Hector, seeing he was now two steps back with his hands on his hips.

"Go get in the shower," he said. It wasn't mean, but it was clear that this wonderful make-out session was over.

I didn't feel the same. "You could join me," I said, taking two steps forward and poking the bear. "Want to?"

"Yes," he replied, but he didn't move an inch. "But the first time I'm inside you, I want to take my time. I need hours, and we don't have that right now."

Hours? My breathing started to pick up as I pictured spending hours with Hector...naked...his hands all over me...and his mouth. Yeah, I wanted to take my time with him too.

"Okay," I grumbled, not really wanting to delay this, but I understood.

"I'll make it up to you," he said, which once again brought me back to my X-rated thoughts.

Oh, the thoughts I had right now.

"Iris," he said, startling me back into the here and now. "How long is your sister staying?"

I stared at him, wondering why he'd asked. "Umm... she, uh...leaves tomorrow afternoon."

"Do you have any immediate plans after she leaves?"

"No, why?" I asked, a bit confused.

"Have dinner with me."

Ohmigod.

"Like, a date?" I asked, perhaps a little too excitedly, because my question elicited a sexy smirk from Hector.

"Yes, Iris, a date," he said, that grin growing bigger as his hands moved from his hips to mine.

"Okay," I whispered and then smiled huge.

"Shower," he commanded and then kissed my forehead. "Go, before both of us get fired for never coming in to work today."

I relented because now I had something to look forward to.

A date. With Hector!

Too giddy to contain my excitement, I leaned up and kissed his mouth quickly and then ran off to take my shower.

This was going to be a great day.

15

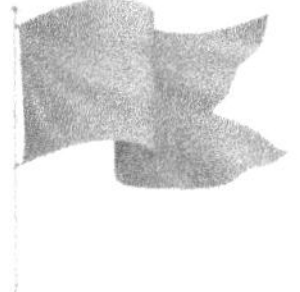

Hector

This was turning out to be a hell of a day.

It started with the worst case of blue balls I'd ever had thanks to Iris. That smile on her face when I'd asked her out on a date was dangerous. Dangerous because I realized—yet again—that I would do just about anything to put that look on her face as often as possible, including possibly getting fired because I chose to stay in bed all day fucking her senseless instead of going in to work.

Instead, we took separate showers—mine being a cold one, which ended up not helping, so I took myself in hand to thoughts of her naked body underneath mine. An hour later, I dropped her off at her apartment after checking to make sure her door had been fixed properly—it had—and then made my way to work.

Then, I'd been volunteered—more like volun-told—to assist with our junior ranger science lesson this morning.

By the time I got back to my office, I ended up eating my lunch at my desk while filling out timecards and schedules. I was mid-bite of my sandwich when my phone rang.

It had better not be anyone else calling in sick. Having Diden out today was already bad enough.

"Madeira," I answered grumpily.

"Good morning, sunshine. It's Agent Andrews," she said on the other line. "Got a minute?"

"Yeah, what's up?" I asked her, hoping she'd skip the chit chat and get to the point.

"Apparently, Steve Stanton decided to showcase our body on his podcast episode last night," she informed me, causing me to roll my eyes.

"What did he say?" I asked, and I knew she couldn't miss the agitation in my tone.

"I'm not entirely sure since I didn't listen to the whole thing," she said. "However, I was informed by no fewer than three people this morning that dear old Steve made a comment about the cotton ball found in Iris's apartment."

She paused, allowing me to take in what she had just said, and I knew why—that information had not been released to the public.

"You thinkin' we got a leak? Or an unintentional confession?" I asked.

"Don't know yet," she said. "I plan to reach out to him today to strike up a conversation, but there's about a dozen people at both the local PD and here at the ISB who knew about it, so a leak isn't entirely out of the question."

"Iris knows, and I also told two of my highest-serving rangers—Diden and Jennings—since they've been on this case since the beginning," I told her so she knew there were a few more.

"I figured," she said. "Do me a favor, though, and start keeping info close to your chest from now on."

"You got it," I told her.

"Alright, have a good one. I'll be in touch," she said and then ended the call.

Great. The last thing I needed was this nut making this case more complicated than it already was.

Going back to my sandwich, I took a big bite...just in time for the phone to ring again.

Dammit.

This time it was my cell, so at least I could see it was Archer, Iris's brother-in-law, calling.

"Hector," I answered.

"Hey, man. Got a heads-up from a buddy still workin' at LVPD letting me know my Iris had her apartment broken into. The report also says you showed up because it might be related to a case you were workin' on. Anything I need to be worried about?"

I knew Iris said she had mentioned the body to her sister, but I wasn't sure if she had mentioned the break-in. I also didn't know how much Anna had shared with her husband.

"How much do you know about the dead body?" I

asked, deciding I better figure that out so I didn't repeat anything.

After a brief pause, Archer spoke. "Did you say a dead body?" He'd asked in a way that I knew this was brand-new news to him.

Well, shit.

I started from the beginning, filling him in on the discovery at Lake Echo all the way up through the break-in. However, after my conversation with Agent Andrews, I opted to leave out the cotton ball part.

"How bad was the break-in?"

"Nothing was taken," I told him, deciding to go with the truth but not the whole truth. "Police still aren't sure if it was a random break-in or related to the body from the lake."

"What do you think?" he asked, because he knew that even if the evidence wasn't always clear, someone in law enforcement usually had hunches about these kinds of things. "Do I need to get her moved to another apartment?"

"She's stayed with me the last few nights. Partly because her landlord took his sweet time getting her locks changed, and partly because I'm leanin' toward it not being a random break-in."

There were a few moments of silence as he took all of that information in.

"She's staying with you?"

This was where the conversation could go one of two ways. I could play it off as no big deal—just me doing a favor for my friend's sister-in-law. Or I could tell him that I planned to make her mine, and while she wasn't sleeping at my place tonight, she would be back at my place soon enough, and I planned to figure out a way to keep her there.

As much as I knew he would understand, it felt weird having that conversation with Archer before I had it with Iris, so I opted for the first option...for now.

"She called me right after it happened because she was concerned about the connection to the case," I said. "After talking with the cops—one of whom I had worked with back at the LVPD—they suggested she not sleep there that first night so they could get everything they needed. So, I offered my guest room, and she took it. It was that or staying with her eighty-year-old neighbor next door."

"She called you right after it happened?" he questioned. "Didn't know you guys were that close."

I heard the accusatory tone in his voice.

"She had my number from the incident at the lake and thought this might be related, so she called," I repeated. "She's staying at her place tonight with her sister Cora, but if I get word of something else going down, I'll let you know, and I'll make sure to keep an eye on her."

"Appreciate it," he said, and I could hear a little bit of relief in his voice. "Thanks, man."

I hung up with the promise to keep him informed of any new updates.

As I finally finished my lunch, my thoughts drifted

right back to Iris—and they stayed there the rest of my shift. Front and center in my mind was kissing her in my kitchen, along with the way her body felt pressed up against mine—soft and supple. I imagined her bare underneath me, begging me not to stop, as I brought both of us intense pleasure for hours on end.

I also thought about our date tomorrow. I wanted her. God, did I want her. But I also wanted to take her out, to show her that I wasn't *just* after sex. She deserved more than that. She deserved better than me, but for some reason, she was willing to overlook that.

Which was dangerous, because the more I thought about her, the more I realized I was already falling hard for her, which was all the more reason I wanted to give this a shot—a real shot.

Over the last few days, I'd noticed she had a hard time accepting a compliment. When I mentioned how gorgeous her body was the other day, she'd accepted the praise with a smile, but there had been some hesitation— a little flicker of doubt in her eyes. I wasn't sure if that was from her upbringing of not having a loving, affec- tionate family in the beginning, or if she'd dated some asshole in the past who'd chipped away at her self-esteem and brought her down so she didn't know her own worth.

By the time I got home, I tried to burn off my excess energy with Sarge, taking him on a long walk. Didn't matter, though. The second we were back, he flopped in front of her bedroom door like he was waiting for her to come back. I couldn't blame him. I felt the same pull.

Clearly, I wasn't the only one in this house thinking of Iris.

I grabbed dinner and dropped onto the couch. I'd eaten in front of the TV for years without a second thought, but after a few nights of sharing the table and meals with Iris, the silence felt lonely for the first time—even hollow.

I had leaned over to grab the remote from the table when I saw her bag of craft supplies. Needle-something, she'd called it.

My fingers itched to text her, to use it as an excuse just to see her name light up on my phone. I pulled it out and then paused—her sister was in town. She deserved that time with her. I could wait until tomorrow.

Tomorrow—a date where I planned to pull out all the stops. In my twenties, I never bothered. Back then, it was all about quick, no-strings, with a woman who wanted the same thing. But I was older now, and Iris wasn't some fling. She was already under my skin, in my head, and in my bed in ways I couldn't stop imagining.

Still, no harm in a little reminder. Maybe even a picture.

ME:

> Hey, Iris. Enjoy your time with your sister.
> Just letting you know you left this here.
> I'll bring it tomorrow when I pick you up.
> 6p okay?

IRIS:

I think I was a little distracted this
morning and totally forgot it. ;)

IRIS:

Thank you. And yes, 6p is perfect.

I really wanted to make a comment about her being distracted, but I chose to let it go. I was a forty-year-old man acting like a teenage boy. I chuckled at the thought. If my teenaged self knew that I had a date with a woman who looked like Iris tomorrow, I think I would have spent the next twenty-something years looking forward to it.

I grinned just thinking about it. And that grin stayed on my face for the rest of the night.

16

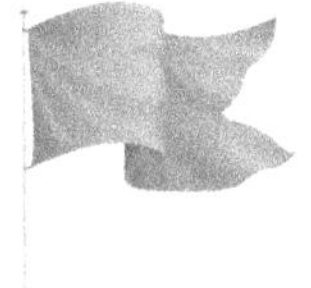

Iris

What a busy day.

It started off fantastic with me making out with Hector and him asking me out on a date—yes, please!

Soon after, it shot off into nonstop busy with me racing to get changed into my work clothes and off to the office and then trying to get all my work done before my sister showed up.

The only problem was everything derailed when I got to work. Apparently, Agent Andrews had called my boss this morning to inform him about the break-in to my apartment and that they weren't entirely sure it was random, which meant they wanted to make sure our building took extra precautions.

I walked into the main room with six people all

standing around as our boss explained the details of our new security measures for everyone. Then, all eyes turned to me.

"You were robbed?" Leah shrieked.

"Technically, they never stole anything," I tried to explain, but Christine cut me off.

"More importantly, why didn't you call me?" Christine asked, looking offended. "You could have stayed with me."

"You were working overnights," I said, trying to justify my reasoning, even though I knew it was a weak excuse.

"No disrespect, but can you really blame her for picking Hector over you?" Calvin chimed in.

"Yes. Yes, I can," Christine answered, still upset.

I tried to soothe things over by giving them the details of what had happened, though it appeared our boss, Stan, had already filled them in on most of the important factors.

Hector had asked—well, ordered—me to tell Stan so that he could be sure someone kept an extra close eye on the security cameras at our office.

"So, you spent multiple nights with Hector the Convector, eh?" Calvin asked, raising his eyebrows up and down suggestively.

Before I could answer though, Stan cut in. "Alright, you got the important info, now get back to work and leave her alone."

Everyone nodded and became fudgels—people who pretended to work but instead got absolutely nothing done—for the few minutes it took him to get out of sight. Once our boss had retreated back to his office, they all swooped back in like vultures.

"Where did you sleep?" Calvin asked.

"Did your clothes happen to fall off randomly at any point in time while you were staying with him?" Christine inquired.

"A lady never kisses and tells," Leah added. "Unless you want to, in which case I am all here for it."

I laughed at all three of them.

"I slept in his guest room. No, my clothes never accidentally fell off in front of him, but..." I paused for dramatic effect. "I do have a date with him tomorrow night."

Leah squealed, Christine clapped, and Calvin tilted his head to the side as if he were thinking very deeply about something.

"Where is he taking you?" he asked.

"Umm...I don't know. He hasn't told me yet," I responded. "Why?"

"Because I think Leah, Christine, and I are due for a friends' dinner tomorrow," Calvin said. "And if it just happens to be at the same place...how convenient!"

"No way," I told them all, shaking my head.

I was not going to let them intrude on what I had hoped would be my last first date. I decided at that moment that even if Hector did text me to tell me where we were going, I would guard that secret with my life.

I decided to change the subject and move on.

"Cora is coming here later today, by the way," I told them, filling them in on the project she was working on.

Thankfully, that pivot worked, and everyone seemed to let go of the topic of Hector—for now.

Apparently, Cora's project down at the bridge ran late, so by the time she was able to meet up, I had already finished for the day, so I just picked her up since it wasn't too far.

I was nervous about having the conversation with her about what had gone down at my apartment, especially since my coworkers had mildly flipped out.

Thankfully, I was spared during the car ride back to my apartment because Cora's supervisor called, trying to arrange for some testing to be done tomorrow where her new equipment was placed.

After we got back to my place, Cora went to take a shower to wash off all the river junk on her body while I changed into comfier clothes and ordered us some takeout from the Italian place down the street. Girls' night tonight was going to be full of deep conversations, so I needed carbs and wine.

Cora came out of the bathroom just as the food was delivered.

"Oh my God, that smells incredible," Cora said, practically drooling as she walked into my small kitchen. "No need to be fancy with plates. I'm good to eat right out of this container."

"Good, cause I wasn't gonna give you one anyway," I teased, handing her a fork, a food container, and the glass of wine I'd poured for her.

We sat at my tiny little table for two just next to the kitchen. It was an epic secondhand find from when I first moved here, with wooden chairs that had a navy-blue stain. They were brushed to look old, but the set probably was only ten years old.

The small table matched and had a half circle that folded up or down on the side, depending on whether you needed more space. Tonight, we propped that semi-circle up so we could spread our food out and share it.

"Okay, girl," Cora said, scooping up a big bite of ravioli. "Start with the dead body and work your way up to staying with a man the past two days, since I have a feeling there is a lot in between those events that I am missing."

Here went nothing.

I started with everything that had happened at Lake Echo, including meeting Hector there. Cora knew a little bit about Hector, having met him at Anna's wedding last year. Then I told her about the letter from Steve.

"Three days ago, I came home from work to find someone had broken into my apartment," I said, trying to tread carefully.

As soon as the words were out of my mouth, hers fell open, along with the pasta that had been inside. Her mouth still wide open, she turned her head slowly as if to scan the room behind her.

Using her fork to point toward my living room behind her, she finally spoke. "Someone broke in here? What did they steal? Was there much damage? Did you call the cops?"

Her rapid-fire questions didn't give me much of a chance to interrupt, but eventually I broke in. "Yes, someone broke in. I don't know if they stole anything or not. There wasn't really any damage to speak of. And yes, I called the cops."

She started to talk again, but I held up my hand to get her to pause. "Let me finish."

I gave her all the details of what had happened at my apartment and told her that I had also called Hector, since not only had he been a former cop, but there was a chance it was related to the body. I also mentioned how the cops had recommended I not stay at my apartment that first night, which was how I ended up staying with Hector.

"Which reminds me, do you mind if I stop by next door after dinner for a minute or two and talk with Nancy? She was here through all of it, and I wanted to give her an update and thank her in person. I brought her some leftover pumpkin spice pancakes."

"Yes, of course. Oh, my God, I love her," Cora said.

She had come over a few times with me to play cards and games at Nancy's apartment and loved her just as much as I did.

As if he knew we were already discussing him, my

phone buzzed with a new text. Seeing Hector's name pop up put a smile on my face.

"Either you just found out you won the lottery, or I'm guessing Hector just texted you," she said, sing-songing his name as she prodded for info.

I looked down to read the text, seeing the photo of my needlework and crochet supplies.

I tried to flirt a little with my response when he mentioned me forgetting my needlepoint supplies, but I also couldn't help the beaming smile that overtook my face as I thought about tomorrow night.

"Yep, definitely Hector putting that disgustingly dreamy smile all over your face," Cora teased.

She sighed loudly and slapped her hands on the table. "Alright, if I eat any more, I'm going to burst. Let's go say hi to Nancy, and then we can come back and sit on the couch. I need to unbutton my pants and let my stomach expand while you tell me all about this hot man you stayed with the last few days."

I grinned, feeling the exact same way. We packed the leftovers up and put them in the fridge, and I grabbed the container full of pancakes before we made our way over to Nancy's.

Cocoa's incessant barking greeted us as soon as we knocked, followed by Nancy's big smile as she opened the door.

"Two O'Hara sisters at once. It must be my lucky day," she greeted and ushered us in.

She offered us food as usual, but we told her we would

explode if we ate anything, so we opted for some decaf coffee she had already brewed.

"I saw Richard over there fixing your door locks the other day. Did he get everything else good over there?" Nancy asked about our maintenance man.

"Yeah, it's all good," I responded.

"I also couldn't help but notice tonight'll be the first night you've been back to sleep here," Nancy mentioned with a sly grin on her face.

"Yeah, I stayed a few extra nights with Hector. Mostly because he wouldn't let me stay until the door was fixed, and Richard had a slight delay with that, and also, because it was his birthday, so I stayed to celebrate with him."

"And how old is that handsome man?" Nancy pried.

"He just turned forty," I replied.

"So, he's...ten years older," Cora said, doing the math out loud.

"That's a good thing, honey," Nancy said. "Men don't mature as fast as women, so it's best to get them a few years older when they are easier to whip into shape."

I chuckled at her reasoning, especially with a man like Hector, who I imagined wouldn't let anyone other than himself decide what he did.

"Do you have any pictures of him?" Cora asked. "I wanna know what he looks like."

"A picture cannot do that man justice," Nancy chimed in. "Let me put it this way...That man will have a successful career as a romance novel cover model if his little ranger thing doesn't work out."

Cora barked out a laugh, and I smiled, picturing Hector hear that she described his job as a "little ranger thing."

Nancy would know, though. She spent more than thirty years as a romance writer, and a bestseller at that. I'd read several of her novels, and they were fantastic.

"I mean it," Nancy continued. "If I had knees that still worked, I'd be chasing him myself."

I smiled at her comment, thinking back to where Hector and I had started and where we were now. I was hopeful about our date tomorrow and what would come after.

"Honey, your relationship life is your business," Nancy said to me. "So, if you aren't interested in him, that's your choice. However, if you do decide to give that boy a chance, I'll give you some of my books so you can casually leave them around your apartment so he can get some hints."

She winked, and Cora chuckled even more.

"I've got a really steamy shower scene in one of them, so we will put that one at the top of the stack," Nancy added, and I nearly spit out my drink.

"I don't have a man, or any potential ones at that, but I wanna read that one just for fun," Cora told her.

"I'll get you your own copy before you leave, dear," Nancy said, pointing at her.

We stayed and chatted with her for another hour, and

she made me promise to ask Hector if he would come over for card night one night just so she could show him off to all her other friends.

I made no promises that he would actually come—because I highly doubted he would—but told her I would try.

"Here, take some cake with you," Nancy said, grabbing some slices from her counter. "Don't worry, ladies. This cake only goes straight to your boobs."

I laughed as Cora reached for the cake. "Iris already has big boobs, so I'll just eat both of them."

We said goodnight and made our way back to my place.

"Change of plans," Cora said as we walked into my living room. "Let's just get our pajamas on and lie in your bed while you give me all the other details about Hector that you wouldn't say in front of Nancy but that I could see written all over your face."

She eyed me, giving me a knowing look.

My lip twitched. We may not be blood related, but she knew me so well. Growing up, I had been closest to Anna since we shared a room together and had moved into the O'Haras' house around the same time. But in the last two years, I had gotten closer to Cora since we lived the closest and her work often allowed her to work side-by-side with me.

Hydrology and meteorology were very closely related, plus we both worked careers where the job didn't stop just because it was a Saturday or Sunday. In fact, Mother

Nature often enjoyed throwing massive storms at us on a weekend or holiday. That meant that I would sometimes get called in to help out, even though I didn't usually work those days.

Despite still being very full, Nancy made amazing cake that should only be eaten while fresh—which was why we decided to eat it in my bed with our stretchy pajama pants on.

"Alright," she mumbled with a mouthful of cake. "Give me the low-down on Hector. You get two to three lines max to describe him and tell me how you feel about him. Then I get to ask more questions."

Only two to three lines? How the heck was I supposed to do that?

"His nickname should be Grumpy McSexypants," I tried to explain as Cora snorted. "He's really tall and handsome, and his smile does things to my ovaries that science can't explain."

She laughed. "Okay, oddly, I like him even more after that very colorful description."

"He also loves my body and told me I was his dream woman," I confessed quietly.

She gazed over at me, and her face softened. She understood how much that meant to me.

I loved my body and how I looked and had no problem ignoring people who felt otherwise about my shape—but I hadn't always felt that way. Kids, and even adults, could be cruel—and they were. It was bad enough growing up in a household where love and encouragement were not given freely. Then, moving into foster care meant a new school and new kids. And all of this happened during my pre-teen and teen years—years when your body changed rapidly and kids were at their peak for cruelty.

But when it came to guys, especially a man you might have a crush on, that cruelty could crush a young girl's self-esteem so fast. I was never going to be tall and skinny, so I needed a guy whose dream woman looked just like me—full of hips, full of tits, and full of attitude.

So now, finding out that Hector thought I had a *dream body* and was his *dream woman*—this changed everything, especially since, if I were being honest with myself, I knew I was already falling hard for this man.

"Then we need to go all out for this date of yours tomorrow," she said, her face gleaming.

I had told her and Nancy about my date earlier. Cora offered to help me pick out my outfit, and Nancy offered to not-so-subtly give Hector a copy of her bestseller when he showed up tomorrow.

"You should wear your red wrap dress," Cora declared, snapping her finger and pointing at me. "The low neckline makes your boobs look great, and the wrap part highlights your waist. Yep...decision made. Now on to shoes."

She quickly hopped off the bed and wandered into my closet, though she was only gone for about thirty seconds.

"These," she said, popping back out of my closet and holding up a pair of strappy black heels. They were my four-inch stilettos and nearly impossible to walk in, but they were also incredibly stunning and looked gorgeous on me—which was why I bought them instantly, even though they weren't on sale.

"Do you have any sexy lingerie to go with it?" she asked.

I thought about what I had in my drawers, and instantly the red lace teddy I had bought a few months ago came to mind. I hadn't actually worn it yet since I hadn't had an occasion for it. It was definitely sexy, and it also had a control panel around the midsection to help suck in and smooth everything out. I loved it, but again, I hadn't had a reason to wear it yet—until now.

I tried to picture what Hector's face would look like if he saw me in it. The same lustful gaze he gave me this morning in the kitchen, perhaps. Maybe a completely new look I hadn't yet experienced. I smiled just picturing it.

I couldn't wait.

17

Iris

I was a nervous wreck.

I hardly got any work done at all today. Partially because Cora came to the office with me in the morning and was chatting it up with everyone, telling them about the new rain and river gauges she was installing. Mostly, though, it was nerves from my upcoming date with Hector.

I chose not to take a lunch break today so that I could leave early. My plan was to rush home, shower quickly, style my hair and makeup, and get dressed all within the hour before Hector arrived.

Things hadn't gone according to plan though—mostly because I had a mild freakout being in my apartment alone. The day before, Hector had walked up with me to make sure my new locks were secure. Then, my sister had been with me last night and this morning. Now, after coming home from work, I was alone for the first time in my apartment since someone had broken in.

It started well. I even made it into the shower and started fixing my hair. But when I was getting dressed and just about to start my makeup routine, I heard a noise. It sounded like someone scratching at my window...or maybe it was my door.

I freaked. I raced into my bedroom, where my phone had been charging on the nightstand, and just as I was about to call 911, the scratching happened again—this time louder. I looked up in the direction of the noise to see the tree branch outside my window scraping against the glass—just like it had done many other times before when it was windy.

I went through all the emotions. Pissed at myself for freaking out over something stupid. Angry that the person who broke in was having this impact on me even days later. Scared because I didn't know what to do since I lived alone and really didn't want to move.

I sat on the bed for a few minutes to calm my nerves and wipe away the tears from my face, but it must have been longer than I thought. Two loud knocks on the door had my body jerking back, startled. I glanced over at my phone to see that it was 5:59.

Hector.

Crap. I hadn't finished my makeup. Or put on my shoes. Did I remember to put on deodorant? I couldn't remember where I had left off. Now, in addition to all the other emotions I had gone through, I could add panicked and frantic to the mix.

Two more loud knocks. I knew I needed to let him in, but I didn't want him to see me like this. Especially since I had been crying and hadn't fixed my makeup yet.

Too late now.

I went to the door, hoping to let him in and turn quickly so he didn't see my face and then finish in the bathroom. Most guys wouldn't care if you needed five more minutes, right? Well, he didn't have a choice.

I looked through my peephole. Dear God. He had on dark jeans and a black dress shirt with the sleeves rolled up. He looked mouthwatering.

Opening the door, I may or may not have openly gawked at him. His chest hair was poking through the top of his shirt where it was unbuttoned, and I may have even drooled a little. And those jeans...They fit him like a glove. Unfortunately, pausing to ogle him was the wrong choice because it gave him a chance to see my face.

His face went from neutral when I opened the door to anger and concerned.

"What's wrong?" he asked, not waiting for me to invite him in, putting his hand on my stomach and pushing me back inside and closing the door behind him before I even had a chance to realize my mistake.

"You were crying. What happened?"

Well, crap. There went my chance of covering up the red splotchiness on my face.

His hands went to cup my face as he tilted my head up. "Iris, talk to me. What's wrong?"

"I heard a noise while I was getting ready and freaked out," I told him, my body slumping in embarrassed defeat. "It was just the tree branch by my bedroom window, but I thought it was someone breaking in, and I panicked."

He pulled me in closer to his body. Feeling his warmth and scent wrap around me made me feel safe, and I just let everything pour out of me.

"Once I realized what it was, I started crying because I hate being that dumb, scared person who is afraid of their own shadow. That made me even more emotional, and I just started freaking out more because I don't want to move apartments, but I feel weird about my space being violated."

"You can stay with me tonight," he said calmly, his fingers stroking my face softly.

"Hector, I love your place—*I do*—but I don't want to be scared of my own place. I need to be able to stay here. I don't want this person to take that away from me."

I sighed again. Both my emotions and my pride felt like they had taken a beating.

"I get that, sweetheart," he said softly. "I don't have Sarge with me, and I can't leave him all night. Let's stay at my place tonight, and then I'll bring him over tomorrow after work, and I'll stay here on the couch. We'll ease you back into your place until you aren't scared anymore."

This man.

"Pack a bag, and we'll go to dinner," he said.

"Okay," I answered, wiping underneath my eyes. "Can I have another five minutes to fix my makeup?"

"Yeah, but you don't need it," he said softly and then kissed my forehead.

I sighed and leaned forward to rest my head on his chest. As I wrapped my arms around him, I whispered, "Thanks."

Not giving him a chance to respond, I turned and started to walk back to my bathroom when he spoke again.

"Iris," he called out, and I looked back at him. "I really like that dress," he said with a small grin, which made me smile, knowing I had made the right call with this outfit.

Hector took me to a really nice Italian restaurant. We sat in a cozy half-circle booth, which allowed us to sit next to each other but at an angle so we didn't have to turn our bodies fully to see each other during conversation.

The restaurant had soft lighting all around, and a blend of Frank Sinatra, Tony Bennett, and Sammy Davis Jr. played in the background.

"You okay with this place?" Hector asked. "I didn't think to check to see if you liked Italian food."

See—super sweet and just didn't realize it.

"Yes, I love Italian food," I responded as a slow grin took over his face.

God, he was already attractive, but when he made that

slow, sexy smile, parts of my brain short-circuited. Unfortunately for me, it short-circuited the part of my brain that regulated speech, because it rendered me incapable of saying anything intelligent for the next sixty seconds. Of course, this happened to be when the waiter came up.

"Could I interest you folks in some wine?" he asked, and Hector looked at me expectantly.

In my defense, my brain was not working fully, so I blurted out the only thing that came to mind.

"I like wine. Italy has one of the best climates for wine, thanks to its sunny, Mediterranean climate."

See, this is what happened when I got nervous. I started to spit out random facts—usually weather or climate related because that was what my brain knew best. But it was also awkward because, most of the time, no one asked for these facts...or cared.

Taking pity on me, Hector ordered a glass of wine and a water for each of us before the waiter walked away.

"Have you been to Italy before?" he asked me.

"No, why? Have you?" I returned the question.

"No. You just seemed to know a lot about it, so I wondered if you'd been there."

"I would love to go there someday, but I really just know facts about places if they are related to my job or weather," I explained as another random thought popped into my head that I had a compulsory need to share.

"Did you know that outside of the U.S., Italy has the most waterspouts of any other country?" I asked, continuing right into my nervous babble without giving him a chance to respond. "Though Spain and Greece also report them every year too. I love waterspouts because even though they are basically just tornadoes over water, unlike tornadoes, you don't have to have a strong thunderstorm to create them. They have what's called fair-weather waterspouts that can happen on sunny days."

I watched as he scooted closer to me and then put his hand to the side of my face, pulling me in for a kiss. It was soft and quick but still just as incredible as his kiss from the other day.

After he pulled back, I realized he had a small grin on his face.

"What was that for?" I asked.

"You're cute when you get nervous and start spouting random facts," he said, the grin on his face growing, which only made him sexier.

"Sorry," I told him, dipping my head.

I was glad to know he wasn't bothered by it but instead found it amusing. It didn't mean I wasn't still semi-embarrassed by it.

"Hey," he said, startling me out of my thoughts, and put two of his fingers under my chin to lift my head. "I'm not much of a talker, Iris, but I enjoy listening to you talk. I don't care if it's about yourself, your family, your job, or just some random thing you find interesting. If it's important or interesting to you, then I want to hear about it."

I was falling deeper and deeper for this man every minute I spent with him. I took his cue and did most of the talking at dinner. Hector just listened with that steady focus of his, adding a word here or there when it suited him. To anyone nearby, he probably looked like his usual grumpy self, while I sat there waving my hands and talking a mile a minute.

We had ordered our food and were just enjoying each other's company. I looked around the restaurant, enjoying the aesthetic, the menu, the waiter, everywhere and every-thing, taking it all in. But every time I looked at Hector, his eyes were always on me—deeply focused.

"What are you thinking about?" I asked as I took a sip of my sparkling water.

"You," he said candidly.

I smiled at him. "Oh yeah? What about me?"

"I like watching you. I like listening to you talk animatedly about things. And I really like what you're wearing tonight."

"You already said that," I replied, giving him an even bigger grin with probably a bit of a blush on my cheeks.

It felt like an oxymoron of sorts, really—something that defied physics. How could I have heat flowing through my whole face, yet chills running through my entire body at the same time?

"Doesn't mean I can't keep appreciating it or admiring you in it."

Okay, if I wasn't blushing before, I definitely was now.

Our waiter brought out our food, and we enjoyed pleasant conversation—again, mostly on my end—for the rest of dinner.

"I had a really good time tonight," I told Hector as we walked out of the restaurant.

His hand was on the small of my back, guiding me out the door. Just as we left, he took a step around, coming to my side and grabbing my hand.

"Me too," he said quietly, squeezing my hand.

He held my hand the whole way back to his SUV, and I smiled, feeling giddy like a teenager again. Hector may not talk much, but his few comments and small gestures like this spoke volumes.

He walked me to my door and opened it. Wanting to show my appreciation, and also my deep desire to touch him and taste him, I turned and leaned up to kiss him.

It didn't take long for him to become an active participant. In fact, within a few seconds, he had all but taken over. His left hand moved around my hips to my lower back, pulling me closer into him. His right hand moved to sift through the hair behind my ear, holding my head tightly as he ravished my lips, allowing my tongue to slip inside and taste him.

I moaned as my senses were overwhelmed—the scent of him, his rough hands rubbing along my soft skin, and his taste on my tongue.

He pulled back, and I immediately wanted to complain.

"Let's go back and let Sarge out before we end up giving people in this parking lot a show," he said.

As much as I hated to stop what we were doing, he was right. If he hadn't stopped us, I likely would have let him take me right here up against the passenger door.

I was learning quickly that when Hector's mouth was on mine, my brain ceased to function. While not a bad problem to have per se, it could definitely get me into trouble.

He rounded the car after closing my door and climbed into the driver's seat. After pulling out of the lot, he reached over to grab my hand, intertwining his fingers with mine, and placed our joined hands on his thigh.

"Sarge will be happy to see you," he said. "He's been camped out just outside the guest bedroom door basically ever since you left."

That sweet little boy.

"Awww, I missed him too," I replied and then looked over at Hector's profile as he drove. "And his owner too."

He didn't say anything back, just squeezed my hand and held on tight.

I spent the rest of the drive filling him in on my sister's visit and our little trip to see Nancy—including the part about how he was invited to her game night so she could show him off to all her friends.

He didn't say no, so I took that as a win for now—especially since he just grinned as I told him the story.

Pulling up his gravel drive, I felt a sense of peacefulness come over me as his cabin came into view. I wasn't entirely sure why, because I was a city girl at heart, but there was just something about his place that made me feel comfortable, safe, and at ease.

I heard Sarge's barks and saw his face in the narrow window by the door as I walked up the front porch. I could see him jumping up and down in excitement as I waited for Hector to open the door. The moment he did, Sarge bolted out and came up to me, sniffing and licking me all over in his excitement.

"Sarge, *platz*," Hector told him, and he reluctantly listened, moving his body off mine but still staying close by, his tail wiggling so fast in excitement.

"Let me take this beast out, and I'll be right in," he said, grabbing Sarge's leash from the entryway.

I walked in and noticed Hector had reached in and set my overnight bag just inside the door. This set the wheels in motion in my brain—where did I put the bag?

Did I go back to the guest room like I had the other nights I slept here? Was the date essentially over? I'd never had a date like this before, so I didn't know what the protocol was.

Okay, think about this rationally.

What if we weren't at his house? What if the night had ended back at my place, like I originally assumed? What would I have done?

I asked myself this and realized I would have invited him in for a drink and hoped that I could convince him to stay the night with me—but not for safety reasons.

Just because the location changed didn't mean the night couldn't end the same—us, in the same bed. Right?

I decided to leave my bag resting near the couch in the living room, and went into the bathroom to freshen up while he walked Sarge. I had just made it back into the living room when they both came back in through the front door.

Sarge immediately ran to me and rolled over, begging for belly rubs. Dogs were such simple creatures. There was no shame in just blatantly asking for what they wanted—pride be damned—even if he looked like an idiot on his back, all spread-eagle and demanding belly rubs.

Why couldn't I do the same? Well, maybe not the belly rub part.

Deciding to be brave—at least on the outside, since on the inside I was a nervous wreck—I walked over to where Hector was in the kitchen, filling up Sarge's water bowl.

"You okay?" he asked as he set the water bowl down in its place. "You look nervous."

Damnit, I needed a new face that didn't give everything away.

I straightened my shoulders to at least give me the look of more confidence. "Where am I sleeping?"

He stared down at me for a few moments. "Where do you *want* to sleep?"

Ugh. Redirecting...really? Fine. I guess I'll be the daring one.

"With you," I told him, standing my ground but also not moving from where I was rooted.

He chose silence again but never broke his gaze from my face.

"I didn't invite you to stay the night just to get you in

my bed and have sex," he added quickly, as if he needed to underline it and wanted no room for misunderstanding.

"I know that, Hector. But if this had been a normal date, and you had walked me back to my place at the end of the night. I um...would have asked if you wanted to stay the night."

He didn't say anything back, so in true awkward and anxious fashion, I just kept babbling like an idiot, waving my hands in front of my face as I talked.

"I'm not saying you had to come in and agree to have a drink, but, um, that's what I would have offered you. The uh...drink part, I mean...for you. I would have offered you a drink."

Okay, I needed to shut up.

"I'm trying to be a gentleman here, Iris," he said, sounding almost pained.

"What if I don't want you to be a gentleman?" I told him, grabbing the sides of his head and forcing him to look into my eyes. "Hector, you not being a *gentleman* does not mean the only other option is an asshole...I just want you to be you."

I took a breath and paused for just a moment. "You don't have to pretend to be who you think I want or think I need when you're around me. I like you the way you are."

I pulled my hands back and moved them to the bow at my waist and began to slowly untie the dress. "Don't be a gentleman, Hector. Just be you."

His gaze moved from my eyes, down my body to

where my hands were currently undoing my dress. Now untied, I pulled at the fabric slowly to open each side like you would a bathrobe. I heard his quick intake of breath as I opened the dress up to where he could finally see my red teddy underneath.

I watched his chest rise and fall as his breathing picked up. Then, I saw the moment he decided to just say fuck it and give into temptation—me being the temptation.

This time his hands moved to cup my face as he tilted my head back so I was looking straight into his eyes.

"Be sure, Iris," he said. His voice held a deep timbre and was slightly raw, as if he needed to clear his throat. There was warmth in his gaze, but there was also a raging fire. "I need you to be really fucking sure. We start this, there's no going back. Not for me."

I thought back to his comment about me being his dream woman, his comments at dinner, and the way he was looking at me at this very moment.

Oh yeah, I was sure.

"Take me to bed, Hector," I whispered back to him. "I need—"

Before I was able to finish my sentence, I was lifted up. He bent at the waist—his shoulder to my stomach—and I was hoisted onto his shoulder.

I shrieked at the sudden movement. "Hector! Put me down, I'm too heavy!"

"Woman, you are not heavy at all. In fact, you are nothing but perfection from top to bottom."

I wanted to disagree with him, but the ease with which he was carrying me into the bedroom—as though I was as light as a feather—was impressive…and I liked it.

We arrived in his bedroom, and this was the first time I had really been in this space. Sure, I had peeked through the door, but now I was in here. He closed the door as I tried to gaze around quickly at the large space, but it was hard since I was upside down.

He once again bent at the waist and then slowly lowered me to the ground, the front of my body sliding against the front of his.

Once my feet were securely on the ground, I stared back up at him as he slid his hands over my shoulders, his fingers underneath the fabric of my dress, and began pushing it over and down my body. I moved my arms slightly behind me so the dress would easily slide off the rest of the way, leaving me with nothing on but my red teddy as I stood in front of him. His eyes were roaming up and down the lacy fabric, taking it all in.

"My eyes are up here, Hector," I teased.

"I know, but I can't look at your eyes right now," he said seriously.

"Why not?" I flirted and gave him a smile.

"Because I'm too busy staring at the most beautiful body I've ever seen in my life," he said reverently as his hands began to roam over my hips and waist, softly caressing me. "Every. Single. Detail. I'm committing it to memory in case you change your mind and this is the only time this happens."

Dear God…This man lit a fire in me like no one else could.

I'd never learned how to just take a compliment. I'd always been so nervous, feeling like even after someone said something nice, there would always be a *but* or some other caveat to go along with it. With Hector, though, it was just him—no bullshit. I needed him now more than ever.

"Hector," I whimpered. "I need you to touch me."

"I am touching you," he said against my skin, and I could hear the smile in his voice.

"I need more. I'm aching. Please."

He growled as his hand moved down my stomach and into the apex of my legs. His fingers grazed across my sensitive bundle of nerves and even through the lacy fabric, I felt electric waves course through my body.

"I have no idea how to take this off, but I really wanna be the one to do it," he said, seemingly fascinated with my teddy as he ran his fingers softly over the lace. His calloused hands scraped delicately along my skin, creating heat all along the surface.

"You just pull the straps down, and then you can slide it off," I informed him, wanting—no…*needing* him to move faster.

"Yeah?" His fingertips skimmed across my collarbone as he lifted the strap and began to slide it over my shoulder.

Goose bumps formed in his wake as he moved to the other shoulder to repeat the move.

The straps now hung loosely near my elbows, and my nipples were barely covered as the lace fabric now left most of my chest exposed.

"Fuck, I can't believe you're real," he said almost reverently.

"I'm real, but I'd really like you to move faster, please," I told him, because as much as I was enjoying this, it was also torture.

His response was to just look down at me and grin. The same devilish grin that he had likely used on so many other people to intimidate them into giving him whatever he wanted—and again, it was working.

That grin came closer to me before it finally touched my own smiling lips. His tongue swiped at my lips asking permission to enter, and I gave it to him. His kiss was slow but full of heat.

His hands slid back to my upper thighs, and he lifted me about a foot off the ground before setting me back down on the bed. Then lowered me slowly to my back—all while never breaking free of my mouth.

He released my lips as he looked down at me, still standing but bent over my body—his heat enveloping me into a cocoon of sorts.

Leaning back, he slowly slid the straps off my arms and down my body, exposing my chest and stomach. He bent down and kissed his way across my body as he drew one of my nipples into his mouth and pulled with his lips as his tongue swirled around it.

Heat and excitement coursed through me. I moaned

and moved my hands behind his head as he tried to lift up from where he was. I needed him to stay. I felt the rumble of his small laugh at my move, but I didn't care. What he was doing felt amazing, and I wanted more.

I won because his mouth stayed where it was and continued to give me bliss as his tongue and mouth worked at my nipple feverishly. At the same time, his hands continued to slide my lace teddy down my body.

I released his head temporarily so I could lift my hips and allow him to remove the obstacle of clothing and keep exploring.

After it was fully removed, he stared down at me, his eyes so intense, I started to get worried.

"Fuck, I can't believe this is real. You are so perfect," he said as his gaze roamed over my entire body.

I had never had a man look at me, let alone use words, like that—such adoration and awe.

"Ummm, you have some catching up to do," I told him, wanting the same opportunity to ogle him.

His eyes broke away from my body and came up to look at mine. I propped myself up on my elbows and smiled.

"I may or may not have a thing for your chest hair, so I'd really like to see all of it up close," I teased.

"My chest hair," he repeated, his left eyebrow lifted in question.

His hands moved up to his shirt, and he slowly unbuttoned from top to bottom, his eyes never breaking their gaze with mine.

That shirt now off, he lifted his white tee that had been underneath, revealing raw beauty. Chiseled abs and the perfect amount of chest hair. Chest hair, I might add, that flowed perfectly down south into the V just above his waistline. I may have licked my lips just thinking about where that happy trail would end.

"Iris," he growled, and I knew he saw me ogling his body.

I didn't care, which was why I continued to stare at him, including his broad shoulders and muscular arms that I couldn't wait to have wrapped around me in this bed.

A bed that was huge, just like him. The king bed had a large wooden headboard and wooden columns at the end of the frame. He had black sheets and a red plaid quilt on top. It looked like something a lumberjack would have on his bed, and it suited Hector perfectly.

The bed was also lofted up at least three feet off the ground, which meant my legs hanging off the side of the mattress were not touching the floor—short people problems. It was, however, the perfect height for Hector. He stood there, slowly working his belt off, and I noticed his hips would line up perfectly to me as I lay here on my back.

I was excited just thinking about it, and I pulled my lip into my mouth—my teeth pinching down on the corner.

"Whatever is going on in your head, I like it," Hector said gruffly.

Without giving me a chance to respond, he leaned

forward, taking my nipple back into his mouth and swirling with his tongue, and a moan escaped me without me even realizing it.

Heat pooled between my legs at his close contact. Every part of me came alive when he touched me. He ignited something inside me that I couldn't control. He set my entire body on fire.

God, if this is what it felt like just to have his tongue and mouth on me, I couldn't wait to see what else he had in store.

18

Hector

I knew without a single doubt in my mind that I would never recover after being inside Iris.

"I wish you could see what I do," I told her, running my hands over her soft skin. "My point of view is incredible."

"My view's not too shabby either," she said with a sly grin.

Just above her hipbone, there was a small sun tattoo with a cloud covering at least half of it. "Didn't take you for a tattoo person," I told her as I ran my fingers over it.

"It's my little reminder that the sun is constantly there, even if you can't always see it," she said softly with a small smile.

Fuck, she was too damn cute for her own good.

"You got any sunshine tattoos?" she asked, smirking at me. "I think maybe I should check all over you, just in case."

She lifted her hands to run over my chest before running her fingers through my hair. She'd mentioned she was into that, which was good because I only had it because I was usually too lazy to shave it off. I tried maybe once a week or every other week, but it was time consuming and I'd rather sleep in. But if she liked it, I'd never shave again.

Her hands roamed over my chest and shoulders and then down my arms on either side of her body.

"Hmm, no tattoos here. Maybe I should check the lower parts." She gave a wink and then an almost seducing grin.

I stood back up, my body between her open legs, and grabbed each of her hands to help pull her up.

Sitting on the edge of the bed, she leaned forward and worked at my pants. My belt already undone, she now navigated the button and zipper of my pants and then slipped her hand inside, rubbing it gently across my throbbing cock.

As her hand continued to work me and make me even harder, I used my hands to grab her face and pull her into me as I took her mouth.

God she tasted divine—fruity and sweet—and I couldn't get enough. I needed to be inside her though.

She must have felt the same because she pulled back, removing her mouth from mine, and stared up at me. "This underwear of yours looks super restrictive. You really should take it off," she said, her eyes glinting with lust-filled humor.

"Is that so?" I asked as I stripped myself of the remaining clothes.

Her eyes widened at my now naked body, and I knew what she was thinking. I was a big dude—tall, bulky frame, just overall a large man—and that included my dick as well.

"It's not a third leg, babe. It'll fit," I told her, teasing her back.

She threw her head back and laughed, and I seized the moment, leaning forward to kiss my way down her neck. My hands moved between her legs, and I barely grazed her, and my fingers were soaked.

I practically growled at how wet she was for me. "*Fuck*, Iris."

"Yes, please fuck Iris. Please," she begged, her voice just above a whisper as she writhed beneath me.

As much as I wanted to draw this out more and enjoy my time, I needed to be inside her...now.

I reached behind myself and grabbed a condom from my nightstand. Putting it on, I stared down at her body as her chest moved up and down rapidly following her increased breathing.

She was leaning back, propped up on her elbows, with her legs spread open and hanging mostly off the bed.

As much as I loved looking at her in this position, it wasn't the greatest given our big height difference.

"Slide back, Iris."

She scooted her body and turned so that her head was now in the middle of my pillows. I moved to follow, positioning myself directly above her.

I leaned forward and took one of her nipples in my mouth, swirling my tongue around her rock-hard nub. She writhed beneath me, arching her back as if she needed more. My fingers slid over her core, rubbing softly but with just enough pressure for her to feel it. She bucked up, gasping my name, as I sank two fingers inside her.

I moved my mouth from her nipple up to her lips, continuing to work her with my fingers. She was drenched, and I couldn't wait to get inside her.

I slid my fingers back out and lined myself up. I leaned my head back, wanting to watch her as I took her. Just in case this never happened again, though I hoped like hell it did—many times—I wanted to catalogue it in my memory.

"Look at me, Iris," I said, swirling the tip of my dick around her entrance, teasing both of us.

The moment her eyes met mine, I eased my way in, filling her slowly. She inhaled a small, ragged breath as I continued to bury myself inside her, stretching her. I pressed all the way to the hilt before pausing to give her a moment to adjust to my size.

"You okay?" I asked, needing to give myself a moment since she was so tight around me.

"More than okay," she said between ragged breaths. "But please move. I need you to move."

I did as commanded, gliding in and out of her, enjoying every single stroke.

"You feel fucking fantastic," I groaned, sliding my free hand around the side of her face, my fingers wrapping around her soft hair as I kissed her like I would never get the chance to kiss her again.

She felt so damn good. She felt like the one place I belonged. I felt rooted in her like she was my anchor, and I never wanted to leave.

I knew I wasn't going to last long, not with her making those needy little whimpers in between every stroke, but there was no way I was coming first.

My finger moved to rub along her clit, causing her to gasp, and her breathing became rough and uneven.

"Hector...I...please...I need," she babbled incoherently.

I continued to stroke her and then bent down to put my mouth near her ear and whispered against it. "Come for me, Iris. I want to feel you come around me."

No sooner had I gotten the words out, and she came, squeezing my cock tight inside her. Her voice was a mix of gasps and mumbled unintelligible words.

I kissed my way down the back of her ear to her neck and chest as I continued to drive inside her, now more erratically as I felt myself getting close.

I took her nipple in my mouth again, not able to get enough of her gorgeous tits, this time kneading them as I worked them with both my hands and mouth.

"Hector," Iris moaned beneath me. "Another...I...I need...I'm so close."

"Mmmm, you're turning into a greedy little fireball, eh?" I teased, but I was more than happy to give her another. It needed to be quick though, because I was on the edge myself.

I moved my hand back to her bundle of nerves to stroke and massage her, only this time, my mouth moved to hers and I devoured her lips, kissing her deeply.

She tumbled over the edge just as I did, her name ripped from my mouth as I ground myself inside her and then collapsed on top of her.

I only let myself stay on top of her for a few moments to catch my breath, so I didn't crush her.

Rolling onto my back, I lay there allowing my heart rate to ease a bit.

She turned into me, and I wrapped my arms around her back to pull her in closer.

We lay there together, her snuggled up against my side, half on top of me for a few moments, and I felt at peace. A peace I hadn't ever known before.

"I was in too much of a hurry to care how we did it just now, but could we maybe try me on top at some point?" she asked, her tone carrying confidence, though her eyes expressed a hint of hesitation.

"Iris, if you want to be on top, you can be on top," I

told her, my brain instantly dreaming of her in that exact position.

"I hope you enjoyed it as much as I did." She spoke quietly against my chest. "Cause I'd like to do that again sometime."

Maybe I was still riding the high of what had just happened and not thinking straight, or maybe she put some sort of spell on me, but my response was to unintentionally unload all my personal inner thoughts.

"Iris, I have never had an orgasm like that in my life, and you aren't the first woman I've slept with."

Her face looked uncomfortable and also a little peeved, so I held up my hand for her to give me a second to explain. "I'm not tellin' you that to start a fight or make you mad. I'm tellin' you so that you understand the magnitude of what I'm saying. I'm a forty-year-old man, Iris. I've been around the block a few times, but I have never, and I mean never, had sex that felt as good as that before. That's all you, woman."

I looked down at her just in time to see a beaming smile on her face.

"Maybe we should do it again. You know, just to make sure it really was that good, and you aren't just putting me on a pedestal."

"Oh, I'm definitely putting you on a pedestal, because that's where you belong. But if you wanna have another go at it, I'm never gonna turn you down."

"Never, eh?" She smiled tauntingly.

"Never," I said seriously, and I meant it.

I kissed the top of her head and relaxed with her at my side.

I took her two more times before we finally slept—both of which involved her being on top—and each time was better than the last.

I was living my best damn life, and I found myself hoping it never ended.

I woke up next to a soft, lush body wrapped around me like a pretzel, and I didn't care one bit.

Despite having sex with Iris three times in the last twenty-four hours, my dick was up and raring to go again.

I ran my hands over the soft skin of her leg, which was wrapped around my waist. The movement must have woken her, because she rustled awake and kissed my neck. I rolled her over and underneath me.

"You're addictive," I said, my hands continuing to roam over her lush curves, my mouth gliding along her skin, peppering her with kiss after kiss.

Just the mere taste of her, and my dick was instantly hard.

"I crave every inch of you, Iris," I told her gruffly.

She arched her back, pushing into me, telling me exactly where she wanted my mouth.

"I should have brought my own car so we could have used that extra time for more fun activities instead of driving," she said, and all I could think of was all the things I could do with those extra minutes.

Jeez. I was forty years old, acting like I was fourteen.

"We can pick this back up again later if you want, but we both have to get to work," I told her, kissing her one last time on her neck—or at least I told myself it was the last time.

"How about I just drop you off at work, and then I'll pick you up when you're done and we'll head back to your place," I suggested.

She agreed, and we reluctantly climbed out of bed, got ready, and made our way to work. The bright spot was knowing we had plans to see each other again that night.

I was mid-bite of my sandwich, daydreaming about Iris's naked body, when there was a hard knock on my half-open door.

"Okay, hear me out," Agent Andrews said from my doorway as she leaned against the frame, with my boss, Superintendent Carl O'Connor, standing beside her.

I braced myself, because people usually said that before they told you something they knew you weren't going to like or agree with.

"I think we should go talk to our podcaster, Steve," Andrews said.

My only response was to roll my eyes in annoyance.

"I decided to listen to the most recent podcast from our guy who wrote the letter," Andrews said.

Internally, I groaned—and also externally. "You've got to be kidding me," I sighed.

If I make it through the day without stabbing someone with a fork, it will be a miracle.

"Again, hear me out," she said, finally walking into the office, O'Connor on her heels as he closed the door behind them. "Yes, he's an eccentric weirdo, but he may actually be onto something."

"Like what?" I asked, wondering if I would regret it.

It was possible, but I also knew she wouldn't blow smoke up my ass unnecessarily, so this had to be leading somewhere.

"Not sure how, but I'm guessing he talked with the parents of the missing girl we found," she explained. "Yesterday, he mentioned on his podcast that the girl was a collegiate athlete and had gone missing at a tournament."

"Okay…" I said, not sure where she was going with this. "He could have looked some of that info up. The name of the woman was announced to all the local TV news stations, so it wasn't a secret."

"I know," she said, holding up her hands as if to tell me to let her talk. "Honestly, the specifics of how he found out aren't the main concern here. It's what he mentioned *after* that got my attention."

She paused, took a deep breath, and dropped a verbal bomb. "He said there were seven other collegiate female athletes who went missing while at tournaments or competitions across the country over the last several years. All of them have never been found. And here's the kicker—all were the same age and same appearance. In fact, three of them could have been doppelgängers for each other."

My head jerked back at the sudden realization that this may not have been a one-off.

"The icing on the cake..." she said, likely pausing for dramatic effect. "All the venues the women were competing at were within ten miles of a large lake."

"Shit," I said, leaning back in my chair.

"So, here's the thing," she said, moving to sit down in the chair across from me at my desk. "Steve is *definitely* a weirdo, but he specifically mentioned the names of all the women in his podcast, so I looked up them and their case files. Each woman went missing roughly six to eight months apart."

"When was the most recent one?" I asked, trying to figure out a timeline here.

"We believe Miss Simpleton from Lake Echo was," Andrews spoke up.

"Okay, but she was reported missing a year ago," O'Connor pointed out.

"Which is why I reached out to the FBI to pull any missing female cases within ten miles of a large body of water within the last year that also match the description of the other athletes," Andrews said.

Damn, she had her work cut out for her.

"How can I help?" I asked, since she clearly wasn't here just to tell me this.

"That's the same question I had for her, but she told me I had to come here to find out in person," O'Connor said, and I noted his mild annoyance that she wouldn't just tell him this information over the phone.

"I want to drop him a bone," she said cryptically. "I want to give Mr. Stanton some info that is not public knowledge."

"To see if he puts it on his podcast?" O'Connor inquired.

"So she can narrow him down as a suspect," I chimed in.

"Yes," she confirmed, smiling at me.

"If Stanton was involved in any way with these crimes, depending on what the information was, he might choose to withhold or alter the information before sharing it to make sure he isn't caught," I explained to O'Connor. "If he's just an overly excited crime nut, he would share all the information as we give it to him."

"So what do you need from us?" O'Connor asked.

"A couple things," she hedged. "First, I want you to send in another dive crew to Lake Echo within 48 hours. And we're going to invite him to come out."

"Hell no," O'Connor interrupted. "We have no reason to bring another dive team in, and that's money and resources we don't have just to appease some weirdo podcaster."

"Second," she continued, ignoring O'Connor's rejection of the first request. "I want you to be there, Hector. You had enough years of working undercover with the LVPD to give you insight into people like this. I want you to watch him while he witnesses the fake search dive. See if you can get a read on him one way or another."

"I appreciate your vote of confidence, but my undercover specialty was the mafia, not potential serial killers."

Her hands waved in front of her as if she were dismissing my comment as trivial. "It's still more insight training than I have. My specialty is dead bodies, not live ones."

She turned to O'Connor and positioned her hands in front of her as if she were about to deal with a petulant child. "And the ISB will cover the cost to bring in a dive team. You just need to provide the park staff."

"Fine. What exactly do you want them to pretend to do?" O'Connor asked.

"They need to pretend to find something—it doesn't matter what," she explained. "Your men will come and talk to Hector and tell him they found *it*. Hector, without telling him what *it* is, will inform Mr. Stanton that it's the break you were looking for in the case, because this piece of evidence could be the smoking gun for who the killer is."

"What if he doesn't believe it?" O'Connor asked.

"He will," I said, and Andrews smiled at me, letting me know she was thinking the same thing I was. "If he's not involved directly in the crime but just doing this to build up his audience or podcast numbers, he'll be so excited to get a scoop for his listeners that there's no way you'll be able to get rid of him. If he's involved, he'll be too paranoid about what it would mean for him, so his desire to get out of there fast should become more important than sticking around to find out what the piece of evidence is."

O'Connor nodded in response. "Alright. You'll have a dive crew for tomorrow."

He left quickly, leaving only Andrews and me in the office.

"By the way…I passed Diden and Jennings on the way in, and they told me to be cautious entering your office because you were acting weird," she said to me with a smirk.

"I've been tucked away in my office most of the day," I said. "I can hardly be a dick if I'm not out there."

"That's just it," she said, getting up from the chair. "Diden said she saw you smiling when you walked in today, and Jennings reported you smiling when he walked by your office."

I groaned. "So first they bitch because I'm grumpy, unapproachable, and don't smile enough. Now they don't like it when I smile?"

"I think they just weren't sure what to make of it," she said, heading toward the door. "Whoever she is…maybe see her again so you can keep that smile. It's a good look for you. I'll be in touch."

With that, she walked out, leaving me to think about what she'd said.

Iris.

That's who'd put the smile on my face. Thinking of her naked. Thinking of her with my dog. Thinking of her in my house.

Jesus, I needed to get my shit together. I was acting like some down-bad Romeo. It wasn't real love—yet. That took time. No, this was just infatuation, a desire to be around her...and only her.

19

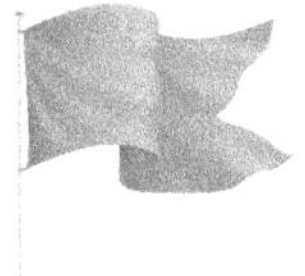

Iris

"I'm guessing you either won the lottery or you got some last night," Ben said, smirking at me when I walked into the office this morning.

"Wait…Who got some? What's happening?" Christine popped up from her desk to see what—and more importantly, who—Ben was talking about.

Ben didn't say a word. He just nodded in my direction, smiled, and went back to work.

Christine gasped after she took a second to look at me. "You did get laid!"

"Shhh!" I snapped and then lowered my tone. "Don't yell that! Besides, how do you know I didn't win the lottery?"

Ben still said nothing, just chuckled while staring at his computer.

Christine, on the other hand, rolled her eyes at me. "If you had won the lottery, you wouldn't have come back to work," she explained. "You would have stayed in bed with Hector all morning instead."

"That's not true," I defended just as Leah walked in. "Besides, he had work too."

Christine snapped her fingers, pointing at me, as Ben laughed even louder. "Ha! Caught you! You *did* have sex with Hector the Convector!"

Well, crap. I'd walked right into that one.

"Maybe we should call him Hector the *Erector* now!" Leah joked, causing Christine to laugh and Ben to groan.

"Tell me all the details," Christine begged as she and Leah produced megawatt smiles.

"Actually, please don't," Ben protested.

I shook my head at all three of them, ignoring Christine's request.

"New controversial topic," Ben interrupted. "Red Flag Warnings should be red, not pink. Why are they bright pink on our maps when they should be red?"

I could have kissed Ben for bringing this up because he was doing it to help me. This was one of those topics that Christine and Leah were divided on and a hill they would each die on—and Ben knew it.

"Thank you!" Leah said. "It literally says red in the name. Why is it not red? Dumbest thing ever."

"Because there are too many other warnings and alerts

that are red," Christine countered. "Tornado warnings, heat warnings, flash flood warnings, and hurricane warnings...The list goes on."

"Then they should switch one of those to pink...since they don't have red in their name," Leah rebutted.

While they argued, I slowly crept to the empty desk in the far corner since it was mostly hidden by the large filing cabinets, hoping they would forget I was in the same room with them and not bring Hector back up again.

It wasn't that I was embarrassed about Hector—quite the opposite. I really liked him, which was why I found myself so protective of him and talking about us, especially since getting Hector to even take a chance on me seemed to ignite some huge internal battle within him.

"Hey!" Christine yelled and then turned her volume down a bit. "You can't leave yet. We have to talk about you sleeping with Hector!"

Leah gasped. "Oh yes!" she asked excitedly.

I turned back around to face them both. "Doesn't matter if I did. We're not talking about it," I said and then slid behind the corner desk, hoping they would take the hint.

"Fine, but that's only because I have to go outside because I think one of the sensors is broken," Christine yelled, clearly disgruntled. "But this conversation is not over—just on pause."

Knowing Christine and Leah likely would never let

this go, I decided to work from one of the private offices today so that I could get the rest of my work done.

Except, it didn't help. I couldn't seem to focus on anything but Hector all day.

I thought about our amazing dinner, him holding my hand the whole drive back to his place, and the incredible sex. I also thought about Hector staying the night at my place tonight. I hated how much I freaked out the other night in my own space. I knew I needed to get over that fear, but it wasn't easy. My hope was that having Hector there would ease me back in and allow me to have that mental security blanket for a few days to conquer my unease. If not, I was going to have to reach out to a therapist to get some advice on how to move forward.

By the time five thirty rolled around, I was giddy with excitement at Hector's impending arrival. He had texted around lunchtime to say he was going to run to his house after work, pick up Sarge, and would meet me at my office.

He arrived just as I walked out of the building, waving to Dorothy. He got out of his car and walked around behind it to greet me.

"Hey," he said, standing near his trunk as I walked up to him.

I wasn't sure if he was going to kiss me, hug me, or just stand there.

"How was work?" I asked him.

"It was all right," he said and then moved his arm to

point to the passenger side of the car. "Here, get in. I left it running so we don't bake Sarge in the car."

I followed him as he opened the passenger side door to let me in.

"Thanks," I told him and decided I would be the one to make the first move.

I leaned in and gave him a quick kiss on the mouth. Even though I really wanted more, I knew Dorothy was likely watching us from the front lobby, and I didn't feel like giving her a show.

I pulled back from the kiss and got into the passenger seat, allowing Hector to close my door. I was immediately assaulted by dog licks and sniffs on my head and face.

I laughed, turning to face him and scratching his head. "Well, hello to you too, Sarge."

His feet tapped excitedly on the back seat as he panted near my face.

"Leave her alone, Sarge," Hector said as he slid into his own seat and put his seat belt on.

I did the same as we pulled out of the parking lot.

We decided to grab some takeout for dinner since we had Sarge with us and then made our way back to my place.

Once we got there, Sarge was very excited to check out a new place. The moment we walked into my apartment, he sniffed his way through my space as though he was on the hunt for something amazing.

An hour later, after eating and taking Sarge for a quick

walk around the building, we were ready to snuggle up on the couch to watch a movie.

I had an L-shaped couch, and Hector was on the long side with his legs stretched out facing the TV. I sat down next to him, my left arm grazing his slightly before he wrapped his arm around my waist and pulled me in closer, all but fusing me to his right side.

"Thank you," I told him softly.

He turned his head and looked down at me. "For what?"

"I feel bad making you stay the night because I freaked out being here by myself, but I'm also really glad because you make me feel safe."

He stared at me for a few moments. "I'm glad I make you feel safer, and I'm happy to do it," he said, taking his hand that wasn't wrapped around me and using it to push one of my loose curls back from my face. "But we'll get you back to where you feel good to stay here alone if you want. It's natural to feel what you're feeling, so don't feel guilty about it. You're strong and resilient. You'll get there."

God, for a man who was usually a grump and mostly quiet, he always seemed to know the perfect thing to say to me.

Wanting to show my gratitude in something other than words, I leaned over and kissed him. I meant for it to be a simple quick kiss, but as often was the case with Hector, that was impossible. He had this magnetic force that was sometimes overwhelming and beyond my ability to ignore.

As the kiss intensified, Hector's hands began to roam over my body in soft, slow movements that both tickled and teased my senses.

He broke the kiss first, pulling back just enough to speak, but close enough that I could feel his breath on my lips. "Christ, Iris. I can't be around you and not touch you."

"I like when you touch me," I told him, hoping he'd touch me some more and kiss me again.

He grinned at my response before shaking his head back and forth. "Damn, woman. I got two hard-ons at work today thinking about you. You're addictive, and I'm not sure I like it. But I also can't help myself."

"So, what are you gonna do about it?" I said, getting up from the couch and walking toward my hallway, adding a little sway to my hips in the process.

I turned to look back at him and smiled. "I think I'm ready for bed. What about you?"

The words were no sooner out of my mouth than three raps on the door sounded. I sucked in a startled breath as I stumbled back a step, knocking into the wall behind me.

Sarge barked as Hector popped up from the couch immediately and came to me. "You okay?"

Still catching my breath, all I could do was nod in response for a moment.

"You expecting anyone?" he asked quietly.

"N—No," I said, stammering over my words as my heart jackhammered inside me. "Sorry for overreacting I just wasn't expecting that."

"Don't apologize," he said. "I'll get the door."

He walked over to it and looked out the peephole before turning back to me. "It's your neighbor, Nancy."

I felt a wave of relief wash over me and also a new wave of embarrassment for how I had reacted.

Sarge came over to my side, half interested in what I was doing and the other half focused on the door Hector was now opening.

"Oh good. You're still here," Nancy announced at seeing Hector.

He moved back to let her into my apartment, and Sarge made his way over to her to determine whether she was friend or foe.

"Oh dear. Are you all right?" Nancy asked, looking at me.

Ugh. I really needed to work on getting a more stoic face.

"And who are you, precious hairy beast?" Nancy said, leaning down to pet Sarge, who had since decided she was his new best friend.

"That's Sarge, Hector's dog," I informed her.

"Before I forget, young man," Nancy said, turning to face Hector. "What are you doing Sunday night? Care to join a bunch of old ladies, plus Iris, in a fun game of cards?"

Hector said nothing at first, but I did briefly see his lip twitch.

"I can't promise it will be the most exciting night of your life, but I can promise dinner and lots of delicious home-baked goodies," she said, showing him her biggest smile.

"I'll check my schedule and let you know," he said, giving her a very small grin.

"You do that," she said, pointing to him. "Anyway, I saw you both out walking that cute dog and decided to come over to remind you about card night and see if Hector could join. Plus, I wanted to give you this."

She handed Hector two books, and even though I couldn't see my face, I could feel the heat taking over and knew it was likely turning pink.

"These are mine," Nancy explained. "Iris likes them a lot, and I thought you might enjoy them too. You know—to see what Iris enjoys."

Oh, dear God, shoot me now.

"Uh, thank you," Hector replied politely, taking the books from her.

"Okay, you two troublemakers. I'll let you go for the night," she said, clapping her hands together. "Behave...or don't."

She ended with a cackle as she moved to the door, Sarge following her, likely hoping for one last pet before she left.

Hector let her out and locked up before turning back to me.

"What's with the books?" he asked, setting them on the kitchen counter as he walked toward me.

I felt my face heat even more because I knew the real reason Nancy had dropped them off.

"Umm...she is a bestselling romance author, and I guess she was just, um, looking to see if you might want to read them. You don't have to," I rushed to add, waving my hands in front of my face. "You can just donate them, or I'll give them to my sister or something."

"What's got you all flustered?" he asked me, a small smirk tugging at his lips.

Did he know what kind of stuff was in those books? I doubted he would think this was funny if he knew.

"I'm not flustered," I lied. "How about we just watch the movie? Or we could just go to bed."

I hoped my redirect would allow us to move on from this topic and maybe pick up from where we left off when Nancy had arrived.

"I'll allow that diversion only because I'm good with taking this to the bed, but just so you know, both my sisters and mom read romance books, so I know what's in them," he said, walking closer to me and grabbing my hips to pull me into him. "So, if there's something in there you enjoy, I'd like to know what it is."

Was it hot in here? It was definitely getting hotter in here.

Clearly unaffected by the increasing temperature in the room, Hector just smiled at me and then kissed my lips. It was soft and quick but held so much promise of what was yet to come.

"Let's go get ready for bed," he murmured against my lips. "Besides, I'm not sure I gave you enough opportunities last night to be on top. Gotta keep you happy if you're gonna let me stick around."

"I think that can be arranged," I said.

A little shriek left my mouth as he lifted me up. I wrapped my legs around him as he carried me back to my bedroom.

Taking his time, he removed his clothes and then mine. He pulled me onto the bed with him—me on top. I sat there, straddling his hips and staring down at the most gorgeous man I had ever laid eyes on. I ran my fingers across his abs and chest hair, enjoying the feel of both— the hard and soft texture creating a gift for my senses.

"What are you thinking about, Iris?" he asked with a grin, running his calloused hands up and down my thighs, triggering goose bumps along the way.

"Give me a new memory in my apartment—a good one—to wash away the bad ones. Make love to me, Hector."

I didn't have to ask twice. He gave me not one but two great new memories in my apartment. The first one wore me out in the best way possible, leading to a great night's sleep snuggled up against him.

The second was the next morning, when Hector woke me with his mouth and tongue all over my body.

I could get used to that.

20

Hector

Once again, I spent most of my day at work thinking about Iris. Whatever spell she had put on me was working, because even innocuous things had me thinking of her.

Books on the shelf in my office? Instantly my brain went to what dirty things were in her neighbor's books that Iris wanted to do.

The new coffee pods at work? Memories flooded my mind of her drinking coffee with me in her kitchen this morning in nothing but my flannel shirt.

Not all my thoughts were of sex, though. Her words last night about how I gave her a sense of safety caused my chest to tighten. Damn, if it hadn't made me feel good that she trusted me like that.

"Look at you..." Diden's voice startled me out of my thoughts, and I looked up to see her in the doorway. "Two days in a row with a smile on your face. You also didn't automatically growl when you walked into the break room this morning. What's gotten into you?"

I knew she was teasing me, but I had definitely felt, I don't know, lighter the last several days, and I knew it was all because of Iris.

"You *want* me to growl?" I asked.

"No, I definitely like this version of you," she said, smiling as she walked farther into the office and sat in the chair across from me on the other side of my desk. "Dare I assume this is because of Iris?"

Jesus, I thought the LVPD was full of gossips...The Park Service wasn't much better.

"What do you need?" I asked, hoping to redirect.

"You're gonna think I'm crazy, but roll with me for a second," she started to say, and I immediately hated where this conversation was going. "I decided to listen to Mr. Stanton last night. It's actually quite good. It's called *Murder, Steve Wrote,* and he details a lot of good cold cases."

"*Murder, Steve Wrote*?" I questioned.

"It's a great name, right?" Diden asked excitedly, although that definitely would not have been the word I'd have used to describe the name.

Cheesy, cringey, overdone—those felt more appropriate.

"Jesus, why do you listen to that kook?" Jennings's voice sounded from my doorway. "The guy's a wannabe cop who probably flunked out of the police academy and lives in his mom's basement."

"Are some of them like that? Yes," Diden admitted. "I'm not sure about this one. He helped solve the cold case from that religious cult in Texas."

"Even a blind squirrel finds a nut every once in a while," Jennings said with a smile on his face, clearly taunting Diden and her love of true crime podcasts. "Honestly, I wouldn't be surprised if you find out some of these podcasters are actually the criminals themselves."

On that note, I chose to intervene. "Speaking of which, there's another dive team set to arrive at Lake Echo in about an hour. Diden, I want you to come with me to help with the crowds or anyone trying to interfere."

"You find another body?" Diden asked, both shock and nervousness written all over her face.

"No bodies," I told her but chose not to give her more info just yet. "You're in charge of the building while we're out, Jennings."

He nodded in response, and the three of us made our way out of my office, Diden following behind me.

I decided to take her with me because I thought it would be good for the podcaster's ego to see someone who actually listened to his podcast. Maybe soften him up.

Diden didn't yet know I had invited Mr. Stanton,

though technically I hadn't invited him personally. Diden had mentioned Steve listened to the police scanners, so I had a buddy of mine back at LVPD make a couple of offhand comments on there about the new dive team we were having come out today at eleven to recover extra evidence we had found.

"Alright, boss, so what's the plan?" she asked as we drove out of the parking lot.

"ISB wants to do one more dive to see if they can find anything else."

As we pulled into a parking space, I knew she saw the same thing I had—Steve Stanton.

"The uh, podcaster, Steve, is here," she mentioned to me.

"I see that," I responded. "As much as he annoys me, he's not standing in a restricted area—yet—so I can't ask him to move. He's free to do what he wants, though if he gets too close, I'll make him leave."

"I'll talk to him," she offered, and that worked perfectly. "I'll make sure he stays where he's supposed to and doesn't interfere."

The tone in her voice was soft, as though she were talking about a friend or someone she admired.

It was perfect timing, as the boat pulled up to the cove in front of us just as I was getting out of the vehicle.

"You go talk to Stanton, and I'll call in to talk to whoever is on command for the boat," I told her and proceeded to call O'Connor from my phone.

After a short discussion, I made sure the walkie talkie

on my belt had the volume turned up extra loud so that both Diden and Stanton could hear it as I walked over to where they were standing.

"I informed him about the dive, and he asked if he could stay and watch," Diden muttered, her voice low so I could hear it, likely just in case I told her no, but the look on Stanton's face showed he heard her too.

"That's fine, but you stay by us, and do not move to the water, as it's now considered a restricted area while they dive," I responded, making sure I was loud enough for both to hear.

"Yes, sir," Stanton replied, nodding emphatically.

I had discussed with O'Connor that his men needed to keep the conversation to a minimum since there would be ears listening to everything they said. The dive team knew they were to get in, swim around for a bit, and then come up to the surface and report they'd found something.

Which was where we were now. Twenty minutes after we had arrived and the divers had made their way into the water, the crackle of static filled the air before a voice chimed in on my two-way radio.

"Command, this is Neptune Two. Copy."

"Neptune Two, this is Command. Go Ahead," O'Connor's voice sounded.

"Be advised, we have found the object. Item is secure. We will bag and surface with it soon. Recommend standby for transfer."

"Affirmative. Chain of custody on contact and awaiting your arrival," O'Connor replied.

They had permission to pull any random piece of debris from the bottom of the lake they wanted, as long as it was small enough to fit in their hands, so as to not be obvious what it was from a short distance.

"They found something?" Diden asked.

"What were they looking for?" Stanton asked, his eyes wide with curiosity.

"It could be the break we've been looking for in the case," I told them, hopefully sounding believable. "We got a credible tip, and as long as it's still intact, it's a piece of evidence that should pinpoint who the killer is."

"What is it?" Stanton asked, trying to sound casual about it, but the gleam in his eye told otherwise.

"Nice try," I said. "I don't mind letting you stand here and watch the crew work, but I'm not telling you details that you could blast to your podcast and potentially let the killer know we're onto him. Just know that your connection may have been right—and this might be the key to connecting this woman to the others."

His eyes bugged out, but only temporarily. If I hadn't already been staring at him while he did it, I may have missed it.

"Understood," he said, but he was clearly disgruntled about it.

We watched the divers reboard the boat and prepare to end their search.

"So how long will you leave this area blocked off?" Stanton asked, aiming for offhand, but there was no mistaking the curiosity in his tone.

"Likely the next day or so, but then it should be open again to the public," I announced, hoping he took the bait.

"Well, um, thank you for letting me watch. I need to get home now," Stanton said to us and then turned to look right at Diden. "If you really do like the podcast, don't forget to leave me a review, please. It helps with the ratings."

"Sure, no problem," Diden responded excitedly.

About thirty minutes later, Diden and I got back in the vehicle to head back to the office, and I hadn't even closed my door before she huffed in frustration.

"You didn't tell me they were looking for something specific," Diden said, and I could tell she was a bit offended I hadn't told her.

"Our office is like a gossip column," I started to explain, giving half-truths the entire time. "I didn't want to have anyone spreading rumors about stuff in case they didn't find anything."

"Fair, but it still would have been nice to know what was at play here."

I knew what she meant, but since technically there wasn't any real item for them to find, the less she knew the better.

The rest of the ride was silent, and I headed straight for my office once we got back so I could call Agent Andrews and fill her in.

"Well, how did it go?" Andrews asked.

"I couldn't get a full read on him, but he's definitely going to do something with that information."

I told her everything that had gone down, including how he asked me what the evidence was and his reactions throughout all of it.

"Alright, well, this sounds like the plan is in motion. We just need to see if he takes the bait, and what he decides to do with that information," she added.

And she was right. He could choose to pounce on the information right away, or he may decide to sit on it for a while.

Now began the waiting game.

21

"You cannot make everyone happy. You are not a taco."
—*It's science*

Hector

It had been two weeks since I'd stayed the night at Iris's place, and we hadn't slept alone since. We mostly stayed at my place because of Sarge, but also because Iris said she liked my place better.

"I love the Thunder Cove area," she had said multiple times. "It's close enough to the city that you get all your amenities and fun things to do, but you're also far enough away that you have some peace and quiet. I love that."

Seeing her happy in my cabin was everything because I enjoyed it too and for the same reasons she did.

Many nights, we found ourselves sitting on my porch just staring off at the lake in the distance, which was what we were doing now. We were both sitting in Adirondack chairs—Iris doing her needlepoint while I was casually throwing a ball to Sarge, which he would fetch and bring back...most of the time.

We had just eaten dinner and were now relaxing. My phone buzzed on the table beside us, bringing me out of my peaceful thoughts.

"Son of a..." I muttered at seeing Jennings's name on the screen.

"What's wrong?" I answered the call.

I was off the clock, so there had to be a good reason for them to call, and it better be, because I was enjoying myself right now.

"Boss, someone called in a report that there was a person digging near the former crime scene of the body, so Lewis and I went to check it out," Jennings started. "Sure enough we found someone doing exactly that. I've got him in cuffs, but the guy claims he will only speak to you."

"You got a name?" I asked, though I had a feeling I knew exactly who it was.

"Yeah, it's Diden's stupid podcast dude," he grumbled.

Bingo.

While I hated having to leave Iris, I had hoped this would happen so we could bring him in for questioning and get some information out of him. The trespassing charge he was about to get would allow me to question him.

"I'll call the ISB and meet you over there," I told him. "Do not do anything or say anything else to him until I get there."

"He's cuffed in the back of my vehicle, so he's not going anywhere," Jennings added, and I could hear the slight smile in his voice. "And Lewis went to block the gated entrance so no one else can get in."

I hung up and turned to Iris, but she spoke before I had the chance to.

"It's okay. I'll hold down the fort and keep Sarge company." She smiled and waved her hands to shoo me away.

I stood from my chair before putting my hands on either side of her chair and leaning down to kiss her.

"I'm sorry, but thank you," I told her. "Hopefully, this won't take long."

She put her hands on each side of my face and pulled me back for another kiss, and once again, I hated that I had to leave.

"Even if it does, I'll still be here when you get back. Don't worry about Sarge and me. We'll have a great time snuggling on the couch or maybe go for a quick walk."

I gave her one last kiss, a longer one this time to hold me over, and then reluctantly left her, grabbing my keys, badge, and gun, before heading out.

On my drive there, I realized how much my life had changed since Iris became a part of it.

A month ago, I never would have minded leaving home to do work-related stuff, even after hours. Now, though, with Iris in my life, I found myself looking for every excuse possible to come home earlier to see her.

By the time I pulled into the lot, I was growing more

agitated by the minute, simply because I had to be here. However, I also knew this was what Agent Andrews and I had hoped for, which was why I'd called her on my way here to let her know.

She planned to meet me there as soon as she could, though it would take longer since she lived farther away. She'd told me I had until she arrived to continue with our plan, and then she would take him into custody.

I waved to Lewis, and he let me in. Lewis was semi-retired and only worked part-time for us, but he was great.

"Hey, man," I said as I pulled up next to him.

"Hey, Madeira," he replied. "Found him knee-deep in the water with some digging tools. He claims you told him he could be here and that digging for scientific samples is allowed. However, he conveniently left his permits at home."

It was true that you could collect samples from a national park as a scientist for research, but you had to have very specific permits for that, and generally the permits only allowed you to collect from a particular area. There was no way in hell I would approve a permit for digging in the area near a former crime scene, so this man didn't *forget* his permits—he didn't have any.

"Thanks, man," I told him. "The ISB will be here soon, so they'll want your statement too."

He nodded, and I continued my way through the gravel lot until I pulled up to the other two Park Service SUVs.

When I pulled up, it was to see Diden and Jennings verbally sparring.

Jesus, I did not need this.

"Hey!" I yelled angrily as I circled the vehicle and made my way to them. "Get your shit together. Both of you."

"He's accusing me of being a traitor and leaking information to Steve!" Diden spouted.

"Steve?" Jennings shot back. "You call him by his first name like you're friends. What the hell, Diden? Why are you trying to help this psychopath?"

"How does calling him by his first name mean I'm helping him?" she snapped. "You're the one who nearly assaulted him."

Great. Just what I needed—an assault charge against one of my staff.

"I didn't assault him!" Jennings spat. "I cuffed him after he lied about you and the boss giving him permission to be here."

That got my attention and had me attempting to break into their heated conversation. "He told you I gave him permission?" I asked, wondering how that conversation went.

"No, he said you and I told him the closed-off area would be re-opening soon, and he thought that meant he could be there," she countered.

"Why the fuck are you defending this guy?" Jennings barked. "You said he mentioned in his podcast that the killer possibly murdered nine other women! How does he know that? He could be the murderer!"

"Enough!" I yelled. "Both of you, take five minutes and walk it off. Now!"

They needed it, but I also needed them to not be around while I asked a few questions of our suspect.

Once they cleared the area, I walked over to the SUV with him inside. Either Jennings or Diden had left the vehicle running with the AC on, but I was about to ruin that. I opened the back door.

"I didn't do anything wrong," he said right out of the gate. "You said it would be open to the public soon after the dive that day. I waited two weeks just to make sure. You can't arrest me for being on public property."

He ended by jutting his chin out in defiance with a level of confidence that was way too high.

"Mr. Stanton, you're not being arrested for trespassing, technically speaking," I informed him. "You're being arrested for digging on federal property without permits."

"I...uh...have them, just not with me," he replied, his confidence breaking just a little. "They're at home."

"You know you are supposed to have them on you, or the permit access is invalid, but..." I held up my hand because I could see he wanted to argue with me. "I'm willing to let that go, but you need to tell me specifically what your conditions and oversight were listed for on your SRCP."

I knew he wouldn't be able to answer that because he didn't have a permit. SRCP stood for Scientific Research and Collecting Permit, but again, most people didn't pay attention to all these details...unless they actually had a permit.

"Look, man, you said the other day while I was here that I couldn't go into these areas while it was an active investigation area, but now it's not, which makes it public access," he argued.

"Public access and public domain are not the same thing," I explained. "This is federal property that we *allow* you to visit. It's like the library. You can go in, read some books, use the space, but you don't get to rip out certain pages of the books and take them home and keep them."

"Okay, but a library also lets you take the books home as long as you bring them back," he argued. "So why can't I just take some samples as long as I agree to bring them back?"

Jeez. Jennings might be right. This guy was a few fries short of a Happy Meal.

"Why does a podcaster need dirt and sand samples?" I asked, getting to the point of the matter.

"For research," he said, sticking his chin out again.

"What kind of research?"

"The criminal justice kind," he shot back, his confidence stretching into arrogance.

We had teams of professionals for that, and he knew that, but I needed him to give me more, so I ignored the fact that he was not a trained professional and moved on.

"What's your specialty?" I inquired. "What do you look for in these circumstances?"

His head jerked back slightly, almost shocked that I'd asked.

"Am I being arrested?" His mood now changed entirely. He was no longer confident but angry. "I want to speak to a lawyer."

"The ISB is on the way, and they will escort you to their office, where you can contact a lawyer," I told him, knowing he would likely just be questioned at the ISB office and then taken to the local sheriff's office for holding.

However, given the sensitivity of this, and the fact that Diden and Jennings had already had a tussle about Stanton, I chose to drive him myself over to Agent Andrews' office.

I'd done my part of the plan. Now it was time for Andrews to do hers, and hopefully we could get some much-needed answers for this case.

22

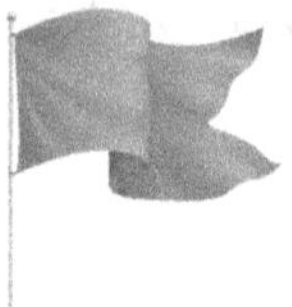

"Love makes your pupils dilate and your brain shut off."
—*It's science*

Iris

A breeze hit my face, akin to what a hairdryer would feel like. Even though it was early evening, it was still hot, and that breeze did nothing to cool me off.

I spent approximately ten minutes after Hector left sitting on the porch before I realized all I was doing was worrying about him since he seemed so stressed when he left.

I knew it had to do with Chantal Simpleton's body found at the lake. I hated that this case—a case that likely wouldn't exist without me—was stressing him out. And that was stressing me out, so I decided to take Sarge for a walk to help me clear my head.

Hector lived so close to one of my favorite spots—the Wash Wetlands park area. It was a little oasis in the desert. Literally. It was a small wetland full of lush plants and bright colors. It was one of those things that you wouldn't think existed in the desert, but it did, and I was grateful for it because my soul needed it today.

I sat on a rock near a stream contemplating the entirety of my existence and the situation I was in, all while Sarge sniffed every square inch of the area around me. There was a narrow trail for people to walk or run on, but Sarge was mostly oblivious to the people, preferring to investigate other critters nearby.

"Iris, is that you?" I heard, looking up to see a man about my age. "It's Lt. Patrick Michaels…You interviewed me at the lake."

Oh yes, now I remembered.

"Oh, yeah, hi," I said to him, turning to shake his hand, which prompted Sarge to want to go and sniff our newcomer.

"I like your dog," he said to me, leaning down to give Sarge some head scratches.

"Oh, he's not mine. He's actually Hector Madeira's."

He stared at me briefly for a moment before speaking. "You walk his dog from time to time or something, or are you dating?"

I knew it was a simple question, but for some reason it felt more personal than that.

"Um, no, I'm not a dog walker," I explained. "We're seeing each other, yes, and I'm staying with him right now, so I decided to bring Sarge down for a walk."

His face went from curiosity to smiling, and then he shook his head and chuckled.

"What?" I asked, not sure why that was funny.

"I'm a little embarrassed to tell you, but that first day we met, I asked Hector if he knew whether you were single," he told me, and I thought back to Christine's comments about her catching Patrick staring at my butt that day. "Hector told me you weren't single, but he didn't tell me that he was the one you were dating. Now I kind of feel like an idiot."

Hector told him what?

That timeline didn't match. We didn't even talk before that day at the lake and for the next week after. Why did Hector tell him we were dating?

"Don't feel like an idiot," I told him. "I'm flattered you even asked."

"Well, tell Hector I said hi. Good seeing you again," he said and then made his way along the trail.

Shortly after Patrick left, Sarge found a frog and was having fun following it along the path and getting excited every time it jumped. His amazement at the little things had me realizing that sometimes joy hides in plain sight, waiting for us to slow down enough to see it.

Much to Sarge's disappointment, we hopped back into the car for the short drive back to the cabin. I had wanted to make sure we were home before Hector returned, just in case things didn't go well for him. Maybe I just needed to offer Hector some joy in plain sight, too, when he got home.

Sarge and I were only home for about fifteen minutes when Hector walked through the door. Sarge greeted him with copious amounts of sniffing and licks before I decided it was my turn.

His head tilted up to me after having bent down to scratch Sarge's head, and I could see the stress lines and exhaustion all over his face. I closed the gap between us and wrapped my arms around his waist and hugged him tight.

"You okay?" he asked me, ever the concerned protector.

"You're my safe space, Hector, and I'm happy to be yours too. If you need to rant, I want you to feel comfortable doing that with me. If you need a hug, advice, or if you need me in other ways, I'm here for that too."

He didn't say anything to me, just stared deeply into my eyes. It was moments like this when I wished he had a super readable face like I did. I would love to know the thoughts swirling deep in those dark eyes.

"You don't need to solve every problem or make sense of everything right away. Sometimes it's just better to take a breath and enjoy what's in front of you."

"You're right in front of me," he replied.

I guess now was the time to try my new tactic. I lowered myself onto my knees in front of him.

"What are you doing?"

"I'm about to take some of your stress away by providing you with some joy," I told him as I stared up at him, my hands going to the waistband of his pants.

"Iris, you take my stress away just by being here," he said, but I saw the heat in his eyes. "You don't need to do that."

See? Good guy.

"I know I don't, but I want to."

His non response was my cue to continue—or at least that was how I was taking it.

I slowly unbuttoned and unzipped his pants, allowing him the time to stop this if he wasn't feeling up to it. Instead, his gaze only intensified.

"Sarge, bed," Hector commanded, and Sarge listened, albeit reluctantly, as he whined the whole way over to his bed.

I pulled the front of his pants and underwear down just enough to free his now growing cock. The man didn't shave his chest, but down here, he groomed to perfection. I ran my fingers over the tip softly before grabbing the rest of him in my fist and stroking him as I looked up. His eyes were sparkling with heat, but I could tell he was trying to control himself and let me be in charge and lead the way.

I was not about to look a gift horse in the mouth, so I seized my opportunity. Tilting my head forward, I took him into my mouth. I slowly made my way down as far as I could before coming back up.

I had no idea what he liked, but I figured this could be a fun way to find out. Clearly I wasn't doing a bad job, because his groans were definitely sending me a message of satisfaction.

"God, your mouth feels so good, Iris," he announced in his husky voice.

His praise made me suck him in even harder. I felt his hands move to my scalp, and he began moving my hair away from my face. I glanced up at him, and his gaze was on me. The deep hunger was clear, but I could tell he was still holding back.

I removed my mouth with a pop as I released him. Then I licked my lips and stared back at him.

"Tell me how you like it?" I asked him.

"Exactly as you are," he replied, but I sensed he was just saying that to appease me.

"Show me, please," I urged.

I saw him fighting the battle mentally and decided to put him back in my mouth while I waited for him to make his decision. I put my lips around the head and sucked lightly while circling my tongue on the tip.

Welp, that did it.

Something in him snapped, because his hands were now firmly around the sides of my head and he was guiding me to take him deeper. I did, making sure to take my time with my tongue as I moved up and down. When he hit the back of my throat, I swallowed, effectively squeezing him and drawing out more gratification from him as he tightened his hold on me.

"Jesus, Iris," he breathed out.

Hector was making so many pleasurable noises that it gave me confidence to try new things. His pleasure was driving up my lust as well, and I could feel myself getting wet between my legs.

To ease my growing need, I moved my legs back and forth while continuing to take him in my mouth. He noticed my movements and pulled my head back so that I released him. In the next moment, I was lifted to a standing position.

"Hector, what are you—I wasn't done," I practically whined.

"Babe, as much as I want to come down the back of your throat, I'd rather be in that tight pussy, having it milk me while I make you scream my name." His words alone sent a tingle through my belly and my legs.

"Bedroom," he said, and he didn't have to tell me twice.

I turned and took off as fast as my legs would take me.

He followed just as quickly behind me, because I no sooner got next to his bed and turned around when he grabbed the sides of my head and captured my mouth in a fevered kiss. His tongue found mine with desperate need. The kiss was rough and real and everything I wanted in that moment.

He lifted me and slid me back so my legs were hanging off the bed and I was on my back. He worked at stripping himself of his shirt, leaving only his black boxer briefs on. They may still be on, but there was no denying what was inside as I stared at the rock-hard bulge fully outlined inside them.

He leaned forward and helped rid me of my own clothes and then his before returning his mouth to mine. He poured everything into that kiss and I never wanted something to last forever like I did this moment.

"Fuck, you have the most perfect body," he said, staring at me dreamily. "It's like you were made for me, Iris. Everything I had on my wish list for a perfect woman is right here in front of me."

When he said stuff like that, I just melted.

The next moment, his mouth was on me, sucking on the bundle of nerves between my legs while his fingers dipped inside and stroked me. His rough beard scratched all the right places, and then his soft tongue soothed. The juxtaposition of those sensations increased my hunger for more. Maybe it was because I was already worked up from earlier, or maybe it was what he'd said to me, but I could already feel that my orgasm was close.

Hector scooted me back farther onto the bed and positioned himself on top. I was so excited for what was about to happen that I didn't care that I wasn't the one on top. I just looked up and admired the sexy man above me.

He joined our hands and lifted them over my head, staring down at me as if he couldn't believe this was real.

"Just so you know, you're my safe space too," he said to me, taking one of his hands and cupping my cheek. "I'm very aware that this is not a level playing field. You are so far out of my league, it's not even funny, but I'm not letting go now. You're mine now. You make me a better person. You've brought me a sense of redemption and atonement I never thought I would get. You taught me that I not only deserve those, but that I can be the man *you* deserve."

Dear God, did he just say that?

"I'm yours?" I asked playfully, checking to see if I'd misheard him.

"Yeah, you are. I fought being with you for too long. But now that I've had perfection, there's no going back."

"I love that you think I'm perfect, Hector, but you're putting me up on a pedestal. I could gain or lose weight. My body could change."

He put his finger to my lips to quiet me. "Iris, yeah, your body is a big part of what attracts me to you, but it's not everything. Your personality is the opposite of mine. You're sunshine to my firestorm. You put a light back inside me. A light that I thought was burned out for good —and so did my family. You brought me out of my shell. You bring me a joy I haven't had in decades. I don't care if you get fatter, skinnier, lose hair, get stretch marks...You will always be the perfect woman for me."

Oh. My. God. Was it hot in here?

"I love knowing other men overlooked you."

"You like knowing other people didn't want to have sex with me?" I asked, not sure I'd heard him correctly.

"No. I like knowing that other people missed out on what's now mine. And I'm gonna revel in the fact that I won out in the end because I get to have the most beautiful woman underneath me."

When he said stuff like that, my heart just turned to mush.

This time, I put my finger to his mouth. "Shut up and fuck me," I said, kissing him fiercely.

He buried himself inside me a fraction of a second later. I gasped and bucked my hips as euphoric sensations coursed through my body.

He drove into me at a fevered pace, and I'd never felt anything better.

Unintelligible noises were all that could be heard, along with the slick sounds of him thrusting back and forth inside me.

"You are the best thing that's ever happened to me, Iris. The best goddamn thing ever."

At his rough voice, I detonated. My orgasm rushed through me, and I could feel the pleasure all over my body. I yelled his name, but my mind was blank.

I knew he followed shortly behind me, but I was in an entirely different universe, on another wavelength.

After my breathing and heart rate stabilized enough to at least reach semi-normal levels, I lay there thinking about the man next to me.

The way he made me feel was different, special. Every time he looked at me, it made my heart swell against my rib cage. He didn't have to speak. His touch, his gestures, spoke volumes.

I was falling for this man, hard and fast, and I realized I didn't care. He was everything I had ever hoped for in a man—steadfast, respectful, loyal...and he worshipped me.

I knew he thought he wasn't good enough for me because of his past, but I saw it differently than he did. He wanted redemption but felt he didn't deserve it, which only made me fall deeper for this handsome man in front of me.

I knew I would spend as much time as I could making him realize he was worthy.

23

Iris

Because it was too hot and windy to be outside today, we had a mostly lazy day inside, and it was wonderful. I say mostly lazy day because there was some physical activity done—the naked kind.

It started when I brought up the conversation I had with Patrick last week, just to see what Hector would say.

"I ran into Patrick the other day—the lieutenant I interviewed with you at the lake," I told him, crossing my arms under my breasts and leaning against the bathroom door while he brushed his teeth. "Funny thing, actually. He mentioned that he'd asked you if I was single, and you'd told him I was seeing someone."

His eyes made contact with mine, but he said nothing, just continued to brush his teeth.

"Except I wasn't seeing anyone, so why did you tell him that?" I asked because the nosy person in me wanted to know.

I gave him a moment to finish washing up but stayed grounded in my position in the doorway.

"He gave me a bad vibe, and I didn't want him asking you out," he said as if it were just as simple as that. Then he turned to me, so close I could feel his breath on my face. "Maybe deep down, I knew you would be mine eventually, so I didn't want him to interfere."

Before I could respond, he kissed me. That kiss led to other things—naked things—and the day progressed happily from there.

Hector watched some baseball on TV while I caught up on my needlepoint. Both of these things were done on the couch, snuggled up next to each other, and I loved every moment of it.

Now, hours later, we were cleaning up the dishes after dinner, and my plan was to finish some laundry and then talk Hector into watching a movie with me in his bed—naked.

We had a nice routine of me washing the dishes and him drying them and putting them away—mostly because he could actually reach all the high cabinets and I couldn't.

I had just handed him a plate when I noticed he was staring at me.

"What? Do I have bubbles on my face or something?" I asked.

"No," he replied, a small grin on his face. "Just admiring how fuckable you look right now."

I snorted in response. I was in an oversized gray T-shirt and cut-off jeans shorts with my hair pulled up into a very messy bun, and I had my glasses on.

"Hector, my glasses are deeply unsexy, and my hair is a hot mess."

"I happen to like the look," he said, grinning back at me.

I rolled my eyes and put my hand on my hip, pausing with the dishes. "Don't tell me you're into that whole sexy librarian thing."

"I'm into *you*," he said, taking a step closer to me and closing the gap between us. "Don't need a librarian. I got a sexy woman right in front of me. But if you wanna pretend to be a librarian, I'm game for whatever you want."

I rolled my eyes at his comment, but I was also going to enjoy the comment and run with it. "Oh yeah?" I asked, leaning into his space and putting my chest up against his abs.

"Yeah," he responded and leaned down to kiss me.

It was a good kiss, too. Soft at first and then more demanding as his mouth moved to take command of mine. He slid his hands into my hair, pulling slightly as he deepened the kiss. My brain began to short-circuit, and he slid his tongue into my mouth as I tasted his minty fresh breath.

Just as we started to get to the good stuff—like groping —his phone rang.

I heard a small whine leave my body as Hector broke away from our kiss. He still held me tight as he looked back at his phone screen on the counter to see who was calling.

His groan let me know it was not a call he could ignore.

We disconnected, and Hector walked to the phone to pick it up.

"Madeira," he answered, sounding irritated already. "Where? Ahhh…shit."

His irritation now seemed to be morphing into pissed off, and I wondered what the call was about.

"Yeah…okay," he continued. "Give me fifteen to get there."

He hung up and turned to me. "That was Jennings. There's a small fire on the north side of the park."

Crap. That wasn't good. We had high winds and very dry conditions, so any fire that started was very likely to spread quickly.

"Is everybody okay?" I asked.

"For now, but Jennings said based on the information he has, it's headed toward the campground, so I need to go over and help try to evacuate those folks," he replied.

"Okay, go do your thing," I told him. "Is it just the two of you?"

"That's the weird thing," he added. "Jennings said he's been trying to get in touch with Diden to go block off the other entrance while he goes and checks it out, but she's not answering her phone, even though she's supposed to be on post. That's not like her to not respond."

Ann definitely struck me as the responsible type, but maybe something had come up.

"Sorry, babe," he said, leaning into me. "I'll try to make this quick."

"It's okay. Be careful," I told him. "I know it's mostly dirt out there on that side of the park, but if there's enough vegetation to burn, it can definitely spread for a few hundred acres before it burns itself out."

"I'm not worried about the park. I'm worried about it spreading into the campground," he said, grabbing his badge and other gear.

"We're under a red flag warning today, so it's not out of the question that some of those embers could get picked up and lofted far away—and quickly," I explained.

"Alright," he said, leaning down to kiss me. "Hopefully, the fire department gets there quickly and I can be back soon."

He walked over to the door to put his shoes on and grab his keys before turning back to me.

"Do not feed him extra treats," he warned.

My only response was to smile back at him as Sarge sat happily at my feet.

He shook his head at me, as though he knew I wouldn't listen.

Once he was out the door, I turned to Sarge and

crouched down to his level. "Daddy says no more treats, but I think we're going to pretend we didn't hear that."

He licked my face—clearly letting me know he agreed with me.

After Hector left, I decided to clean up the kitchen and get some laundry going. That way half the to-do list would already be done by the time he got back, allowing us to focus on picking up from where we'd left off. Priorities.

My phone rang in the kitchen, and I rushed to get it, hoping it was Hector saying he was on his way home. It wasn't, but I still smiled seeing Christine's name pop up on the screen.

"Hey girl," I greeted her. "I thought you were working today. I figured you'd be busy already."

"I'm actually about to leave here in ten minutes, but I wanted to ask if I could borrow your black sequin dress for my cousin's wedding next weekend," she asked me.

"Yeah, totally," I told her.

"Can I swing by on my way home and grab it?"

"I'm actually at Hector's place right now, waiting for him to get back, but I can bring it to work tomorrow if you want."

"Yeah, that works," she said. "Why are you there if he isn't?"

"He went to check out the fire on the north side of the park," I told her.

"There's a fire?" she asked, seeming genuinely confused. "No one reported anything."

"Really?" I asked, because it was usual standard protocol to report it to the weather service because it affected our warning products and the alerts we would send out to the public.

Sarge started to bark, followed by a knock on the door.

"Here, I'll text you his number," I told her. "Call him because he may still be driving, but he can get you some coordinates of the fire so you can get it on the maps ASAP."

"Thanks," she said. "I'd like to get it on there before I finish my shift."

I looked out the narrow window on the side of the door and saw Ranger Diden's face.

"Okay, I gotta go. Hector's co-worker, Ann, is here," I told her.

"No problem. I'll see you tomorrow!" she said, and I hung up just as I swung the door open.

24

"Red Flag Warnings mean dangerous conditions ahead. Same for Tinder dates."
—*It's science*

Hector

Hell, I did not want to be doing this.

I'd rather be back at my house enjoying Iris and the good time we were working our way up to. Instead, here I was, on my way to check out a wildfire—likely set by some dumbass camper. Jennings was super vague on the phone about where it was, but he said he hadn't fully scoped it out yet and spent most of his time, unsuccessfully, trying to get in touch with Diden to help set the perimeter.

I also tried calling Diden, but it went straight to voicemail three times in a row.

I'd only been in the car driving for at most fifteen minutes when my phone rang. I didn't recognize the number but knew it could be someone from the fire department, so I grabbed it.

"Madeira," I answered.

"Hi, Hector. This is Christine from the weather service," the woman responded. "I was just talking with Iris, and she mentioned the fire you were headed to, but we have no report of it. I was hoping you could give me some coordinates so we could get our warnings updated and alerts sent out."

Of course, Jennings would forget to fucking call this in.

"Christine, I'm not entirely sure where it is yet, but it's on the northern edge of the lake according to my other ranger," I explained. "If you give me about ten more minutes, I should be up there and can give you a better estimate of the coordinates. Does that work?"

"Yeah, that's fine," she responded.

"Good, and if this gets bad and you see it start spreading southwest, will you call Iris and tell her to evacuate my house, please?" I asked, hoping it didn't come to that, but I wanted her to have someone watching out for her since I would likely be stuck up here on the north side until this was contained.

"Yeah, no problem, although one of your other rangers had just gotten there when I called her," she mentioned.

What?

"Did you say another ranger was at my house?" I asked.

"Yeah, when I was hanging up with her, she said someone named Ann, I think, had shown up."

Diden? What the hell was Diden doing at my house?

"Thanks. Appreciate it," I told her and hung up.

I tried calling Diden's phone again, now more confused than ever. Again, it went straight to voicemail, but before I could try calling Iris, my phone vibrated with another new call, this time from Agent Andrews.

"I'm headed to a fire, so you gotta make this quick," I said instead of a traditional greeting.

There was a short pause before she spoke. "What did you just say?"

"Jennings called about a fire on the north side of the lake I'm headed to, so you need to make this quick."

"Where's Iris?" she asked me, her voice serious and grave.

"At my place. Why?"

"Shit," she said the sound of shuffling papers in the background.

"Andrews, what's up?" I asked, getting a little peeved at her frenzied tone.

"Ranger Diden just called me twenty minutes ago, frantic," she said. "She was rambling on and on about Jennings working for multiple different parks over the last few years and never staying at more than one for longer than a year. Then she blabbered on about the missing women. It was honestly hard to keep up. The last thing she said before her phone died was that she was headed to your place so you could get Iris safe because Jennings was after her."

What the fuck? What was going on?

"I've spent the last twenty minutes going over everything she said in my head and checking a few databases for information," she added quickly. "Diden believes Jennings is our serial killer, and I can't disprove that theory."

"Are you serious?" I asked her in disbelief.

"After Diden's tip, I checked the dates," she said. "The seven women who went missing in the last six years—the ones Steve mentioned in his podcast—were all in places where Jennings was working nearby. Seven different national parks, all of which were fewer than ten miles from the last known location of the women."

Rage built inside me, but I tamped it down, letting my police training kick into gear. "That could just be a coincidence."

"Yes, but right before she got off the phone, she mentioned she found something at his house about blaming Iris for stealing evidence and giving it to the podcaster. Her phone dropped out after that."

My stomach dropped, and I pulled the car to the side of the road and stopped.

"I didn't think anything of it until you just mentioned the fire," Andrews added.

"Supposedly Diden is at my house," I told her, remembering what Christine had told me and relaying that to Andrews.

"I'm turning around and heading back to my place. Can you call people in and send them up to the north side of the lake to meet Jennings just in case this is a legit fire?" I asked, though the likelihood of that being true was diminishing by the second. "And have someone track their cars. All our vehicles have trackers on them."

"Got it. Go. And report back," she said quickly and then hung up.

I spun my car around and sped as fast as my vehicle would take me in the direction of home.

I needed to get to Iris. I needed to make sure she was safe. There were too many unknowns right now.

I didn't have a good feeling about this, which was why I called the fire department myself to report the fire. If there really was one, they needed to know about it, and they could get to it quickly.

At my call, the dispatch agent informed me they were aware of the large fire and had sent several crews.

Hearing her say that only made my panic ease slightly.

I continued to race toward my house, and as I got closer, I began to see a faint orange glow in the distance.

I grabbed my phone and dialed Andrews as I drove impossibly faster to my house.

"Hey, I've got a..." she started to say, but I cut her off.

"There's another fire up ahead. I can see the faint glow, and if I'm judging it right, it's damn close to my house," I told her. "I just called dispatch, and they said someone had reported a very large fire and they had sent several crews."

She paused for a moment before what I had said sank in. "The other fire wasn't just a distraction to get you away from the house."

"It was also to divert resources," I confirmed.

"I'll call it in and have the crews move to your house ASAP," she said. "Do not go too close to the house, Hector. Wait until crews can get there."

"I gotta go," I told her, hanging up the phone.

There was no way I was standing by if my house was on fire.

25

—*It's science*

Iris

"Hey, Ann. How are—" I started to say, but she shoved her way in and interrupted me.

"Are you alone? Where's Hector?" she asked, very jittery and clearly on edge.

Before I could answer, a second person slid in through the front door and closed it quickly.

Sarge barked at the newcomer and then began to sniff him up and down as though he held a thousand snacks in his pants.

"Iris, this is Steve Stanton, the podcaster who wrote you the letter." Ann waved her hand to point at him quickly.

I felt my eyes bug out of my sockets as she introduced

him. "Who...What..." I started to speak, but Ann cut me off again.

"Where is Hector? Did he already leave?"

Now was about when my Spidey-senses started to go off. How did she know Hector was leaving? And why did she come here if she knew he might not be here? And why was the weirdo podcaster here?

"Ann, what's going on?" I asked her.

"Please, I promise I will tell you everything, but I need to know how long ago Hector left," she begged.

"About ten, maybe fifteen minutes ago for the fire," I told her, although I was a bit confused because she would have known that if she had answered her phone.

She had brushed past me in her quest to search the house for Hector, and Steve was standing just inside the door. I was going to ask him what was going on, but Ann had quickly returned and was now facing me.

"Where?" she asked, both unsettled and a bit distracted.

"Ranger Jennings called to tell him there was a fire somewhere on the north side, up near the campgrounds," I told her. "It must be new because they hadn't called it in yet."

"How do you know they hadn't called it in yet?" she asked anxiously.

"I was just on the phone with my colleague Christine at the weather service, and she said no one had reported it yet. She was going to call Hector as soon as she got off the phone with me."

She stood there staring off into the living room instead of responding. Her breathing was very fast, and she seemed flushed. I started to get a little worried. Even Sarge was a bit apprehensive. He normally went up to anyone who came in the house to see if he could get some free belly rubs out of them, but he had chosen to return to my side instead, watching warily as the scene in front of me unfolded.

"Okay, this is good," she said, nodding, and then she turned to Steve. "We all need to go. Now. And bring your phone because mine died."

"What's going on?" I asked, starting to get a little scared.

"It's Jennings," she said, looking around the kitchen like she was searching for something. "Where is Sarge's leash? We need to go and get you somewhere safe."

"I don't understand. What's wrong with Jennings?"

"Let's get in my car, and I'll tell you everything, but I'm guessing the reason the fire wasn't reported is because the fire isn't actually real. It was a diversion to get Hector away from you."

"Ann, I'm not trying to be difficult, but I'm not leaving until you give me more information. What is going on?"

"Steve and I were on our way to the ISB office to meet with Agent Andrews with some new information we had, when my phone died," she said quickly. "I turned on our radios in our vehicles to see if I could reach out to Hector that way, but that's when I heard Jennings get on and report the fire over our Park Service radios. He alerted everyone to get up there quickly and mentioned that he called me and couldn't get ahold of me."

"Just like we talked about," Steve broke in to speak for the first time, looking at Ann.

Ann nodded at him and then turned to me. "Steve and I were going over some things at his place last night, and it occurred to me while we were in bed that Jennings had suspected *I* was the one who was leaking the info to Steve and he might try to come after me."

What did she just say? She leaked information? She was also lying in bed with Steve? What in the world was happening right now?

"But then I heard Jennings say on the scanner that Hector would be heading up that way too, and I knew something was wrong."

"A trap," Steve interrupted. "There is no fire."

"That's when it hit me that you, Iris, were his real target. Not me," Ann said. "So Steve and I diverted and drove here to check on you instead of driving to the ISB. But we still need to go there. So please grab your things and Sarge, and we will all head there together. Please."

She pleaded that last part, and I believed her. I nodded and was about to grab Sarge's leash, when he began barking again.

Ann and I both turned around at the same moment to see Ranger Jennings standing in the doorway.

"Ann, what are you doing here?" Jennings said, as calm as could be.

"It's you," Ann growled at him. "You're the one who murdered those girls!"

"Now, Ann, you've been listening to this crackhead podcaster too much," Jennings said as he nodded in Steve's direction.

Steve had moved just to the side of the door, barely even in the house, and now stared wide-eyes at Jennings.

As Jennings stepped farther into the room, Steve bolted out the front door and took off. Jennings, realizing his mistake, reached around and pulled a gun from his back, pointing it straight at Ann.

"Now, we're all going to take a seat and talk about this calmly," he said, very composed but also detached and unfazed.

Sarge, however, had read the room and was now growling low at Jennings from where he had returned to my side. I saw the moment his eyes met the dog's and realized Sarge may be a threat. His eyes changed from stoic to icy in one blink.

I stepped around Sarge, putting myself in front of him. "Do not harm him," I told Jennings.

"Why are you doing this?" Ann asked him, bringing the attention back to her.

"Well, because this one couldn't keep her mouth shut," Jennings said, pointing at me. "I assumed she lied and had gone and told the podcaster all kinds of confidential information and he started to connect too many dots."

What the hell was he talking about?

"I never talked to the podcaster!" I announced.

Jennings now turned to Ann, his voice rising. "But now...now I realize it was you. Because he knew about things that the public was not privy to."

"It was me. I told him," Ann said from beside me, shocking the hell out of me. "I also told the ISB, so you won't get away with this."

"You bitch," he snarled, lifting his gun and firing at her.

The shot was deafening as it echoed through the house. I looked over to see Ann drop to the ground, moaning and grabbing her side. I jerked around to look at Jennings, who took the side of the gun and swung it my way. I wasn't fast enough to react, though, and I felt a sharp blow to the side of my head. The next thing I knew, everything went black.

My head hurt so bad—it felt as though it was about to explode if I moved even the slightest bit.

I tried to close my eyes again to dull the pain, but something cool and wet hit my face. I opened my eyes to see Sarge staring back at me, looking very worried.

His feet were tap dancing around the floor, but he was staying in place. He whined and licked my face again. I tried opening my eyes wider and looked around.

I was in Hector's house. Where weas Hector?

I was lying on the floor on my side. I tried to sit upright, but that caused a wave of nausea to roll through me. I tried to hold myself steady in the sitting position as I looked around. From where I sat on the floor, I saw the front door was ajar, and it was getting darker outside, as if the sun were about to set.

I moved my head slowly to the right and saw red on the hardwood floors. It took a moment to register that it was blood. A lot of blood.

Ann!

Memories of what happened flooded back to me.

Hector! I needed to warn Hector.

I tried to get up, but the feeling of both passing out and throwing up overtook me. I paused in my effort to get up, trying to scan the room for my phone. At the same time, Sarge, who had been at my side, was now by the door, barking in my direction and pacing.

Was he trying to warn me of something? His mix of whining and high-pitched barks along with his frantic movements had me worried that Jennings might still be nearby.

I needed to get to my phone and call Hector. Or 911. Or both.

Just as I tried again, slowly, to lift myself up, Sarge barked again, but this time, he took off out the front door.

Mild panic set in—I had no idea where he was going —but I forced myself to focus and find my phone. Standing was too much, so I crawled over to the kitchen— the spot I remembered setting my phone down when Ann had arrived.

I made it about halfway when Sarge came sprinting

back inside and raced toward me, barking incessantly once he made it to me.

His barks made my head hurt even more. I turned to tell him to be quiet so I could concentrate, when I saw Hector's frame in the doorway.

"Jesus Christ," he muttered and then bolted to my side.

26

—*It's science*

Hector

The flames kept getting brighter as I approached my house. When I pulled up, I saw two extra vehicles next to Iris's—the first was one of our standard-issue SUVs, but I had no idea who the other vehicle belonged to. It could be Diden's or Jennings's or anyone else's. Nothing was off the table at this point.

I opted to leave my car at the end of the drive and walk up to the house instead. Yes, that would be slower, but it would also allow me to be quieter if I needed to launch a surprise attack. I could see flames off in the distance to the northwest of my house, but they were still far enough away that I had time to go in and see if anyone was still in the house.

My heart was beating faster than it ever had before. I'd

fought overseas with the Army and gone undercover on several operations with the LVPD—some of which had involved incredibly close calls—but none had terrified me like this. The thought of Iris being hurt or scared boiled my blood.

Just as I left my vehicle, I heard a soft voice call out. "Ranger Madeira. Ranger Madeira. Over here."

I turned, putting my hand at my hip where my service weapon was.

A shadow appeared from behind the shrubs along the ridge. It was Steve.

"What the fuck are you doing here?" I hissed at him.

"I'm trying to help," he said frantically, holding his hands up. "Jennings is in there with Iris and Ann. He shot Ann and hit Iris over the head."

"Why didn't he hurt you?" I questioned him, noting he looked perfectly fine to me.

"I…uhh…was watching through a side window," he sputtered and looked down. "I was going to call for help, but I dropped my phone on the way out here, and now it doesn't work."

He held out his phone with a cracked screen as proof.

"Give me the basics of what happened as fast as you can," I demanded.

"Ann and I showed up because we were coming to get Iris and take her to some special agent lady that Ann knew because we suspected Jennings," he started to rattle off. "Jennings must have been not far behind because he showed up. He shot Ann when she tried to go after him, and then turned and went for Iris. He hit her over the head with his gun, and she went down. He was so caught up with all the others, I slipped out the door. I was going to get in the car and drive to get help, but he'd slashed all the tires of the vehicles. I came down here hoping someone would come by and call for help."

Shit. I needed to get up there and check the situation.

"Is he still in there?"

"I...I don't know," he responded. "I heard another shot fired, but then I noticed the fire and wasn't sure what to do."

"Here's what's going to happen," I directed. "If both women are injured, I can't carry them both, so I need you to come with me. But you are going to stay by my side the entire time. Do you understand?"

I didn't fully trust him yet, so there was no way I was having him at my back.

He quickly held up his hands in surrender with a panicked look on his face. "Yes, got it."

"I've already called in for backup and help, so it should be on the way, but we need to get those women and my dog out of there before the fire gets to the house."

He nodded, and we began walking up to the house.

"No talking, and no noises. Understood?" I instructed.

He nodded again, and we quietly walked up my dirt path just to the side of my gravel driveway.

We passed all three vehicles and noticed that they did in fact have all their tires slashed. As we crept closer to the house, I could see that the front door was open.

A moment later, something bolted out, and I heard a low bark. Sarge came rushing toward me, barking again and doing circles. This was his alert bark—his recall signal—to let me know he'd found something important and I needed to follow him.

I gave Steve the universal signal to be quiet with my finger over my lips, and he nodded. I pulled out my gun as I approached the doorway...and then I saw blood. Not a lot, but drips and streaks scattered along my living room and hallway. That's when I saw her—Iris—sitting half upright and holding her head.

"Jesus Christ," I muttered, bolting into the house and crouching down beside her.

"Are you okay?" I asked, running my hands over her body to check for blood.

"I'm okay," she said, her voice very raspy.

Sarge came to sit right next to her.

"Is there anyone else here?" I asked as I scanned the house quickly.

"I...I don't think so," she said. "Jennings shot Ann, but then he hit me over the head and I blacked out. I...I don't know where they are."

That explained the blood. My guess was he dragged Ann somewhere, but he wouldn't just leave Iris here for good. He would come back.

"Steve," I called out to him but in a quieter tone.

He popped his head through the doorway immediately as I waved for him to come over to where Iris and I were. To his credit, he came over immediately.

"He's one of the good guys, Hector," Iris said to me, likely sensing my hesitation around him.

"Can you walk, or do I need to carry you?" I asked her, knowing we needed to leave now.

"I just need to sit here for a moment and let my head stop spinning."

"We can't do that, Iris," I told her. "We need to leave now. I'll carry you."

I started to scoop her up when she turned to me, holding her hands up. "Just give me a few minutes."

"We don't have a few minutes, Iris," I said gravely. "The area around the house is on fire, and the wind is causing it to spread quickly. We need to go now."

I lifted her up and set her on the edge of my living room chair.

"You have sixty seconds to determine whether I carry you or you walk," I told her. "I'm going to go scan the rest of the house for Ann, and then we are leaving."

I turned to Steve. "You watch her while I check the house. If something feels off or Sarge starts to growl, you yell out as loud as you can. Got it?"

He nodded feverishly and stayed right where he was.

Less than sixty seconds later, I had passed through two other rooms and then finally made it to my master bedroom, where several drops of blood had led.

My gun was up as I entered. I found Ann slumped on the floor next to my bed. I quickly scanned the rest of the room and noticed my bedroom window on the far wall was wide open. I never opened those—ever. My guess was

Jennings either left on his own, thinking neither woman would wake up, or he heard Sarge bark and took off, thinking backup was arriving.

Out that same window, I could see the flames edging closer to the house. I walked in and bent at Ann's side.

"Ann, are you okay?" I whispered to her as I checked for a pulse and scanned her body for injuries.

"Not really." Her voice was pained as she spoke.

She had blood coming from what looked like a bullet wound in her side, but as I looked closer, it appeared to be just a superficial wound. It seemed like a lot of blood loss for her injury, but maybe Jennings was also injured.

"I'm going to carry you out, okay? But this might hurt because we need to move quickly," I told her, scooping her up while scanning the room once more before we slid out into the hallway.

When I returned to the living room, Iris was now standing, though she looked like she could keel over at any moment.

"I can carry her," Steve offered when he saw Ann in my arms.

I doubted that, given he was roughly five foot eleven and maybe one hundred eighty pounds, but I'd let him try.

Plus, I'd rather have my focus on Iris and have a hand ready to use my gun if needed.

I handed her off to Steve, wrapping her over his back like you would carry a child—piggyback style. To his credit, he supported her and seemed to have a good grip.

"Let's go," I said, needing to get everyone out ASAP.

Iris was being really strong now, even though she was obviously in pain.

Just as I reached out for her to take my hand, a massive boom shook the house. I heard a few windows break, but the house itself was fine.

"What was that?" Steve asked, clearly panicked.

"I'm guessing it was my shed," I said, scanning the room since we had all flinched, ducked down, or at least shifted during the noise.

"Your shed?" Iris asked.

"I have propane tanks in there, which are highly flammable," I told them. "Which means either the fire has now made it to my property, or someone lit the shed on fire so that it would explode.

"Steve, you still good with Ann?" I asked him, and he nodded.

"Sarge, *hier*," I called, telling him I wanted him to come near me. Mostly because I wanted him near Iris in case something bad happened.

"Sarge, *schutz*," I told him, pointing at Iris.

"What did you tell him?" Iris asked beside me as we walked as quickly as she could, given her head injury.

"I told him to protect and guard you. I have a gun and you don't, so I want him to make you his focus," I said as we walked down my front steps.

I kept my grip on her hand and wanted to get to my vehicle quickly, but I knew Iris needed to walk slower. I used that to my advantage and scanned the area around us, which was getting harder now that sunset had passed.

Behind me, flames were shooting high in the sky—both from the roof of my house and what was left of my shed.

"I parked at the end of the driveway because I had no idea who was here. Are you okay to walk?" I asked Iris. "It's about another sixty yards."

"I've got it," she said, her tenacious attitude—and some stubbornness—powering her through the rest of the walk down the driveway.

Rounding the car to the passenger side so I could help her in, I glanced down and saw the wheels of my SUV bulging out along the gravel, deflated with the rubber gaping open.

Slashed, and recently if the quiet hiss of air leaking out was any indication.

Jennings was still here—nearby—but where?

27

Iris

We walked as quickly as I could manage down the drive, though his long driveway felt even longer when you were trying not to throw up the entire way.

Just as I was about to open my door, Hector called out, "Iris, Steve, go to the trunk."

I looked up, not understanding, when he turned and spoke to Sarge.

"*Pass auf,*" he said, his voice stern and authoritative.

I didn't know that particular command, but I watched as Hector and Sarge both walked back to the trunk with me. Sarge's body was lowered to the ground, and his eyes were scanning everywhere quickly, as if looking for something.

"What does that mean?" I asked.

He didn't respond at first, just opened the hatch and reached in to grab a few small items. He spoke quietly as he handed me a flashlight. "New plan. We leave on foot. The tires on the car have been slashed. We need to be cautious as we make our way out of here, because Jennings likely did it, and that means he's close."

It took a few moments for his comments to process in my brain. I just stood there while Hector grabbed a few more things from the back of his vehicle before finally closing it.

"I gave Sarge the *be alert* command so he'll be watching, but I don't know who or what is out there, so I need you to pay attention, and if I ask you to do something, I need you to do it without hesitation. Understood?"

"Yeah," I responded. I wasn't stupid. He was definitely the only trained one of the two of us when it came to situations like this.

"We'll head over the tree line there and make our way quickly up the road," Hector said as he pushed me in that direction. "There should be help on the way, so we just need to get going in that direction, and maybe we'll pass an emergency vehicle before the fire can get there."

That brought my brain back to the here and now. The fire.

"No," I told him, grabbing his arm to stop him and then pointing to the other side. "We're safer going down that hill over there rather than up the road along the ridge."

"No, that will take too long," Hector countered. "The

fastest route is just up that small hill beyond the trees. We can get to the road faster and hopefully outrun the fire."

He tried pulling me again, but I resisted. "Hector, listen to me. I may not know evasive maneuvers and tactical stuff like you, but I know fires. We're actually more at risk going up that hill because fire spreads faster uphill because both heat and fire rise, which dries out the vegetation before the full flames get there, spreading it faster," I explained, pointing to the area I would prefer to evacuate to. "This is a longer route, yes, but it's also down-hill and has less vegetation, meaning the fire won't spread as fast, giving us more time."

I watched him chew the inside of his cheek as he looked around, assessing the situation.

"Okay, let's go." He grabbed my hand and called for Sarge to follow, Steve and Ann not far behind.

The flames continued to spread rapidly, and I just hoped that my plan worked and we made it out of here safely.

I scanned the area around us as we quickly worked our way through the rough terrain in the dark. This area wasn't a forest in the traditional sense, but we had Joshua trees and palm trees, along with lots of sagebrush, cacti, and yucca plants. None of those would feel pleasant if you tripped and fell into them.

I kept looking back at Steve, who was still carrying Ann, though he was beginning to show signs of struggling.

Hector's right hand held his gun, ready to use it, while

his other hand was outstretched, ready to catch me if I went down. I was holding my own, but I loved that he was there if I needed him.

"Now where?" I asked several minutes later as we finally made it to the bottom of the ridge. "I'm not familiar with this area, and it's so dark."

I turned to look back up the large hill we had just come down to see the glowing orange color behind it from the fire. We'd made it to the bottom safely, but those flames would catch up to us sooner rather than later.

"Follow me," Hector answered simply as he pulled out his phone.

"Andrews. Change of plans. I need a pickup. You got anybody close by? I've got one person with a gunshot wound, another with a head injury, and my tires were slashed, so Iris, Sarge, Stanton, Diden, and I are all on foot. The cabin and surrounding area are on fire, so we came down the bluff and will head down Highway Three moving east. Can you have someone meet us there?"

I listened to what he was saying but also kept turning back to look behind us.

"Thanks," Hector said, finishing his call, and then he turned back to both Steve and me.

"The main road should be about a quarter mile over there," he said, pointing. "There's an outpost on that road about another half mile down that we'll get picked up at, but we need to move before the flames get to us."

Steve and I both nodded before Hector handed me his gun.

"Do you know how to shoot?" he asked, and I nodded. Auntie had taught me in case we ever had a bear or coyote come on the farm to try to get our animals, though it had been years since I'd fired a gun.

Hector turned to Steve. "Give me Diden for a bit. You walk with Iris and set the pace faster so we can meet the sheriff."

They carefully hoisted Ann onto Hector's back, and we took off toward Highway Three.

A quarter mile was a long way to walk. When I glanced back at the fire, I wondered if we should have gone toward the lake instead of the highway. The fire wasn't likely to make it all the way there since there wasn't much vegetation near the beach, but if it did, at least we could have had safety in the water.

But this was Hector's specialty, and his confidence helped steady me. He knew this area like the back of his hand, so I had to trust him that he knew where he was taking us.

Unlike big cities, we didn't have a lot of buildings or homes out here in the national park area to help light up the sky, so it was very dark. There was barely a crescent moon to cut through the dark above us and guide our way. This made it difficult for us to navigate our way down the road, but it would also make it difficult for Jennings to find us if he was following behind.

I was counting on that because I knew with Ann being shot and me having a raging headache, our group wasn't exactly in tip-top shape. We moved as quietly and quickly as we could, taking every small advantage towards safety.

Not even five minutes later, we saw the lights and heard the sirens as two police vehicles and one ambulance raced toward us.

We loaded Ann into the ambulance first, and Steve demanded he go with her.

I refused to go to the hospital since we couldn't take Sarge with us, and there was no way I was making Hector leave Sarge. I did, however, agree to go to the ISB office and have an EMT check me out there. The sheriff and fire department showed up shortly after, and Hector filled them in on Jennings, who was armed and missing.

"Secure the perimeter so the fire doesn't spread, but do not approach the house," Hector told them, and I hated what that meant. Because if they couldn't get too close, they likely wouldn't be able to save the cabin.

An hour later, we were in Agent Andrews's personal office while she barked out orders on both her phone and two-way radio, giving guidance to all the emergency personnel surrounding the park.

She had a nice couch that we were both sitting on, with Sarge at our feet on the floor. He, too, had been checked out and was all good according to the vet.

Hector had sent one of his other rangers, Lewis, over to the hospital to find out Ann's condition and report back. Hector had put the call on speaker so I could hear too, since I was worried about her.

"Diden's in surgery now, but the nurse said it shouldn't take long," Lewis told us. "The bullet just grazed her, but they found bullet fragments still inside, so they are going to remove those and stitch her up. I'll let you know when she's out and in recovery."

"Thanks, man," Hector told him.

"And, uh...boss..." Lewis added, lowering his voice a bit. "That podcaster guy, Steve, is here saying he's her boyfriend. You think that's true? Or do you want me to tell the cop who's here to have him removed?"

The ISB had requested an LVPD officer be sent to the hospital for protection in case Jennings showed up.

"All the evidence we have shows he's not the bad guy," Hector told him, and they hung up before Hector settled back against me.

I'd finally let an EMT check me out from top to bottom. He'd informed me I likely had a mild concussion and recommended I go to the hospital, but I was feeling much better and hadn't wanted to leave Hector's side, so I'd stayed in Agent Andrews's office.

Agent Andrews had been by to fill us in on what Ann had told her before she had come to Hector's cabin.

The best phone call had come in about half an hour ago when the sheriff reported they had found Jennings. He had found himself trapped between the fire and the sheriff—the only way out was to turn himself in.

Apparently, when having to choose between death and prison, he chose the latter.

The craziest thing was when Andrews filled us in on how Steve had pieced it all together.

"According to Stanton, it wasn't until the incident at the lake, where he'd been caught trespassing, that he finally started to suspect Jennings," Andrews said.

"Why that moment?" I asked, trying to remember what Hector had told me about that night.

"Diden and Jennings had been arguing about Mr. Stanton while he sat in the back seat of the SUV just a few feet away," she told me. "Because Diden was a huge fan of Stanton's, she was defending him when Jennings mentioned Steve possibly being the killer of the other nine missing women, and Stanton overheard it."

She and Hector exchanged a look, and I felt totally out of the loop.

"I'm sorry...I'm obviously missing something," I added. "What does that mean exactly?"

"On his podcast, Steve only mentioned *seven* other women, not nine," Andrews pointed out, "which had him digging into it more. Plus, then he asked Diden more about Jennings and where he had lived. Once she gave him the backstory of how he'd moved around a lot, Stanton started to put the pieces together."

Wow.

Hector leaned forward, his elbows landing on his knees with his hands clasped together.

"Now, on the topic of your cabin," Andrews said, looking sympathetic. "The good news is it's not a complete loss. The bad news is you won't be able to move back anytime soon."

I turned to look at Hector, but his face was as stoic as ever. Still, I placed my hand on his forearm, squeezing gently.

"It's just a cabin," he said. "It can be rebuilt."

I knew he was right, but I still felt bad. Not just because it was his home, but because I loved it there. It gave me peace and serenity that I had only ever felt in one other place in my life—the O'Haras' farm.

"You got a place to stay in the meantime?" Andrews asked. "I know the fire makes it unlivable, but even if it was, being that it's part of a crime scene, we wouldn't let you back in for a few days. So I can help you get a hotel for a few days until you figure something out."

"You can stay with me," I told him.

I knew my place was smaller, but I liked having him there, and Sarge too.

"Thanks," he said to me and then turned back to Andrews. "I'll be with Iris if you need anything."

Andrews just smiled at the two of us and then started listing off a few procedural things.

The adrenaline must have finally worn off, because the next thing I knew, Hector was waking me up.

"Iris," he said softly to me while stroking the side of my face. "Wake up, babe. It's time to head back to your place and get some sleep."

"Mmmhmmm," I mumbled groggily as I slowly woke up.

Hector helped walk me to a silver sedan that Agent Andrews apparently was loaning us for the night until we could make arrangements to get new vehicles, since both of ours were goners.

I must have fallen asleep again, because I came to as Hector was trying to lift me out of the seat to carry me up the stairs.

"I can walk, Hector," I told him.

"You sure?" he asked.

"Yeah," I told him, and he held my hand as we walked up to my unit.

While Hector made one last phone call to his boss, I hopped into the shower, needing to get rid of the smoke smell and bad juju from the day.

I had been standing under the hot water for a few minutes when Hector climbed into the shower with me, naked and gloriously good-looking.

Needing a pull from his energy and strength, I took a step forward and wrapped my arms around him, pressing my forehead to his chest.

"You doing okay?" he asked, rubbing his hands up and down my back soothingly.

"Yeah, why?" I muttered, enjoying the comfort that he gave me.

"Because you're going through an adrenaline dump, and sometimes that can stir things up in people after a traumatizing event," he mentioned, and I realized he was right.

I hadn't really given myself the time or space to think about everything we had been through, but the thing my mind seemed to focus on first was the cabin fire.

"Hector, I'm sorry I didn't think to grab some of your important things from your house to save." My voice strained as guilt washed over me that I hadn't grabbed at least some photos or something.

"The only things in that house I wanted to save were you and Sarge," he said, tilting my head back to look at me. "Nothing else matters—nothing."

He leaned down and kissed me, gently but with conviction, as though he knew he'd almost lost me tonight.

Pulling back, he looked down into my eyes. "Did you wash your hair yet?"

I shook my head, and he reached down to grab my shampoo bottle. "I'll do it. Tilt back."

He lathered his hands up and began to massage it through my hair and scalp in a way that sent tingles through my whole body.

"Oh, my God. Why are you so good at that?" I asked, tilting my head back and enjoying the feel of his fingers kneading my scalp.

"I used to have longer hair, remember?" he said, and I vaguely remembered that, but then my mind blanked as his fingers continued to work their magic through my hair.

"Woman, you keep making those noises, and we're never gonna leave here," he said in a gruff, throaty tone.

I hadn't even realized I was making any noises, but that was what Hector did to me. My brain ceased to function whenever his hands were on me.

"Iris," he said, but it was a warning. "Let's finish up in here, and we can go to bed."

I hope he didn't mean to just sleep. I wanted sleep, but I also wanted his hands and mouth all over me.

With that thought, I hurried up in the shower. After drying off and brushing my hair and teeth, I climbed into bed to wait for Hector, who was taking Sarge out for the last time.

Despite my best efforts, exhaustion overtook me, and moments later, all snuggled in bed, I was lulled into dreamland.

That dreamland was a wonderful place that included snuggling with Hector and Sarge. Being lost to that dreamworld—as good as it was—was how I almost missed hearing Hector tell me he loved me for the first time as he drifted to sleep with me tucked up against his side.

28

Hector

It took two weeks for Jennings to get out of the hospital due to his severe burns and smoke inhalation. Personally, I was glad he'd suffered.

I had gone to visit him, unfortunately with Andrews supervising me. I knew she likely hadn't trusted me to be alone with him—smart on her part. As someone who had more than once in the past blurred the lines between right and wrong, this likely would have been another situation to add to that list.

I had never felt more rage in my body than I did listening to Jennings carelessly and callously discuss how this was all Iris's fault for finding the body in the first place. Knowing he'd planned to kill her simply because she was in the wrong place at the wrong time and ruined his chances of getting away with his crimes had me contemplating how to cross a few of his medical wires to make him suffer a bit more. Andrews's presence had prevented that.

I had also gone to visit Diden at the hospital and learned that once she heard Steve's podcast linking the body we found to other collegiate athletes, she had become fixated on the case. Having been a collegiate athlete herself, she'd taken this case personally, even though she hadn't known any of the victims. She'd begun feeding Steve inside information to help him, and somewhere along the way, the two of them became involved, which blurred the lines even more.

We'd learned a lot in these past two weeks, including that our podcaster, Steve, was correct. We'd confirmed the woman's body we had found in Lake Echo had not been his only victim. Jennings was a roving ranger, meaning he moved from one park to the next depending on where the need was the greatest. A summer in a national park in Montana to help with the busy season, and then when that slowed down, he did a six-month stint in Florida.

He moved roughly every six to twelve months, allowing him the perfect opportunity to learn the lay of the land, find a lake, find a victim, and then leave before most of the bodies were ever even found.

Several of the women Steve suspected Jennings of killing had their cases reopened to search nearby lakes.

Andrews had filled me in this afternoon with the latest information.

"The women were indeed all collegiate athletes," she said. *"Apparently, Jennings had a high school sweetheart who went to college on an athletic scholarship. He couldn't get into that same university, so he traveled to see her, only to find out that when she was at a tournament, she had cheated on him."*

Bingo, I thought. That's what had set off his fixation on female athletes.

"After hours of interrogation, he'd finally confessed that he would meet the athletes, flirt with them, and then casually ask if they were seeing someone," she continued. *"If they said yes, he drugged their drinks and lured them away. He usually killed them nearby and then took them to the nearest body of water."*

In the case of Lake Echo—which was more a reservoir than a traditional lake—he hadn't taken into account that in nine months, we would receive almost no rain. That meant the lake levels dropped so low that the water was much shallower than when he had dumped the body, making it easier to find.

As for Iris, his plan was to kill her and set my cabin on fire, leaving her body in there. When Diden and Steve had shown up, his plan was to add them to the body count as well. He had been dragging Diden's body back to my room, where he planned to tie them up and then set the fire. But when he heard me come in, he made a quick escape out the window and ran to the shed. He saw the butane tanks in there and used the rest of his fire starters on the shed so it would ignite and hopefully trap us all in the house.

"Unfortunately for him, they ignited faster than he thought," Andrews added. *"That meant he had injured himself in the process, slowing down his ability to chase after all of you."*

Especially since he hadn't planned on us going the weird route down the mountain that Iris took us—which, God love her, not only saved us from the flames but also from Jennings.

He was also the one who had broken into Iris's apartment. After the letter had been dropped off, Jennings had convinced himself that Iris really did take something from the crime scene, so he wanted to search her place to see if he could find it.

"The cotton ball that was found at the scene had a forensic chemical preservative solution on it," Andrews explained. *"He wanted to look for any other evidence left on her clothes after she washed them from the lake. He used some kind of ethanol agent to slow down evaporation until he could get it home, where he had a full forensic kit ready."*

"Damn," I responded, pissed, but also mildly impressed Jennings was this elaborate in his execution.

"Our forensic team knew what the solution was on the cotton ball very quickly, but we just didn't know why they used it, or who," Andrews pointed out.

He'd thought he had done a good enough job of cleaning up and leaving no trace behind, but he'd failed.

Especially the part where he'd broken her lock as he kicked in the door—which apparently had happened in haste because he'd heard voices coming around the corner.

Given his medical condition, Jennings had been arraigned from the hospital with a police guard twenty-four-seven since he was deemed a flight risk. He was also denied bail for the very same reason. It would likely be months before his actual trial, but knowing he would be in jail the entire time was a small blessing.

I had been staying at Iris's apartment since my cabin was condemned. She hadn't asked me to leave. and I hadn't wanted to. She needed a bigger bed because my body—especially with hers next to me—was too much for a queen bed.

I had ordered a king bed to be delivered today, and we'd move hers to storage if she wanted to keep it.

I had just pulled up to her apartment complex when the delivery company called to say they were ten minutes out.

Iris was working from home today since she had done a career day event at UNLV this morning. When I walked in, her gaze moved straight to me, and she smiled from her position on the floor as she played with Sarge.

He came to greet me as I walked in, and Iris rose from the floor to join him.

"So, I have a surprise," I told her as she leaned up to kiss me.

"Is this one of those 'I have a surprise for you in my

pants' kind of surprises, or more like a 'I finally decided to take Nancy up on her offer and come play cards with you and her friends tomorrow night' kind of surprise?" she asked, causing me to laugh.

"Neither, though I like the first idea a lot better than the second," I told her, pulling her into me and wrapping my arms around her waist.

"Okay, I'll bite." She smirked. "What is it?"

"I talked to my boss, and he agreed to let me buy the property on the other side of the ridge near the Wash Wetlands, so long as if I decide to sell it later, I allow the Parks Service to make the first offer," I told her.

We had been looking to sell off some property near the edge of the park where the old ranger outposts had been but had held back for fear a large developer would come in and put in a strip mall.

I promised O'Connor I just wanted to build my cabin near where I was before, but not in the exact same spot because I hadn't wanted any issues with PTSD for Iris or anyone else. He agreed, and we would sign the paperwork next week.

She beamed at me, and it was too irresistible to ignore. I crushed my mouth to hers, devouring her, enjoying the soft little noises she never seemed to know she made when I kissed her like this.

Sarge barked, breaking me out of my lustful thoughts, followed by a knock at the door.

Shit. I had gotten so caught up in her that I hadn't finished telling her the rest of the surprise.

"There's one more part of the surprise, and I think it's here," I said, turning to go answer the door.

"Well, that's not cryptic at all," she muttered behind me.

Expecting the delivery people, I chose not to look at the peephole and just opened the door, which was why I was shocked to see Nancy on the other side.

"Unless you've suddenly decided I'm your dream girl instead of Iris and you're proposing a sleepover, I think this bed was delivered to the wrong door," she said with a lopsided smile.

Crap.

"Uh, yeah, that's meant for Iris," I told her.

"No worries, big guy. You can make it up to me by coming to game night tomorrow," she said, and I realized she'd conned me right into that one. "I'm thinkin' we might play strip poker."

Usually, I was very good at keeping my reactions hidden, but in this case, I must not have been as fast to cover my face, because she cackled and then turned around and spoke to someone behind her.

"In here, boys. This is the unit you really want," she said, and two men carrying a huge box walked over to the door I was standing in front of.

I moved out of the way, telling them where to put it.

"A new bed, eh?" Iris looked at me, her arms crossed, head tilted back to look up at me with a small grin tugging at her lips.

Lips that I wanted to kiss the ever-loving hell out of.

"Surprise," I said, giving her a small smile in return.

"And what's going to happen to my current bed?" she asked.

"If you want to keep it, we can, but these guys offered to take it to the local women's shelter for free if you don't want it."

Her face softened, and she nodded. "Yeah, let's have them donate it."

An hour later, the new bed and mattress were all delivered and set up and the old one was on its way to the shelter. I finally had her alone again and was looking forward to trying out that new bed.

After signing the paperwork for everything, I walked back into her apartment and found her snuggled up on the couch with Sarge in her lap and a book in her hand. Her glasses were perched on top of her nose, and her hair was up in some messy bun with a few stray curls around her face. She looked perfect.

This woman was it for me. I loved her. The words had fallen from my lips a few weeks ago after everything had happened, but I hadn't said them again since, not sure if I was just caught up in the adrenaline of the day, or if my brain really knew what the rest of my body was feeling.

I knew we hadn't known each other for long, but some things you just knew, and this was one of them.

I loved how brave and strong she was—how caring, loyal, and compassionate. I felt deep down like she was my other half. She was the answer I didn't know I had been searching for.

I hadn't realized how long I had been standing there staring at her until she spoke, though her eyes were still trained on her book. "How long you gonna stand there and gawk at me?"

She looked up at me and smiled. When she smiled at me like that, I knew I would give her the world if she asked. Not being one to beat around the bush, I realized I wanted her to hear me say it this time, not just when she was asleep.

"I love you, Iris," I said, walking over to the couch and squatting in front of her. "You're it for me. You have been since the day I met you. I just didn't know it yet."

She didn't say anything, but her face was an open book, so the emotions swirling through her were clearly visible.

"Hector," she said, her breath hitching. "I love you, too."

I leaned forward to kiss her, but Sarge grumbled at me for invading his comfy pillow—also known as Iris's lap.

"Why don't I help you christen this new bed you got us...you know...just to make sure it doesn't suck," she said, smiling at me while giving me a little wink.

I chose not to respond verbally. I simply picked her up, put her over my shoulder, and carried her straight to the bedroom. I did it to the sound of her laughter—a sound I would never tire of hearing.

A sound I hoped to hear for the rest of my life.

EPILOGUE

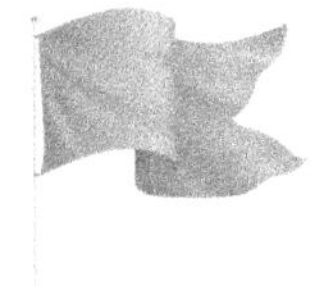

Iris

Three Months Later

"You always said you wanted to get married on the farm, surrounded by the animals," my sister Anna said as we looked out the window at all the people taking their seats. "I'm just happy Auntie hosed them all down and gave them a bath so they didn't ruin your wedding with their... umm...pleasant smell."

I laughed. She was correct. Farm animals weren't exactly known for their fragrant aroma, but they felt like family to me.

Ever since I was a teenage girl living at the O'Hara farm, I always knew the farm was where I wanted to get married. It was a beautiful piece of land and I would be surrounded by family and friends—and yes, that included the animals.

The animals became my sanctuary. Animals didn't

care where you came from or what your past was like. They only cared if you were friendly and kind, so they had been some of the first friends I'd made here, and I wanted them to be a part of the wedding too.

It was the very end of summer, which was the dry season here—as a meteorologist, I had to make sure I didn't have rain on my wedding day. So, naturally, I picked the climatologically driest part of the year. Plus, this was Northern California along the coast, so it never really got too hot here like it did in Vegas.

Hector had proposed only a month after he moved in with me.

"Iris, I'm forty years old," he said to me after I said yes but questioned whether it was too soon. "I've lived through enough to know what feels right and not to waste my time when I find the person I want to spend the rest of my life with."

"Okay," I responded with happy tears. "But I want to get married on the farm in the summer."

"Then call your moms and see if they can get it ready in two months, because I'm not waiting till next year to make you officially mine."

After we celebrated, with him showing me how much he loved me with his hands and mouth, I called my moms to tell them the great news.

Mom was nervous we wouldn't have enough time, but Auntie—who was very much a fly-by-the-seat-of-her-pants woman—assured me everything would be ready and to start telling everyone so they had enough time to plan for traveling.

There was a knock at the door, bringing me back to the present, and Anna opened it.

"Is it okay if Hazel and I come in really quick?" I heard my sister Cora's voice behind the door.

"It's fine, Sissy. Let them in," I told Anna.

"You look beautiful, Iris," Cora said, smiling.

"You really do look stunning," Hazel said to me, beaming.

"Thanks, ladies."

"Gale is keeping an eye on the animals but promised to make an appearance in time for the ceremony," Hazel said.

Gale—our very own poster child for introverts—did not do large crowds of people, and even though we only had about fifty people in attendance, that was too many for her. She had already talked with me about it because she was afraid that I would be offended if she wasn't around much, but I knew her, and I knew things like this were hard for her.

She was in charge of the animals, but she would show up for some of the ceremony, family photos, and a little bit of the reception, and that was perfectly fine with me.

"You ready to get this show on the road?" Anna asked.

"Absolutely," I responded, staring at myself one last time in the mirror to make sure everything looked as I wanted it.

I had a very simple white dress made of crepe and

satin fabrics draped with a little bit of lace. It was a one-shoulder gown that had a high split up to my thigh. The fabric was draped and weaved in a way that highlighted the curves I wanted to show and hid the others.

Hector said he adored my curly hair, especially when it was wild, so I'd left it mostly down, only pinning a few pieces right near my face so they wouldn't fall into my eyes.

My sisters had all gone in together and gotten me the most beautiful pale-blue undergarments, including custom underwear that said "All for Hector" on the back.

Rita let me borrow her dangly teardrop ruby earrings, which were stunning.

With everything checked and perfected, Anna and I made our way outside for the ceremony. Anna was my matron of honor, and Hector's father was his best man. Since I didn't have a dad, both Mom and Auntie were going to walk me down the aisle—each holding one arm.

Hector's dad also served as our sign language interpreter so that Dani could follow along with everything that was said at the wedding.

Even Sarge was here as our ring bearer, though when he walked down the aisle toward Hector, he kept stopping every five feet to let people pet him.

The music began, and that was my cue.

"Thanks for doing this," I said to Mom and Auntie as they each latched on to one of my arms.

"Sweetheart, we are honored you would even ask," Mom said with unshed tears in her eyes.

"Do you need one of us to have the famous 'honor my daughter or I'll kill you' type of dad talks with Hector? Cause I'll definitely do it," Auntie offered, and I laughed.

"Your turn," Hazel said, letting me know to start walking down the aisle.

I walked around the giant plants that were being used to hide us—as well as they could on an open farm—and walked under the flower arch covered in irises.

It matched the bouquet of blue and purple irises in my hand. Was it cheesy? Yes. Did I care? No.

My parents had only ever given me one thing that I loved, and that was my name, so I leaned into it and had irises all over the ceremony and even the reception tables.

I looked up and stared right at Hector as I walked down the aisle. God, he was a five-alarm fire in his three-piece suit. It was a dark cream that showed off his tanned skin and dark hair. He had on a periwinkle dress shirt to match my flowers.

I couldn't believe this was the man I was about to marry. He was sexy as hell, yes, but he was also humble, loyal, protective, and treated me like I was the best thing to ever happen in his life. Everyone needed a partner like that in their life. Someone who supported you in every facet of your journey.

His gaze was on me the entire time I walked, and for the 4,973rd time, I wished I knew what he was thinking. I may not know his exact thoughts, but I saw the happiness mixed with lust in his eyes.

When we made it to the front, he walked down to take my hand from Mom and Auntie.

"Congratulations, and welcome to the family," Mom whispered to him.

"You hurt her, I'll kill you in your sleep," Auntie also whispered but with a smile on her face as she gave him my hand.

Hector snorted as he thanked Mom and then moved to Auntie. "You have my permission."

He then leaned down to kiss my cheek and whisper in my ear. "You look absolutely stunning, and sexy, and all mine."

I smiled at him as we made our way to the front.

I looked out at all the people who had come to celebrate our special day and smiled.

My sisters, foster mothers, my coworkers, as well as all of Hector's friends and family.

Ann and Steve had also come to the wedding—as a couple. Hector thought I was a little crazy for inviting them, but I simply reminded him that we wouldn't be able to have this moment without them. If they hadn't come to my rescue, I may not have been here today. He'd quickly relented.

I may not have a biological family, but my found family was better than I could have ever imagined.

An hour later, I was staring out at the valley in the distance as the dusk light started to spread beautiful colors everywhere. We had just finished with our pictures, and I was enjoying the moment and the views.

"Hello, *wife*," Hector's voice sounded behind me just as he wrapped his arms around my waist.

His body heat felt like a blanket at my back, and his warm breath and beard tickled my cheek.

"Hello, *husband*," I responded as he nuzzled into my neck, peppering me with kisses.

"I can't wait to take this dress off with my teeth."

Shivers rolled through my body, and I knew he felt it too.

"Hmm…You like that idea, don't you?"

"Do you think we could just sneak away and leave now and no one would notice?" I asked as I turned to face him.

He leaned down, putting his forehead against mine. "I like where your mind is headed, sweetheart, but I'm starving, and I need you to have energy for later—lots of energy."

He tilted my head back, and his mouth found mine with desperate need.

I had no idea how much time passed, but eventually we came up for air, my mind dizzy from his kiss, along with my labored breathing.

"Let's go feed you, *wife*," he said to me, smiling. "I also want to dance with you and enjoy you in public for a bit before I take you back to the hotel and keep you there, possibly for twenty-four hours straight while I ravish your body from top to bottom."

There were those damn shivers again.

I joined my hand with his, and we made our way to

the reception tent, but it was the promise of what was to come that had me most excited.

Eight Months Later

It was moving day today.

We were all set to move into our new home not far from where Hector's old cabin had been, but this one would be ours. We'd played a role in the design of the home from the very beginning, and I couldn't be happier with how it had turned out. It still had the cabin aesthetic, with a stone fireplace, natural wood elements throughout, and rustic touches right alongside modern features. I loved it.

The best part was the wraparound porch that had views similar to the old cabin, so we could sit out and enjoy many nights and mornings together when the sun wasn't too intense.

The house had four bedrooms instead of three like the last one, because we wanted one extra in case my family wanted to come visit their grandchildren or nieces and nephews in the future.

I was standing in the doorway of one of those spare bedrooms when Hector came up behind me and hugged his arms around me. I smelled his freshly washed hair and soapy scent wrap around me and sighed.

"You thinking about what you want in this space?" he asked, noting that I had just been standing in the doorway staring.

That was because I had a secret. A secret I'd only found out about yesterday, but had been too busy to tell him because of all the last-minute packing and such.

I turned in his arms, wanting to keep his arms around me but needing to face him.

"Do you want to paint it blue or pink, or should we go with a more neutral color?" I asked, smirking at him.

He stared down at me with that impassive, silent-as-snowfall facial expression.

"You don't need to decide right now," I told him, smiling even bigger. "You've got about six more months to figure it out."

Still silent, but his eyes got bigger, and I could feel his heart racing faster now.

"You're pregnant?" he asked, his voice barely above a whisper.

I nodded. "I just went to the doctor yesterday and got it confirmed."

"Is it a boy or a girl?" he asked and then quickly waved his hand. "Never mind. Don't care."

He smiled down at me, and I was so happy that he was just as excited as I was.

"A baby...really?" he asked again, as if he couldn't believe it.

I nodded and kissed him gently on the lips before pulling back. "You okay with this?"

"I know this is kind of fast, but I'm happy about that," he responded. "I'm already in my forties, and I don't want to be a super old dad."

"You're not old, but I get it," I told him.

"No, but I don't want to be fifty and still having kids, so you better get used to being pregnant, because I'm gonna keep giving you more babies until either you hit a number you're happy with, or I hit fifty—whichever happens first."

I laughed. "Two or three is fine with me."

"I'm happy with that too," he said, leaning down to kiss me, more intensely this time.

"You are the best thing that's ever happened to me, Iris, and I will spend every day of the rest of my life showing you how much I love you."

He started right then and there—lifting me and carrying me back to the bedroom so we could break in the new bed in the new house, followed by the couch, and then the shower. It took a lot longer to unpack the boxes, but it was totally worth it in the end.

Four Weeks Later

"Can you hear that?" our cheerful ultrasound technician said. "That's baby's heartbeat. It's a little fast but sounds strong."

Hector was next to me, holding my hand as she moved the wand over my growing belly.

"Now, let's see if baby wants to cooperate so we can get some good pictures," she added. "Do you want to know the sex?"

"Yes, please," I told her.

Hector didn't care, but I did. I was a planner and needed to know for planning purposes.

She moved her wand back and forth, taking a few pictures here and there, but mostly remained silent as Hector and I just watched her, fascinated by everything.

Then I noticed the puzzled look on her face, and I began to get worried.

"Is everything okay?" I finally worked up the nerve to ask her.

"Yes, everything is fine," she started, but there was a hesitation in her voice. "I'm just trying to check something, and baby is not cooperating."

I knew I just needed to trust her for now and let her do her thing, but Hector obviously sensed my nerves and began to stroke my hand and arm, and then he leaned down and kissed me on my forehead. This man was my rock—my everything.

"Aha!" the tech called out. "I had a feeling because of the super-fast heartbeat. Congratulations, Mr. and Mrs. Madeira. You are having twins."

My mouth dropped open as I stared at her in awe, trying to process what she had just announced.

"What did you say?" Hector asked before my own mouth could form words.

"Oh...wait...nope...sorry," she apologized, and I about died from having held my breath for so long. "Okay, I was wrong. It's not two heartbeats...I think...yep...There's the third set of legs. Congrats! You're having triplets!"

I didn't think my mouth could have opened any bigger.

"Excuse me?" Hector choked out, his voice barely above a whisper.

"Triplets," she repeated. "That would explain why the heartbeat was so fast. It was actually just more than one heartbeat. But everything looks great—six arms, six legs, everything is exactly as it should be."

"I guess you're getting your wish after all," I turned to tell Hector.

"What?" he looked at me, still a bit dazed from the news.

"You didn't want to be an old dad, so I guess we're just going to get them all at once and then be done," I reminded him.

He chuckled nervously and then turned back to me and smiled. "I guess all my wishes came true. Thank you, Iris, for giving me everything I could have ever wanted—a beautiful, smart, and caring wife and now a family of our own."

THE END

AFTERWORD

Thank you for reading *Red Flag Warning*.
I hope you enjoyed it.

There's a steamy bonus scene featuring Hector & Iris.
Grab it here:

https://dl.bookfunnel.com/o7586n1zgv

Want more of the Cupid Meets Crime Scene series?
Don't worry—you don't have to wait long.
The second book in the series, HEAT ADVISORY,
will be out on May 21, 2026.
Keep reading for a sneak peek...

* * *

Be sure to sign up for my newsletter at AllisonBettes.com
to stay up to date on all the latest news about my
upcoming releases.

**First date? He ghosted.
Second date? He threw up on her.
Third date? He proposed.**

Back in high school, Cora O'Hara was the invisible book nerd. Jay was the golden-boy star athlete who actually saw her—then broke her heart.

Now Cora is the Nevada state hydrologist, knee-deep in data and happily single. But Jay moves to town as the new firefighter with way too much charm and a dangerously flammable smile.

When a flash flood threatens their town, their worlds —and their unresolved chemistry—collide head on. She works in facts and forecasts...he thrives on instinct and adrenaline. But in the middle of the storm, they discover that opposites don't just attract—they ignite. And as the danger rises around them, they'll have to decide if they can keep their heads above water...or drown in something far more unpredictable.

1

"Dams break under intense pressure. So do I."
—It's science

Cora

Have you ever had a kiss that was so incredibly good, it ruined you for all other men?

For me, that was my high school crush, Jay Rainer.

He was the epitome of handsome, everything my teenage brain had imagined. That first kiss didn't disappoint—it sailed past the usual cliches of stars and butterflies and landed somewhere deeper. I felt desired—truly wanted—in a way I had never felt before.

The only problem was he left two days after that kiss, never to speak to me again.

What was worse, his sister, Morgan, was my best friend, so I still heard everything about him through her, which only dug the knife in deeper. Just like I filled her in on what was happening with all my sisters, she did the same about her brother.

It wasn't her fault. Morgan didn't know that her brother and I had kissed. So how would she know that every time she brought him up, it was both information I craved and loathed at the same time?

Jay had left school right after graduating because he

was drafted to play for a minor league baseball team in Texas. He played for them for two years, and just before he got his big break, he suffered an ulnar collateral ligament tear and had Tommy John surgery. According to Morgan, the surgery went well, but his baseball career was over.

He stayed in Texas, choosing to become a firefighter instead.

She mentioned about a year ago that the heat was getting to him, so he'd moved north to become a firefighter in Colorado. She missed him and wished he would move back home, but she thought he was embarrassed because of how his career had turned out. Especially because their dad pushed the major league dream so hard.

So, color me shocked when I was in Las Vegas at a training exercise and saw Jay across the room.

The same man who, even years later, still occupied an enormous amount of space in my mind.

My sister Iris's voice cut into my thoughts. "What do you keep staring at?"

"Umm...nothing," I lied to her, shaking my head to help clear my brain. "Did you get that thing to load yet?"

My sister was a meteorologist with the National Weather Service in Las Vegas, and I was the Nevada state hydrologist, and we were here to do a fire and flood safety training event.

"Yeah, it just took a little magic, sweet talk, and a full reset of the program," Iris's coworker Christine responded. "PowerPoint is up and running—finally."

The event included the three of us, plus some local firefighters, the fire marshal, EMTs, the Public Works Department, Nevada Highway Patrol, a Public Information Officer from the Las Vegas PD, emergency managers, and a few local TV meteorologists. It was a large group to make sure everything went smoothly—prepare for the worst but hope for the best.

My hope, however, was dwindling that the man across the large conference room was just a Jay lookalike when he finally looked my way and our eyes connected.

Okay, be cool. He's looking at you. Do not look nervous. Maybe he won't recognize you.

That prayer went right out the window as he smiled and began walking my way.

"Oh, no," I mumbled.

"What's wrong?" Iris asked as she looked up to follow where my gaze was aimed. "Do you know that guy walking toward us?"

She mumbled that last part under her breath so only the three of us at our table could hear it.

"Who are we looking at?" Christine said, causing me to close my eyes and hope that this was just a dream I would wake up from.

"Hey, Cora," the smooth, masculine voice said.

I opened my eyes to see him smiling at me, but no words came out of my mouth.

Cora, you're an adult. Act like it.

At my lack of response, his attention turned to my

sister. "Hey, Iris. Jay Rainer. We graduated from high school together."

"Oh yes, Jay!" Iris exclaimed, nodding as she realized that she remembered him. "You were voted 'most likely to become famous'."

"Yeah, well, I have some disappointing news regarding that," he replied with a somber tone but a smirk on his face.

"Oh, it's okay," Iris replied and pointed to me. "People voted Cora, most likely to own and operate the Scholastic book fair, and that never came true either."

It was true. I was a book nerd in school. When I wasn't studying, tutoring someone, or helping out on the family farm, I was at the library. It was my sanctuary. My escape.

"I think Morgan might have mentioned that," Jay said, a small grin tugging at his mouth—a mouth that was just as sexy as the rest of his body. "It's good to see you both."

He'd always had an athletic build, but he looked even more handsome now. He had short brown hair that was practically buzzed on the sides, sun-kissed skin, and muscles upon muscles built into his tall frame. He also had stunning whiskey-colored eyes—eyes that were darkly romantic and boring into me.

Was it getting hot in here? It felt like it.

It was hotter than hell outside, so maybe the air conditioner had stopped working. That must be why I was sweating in places I had no right to be sweating.

"So, you both live in Vegas now?" he asked, but before I could respond, Iris chimed in first.

"I do, but Cora lives up near Reno. She travels all over the state for her job, so she's here for this event. You live here too?"

His eyes flared a bit but then just as quickly went back to normal. If I hadn't been staring at him, I likely would have missed it.

"I'm actually up in the Reno area as well," he responded, a growing smile taking over his face. "Just took a job there. This event helps me complete my fire investigator certification."

There was a lot to break down there, but I focused on one thing. *He lived in Reno now? Why hadn't Morgan told me?*

"Oh, my gosh. That's so cool," Iris said, excitedly clapping her hands. "You and Cora should get lunch sometime."

Oh. My. God. She did not just say that.

He stared at me for a second, his gaze burning a hole through me with its intensity. I knew there was no way my face was not turning fifty shades of pink.

"I'd actually like that," he said to me as mischief lit his eyes. "I just moved there earlier this year, so I haven't quite learned my way around. I'd love a tour guide."

"Um…I'm not sure I would…umm…have the time," I told him, stuttering my way through this bullshit made-up excuse.

"You just said you have next week off, so you should show him around," Iris said, smiling slyly at me.

Oh, my God. I was going to kill her later.

"Great," Jay said excitedly. "Let me get your phone number so we can connect."

He pulled his phone out to type my number into it.

Oh, my God. He asked for my phone number. Breathe. Normal breathing.

I did my best to look casual as I rattled off my phone number and he typed it in.

"Perfect. I'll send you a text so you have my number too," he said to me. "I'll let you go since I'm sure you ladies are busy. Good to see you both."

"You too, Jay," Iris said gleefully.

"Oh, I'm sorry. I forgot to introduce myself," he said to Christine, holding out his hand. "I'm Jay Rainer."

"Nice to meet you," she responded as she shook his hand.

"Have a great night, ladies," he said.

I silently waved, like a moron, with a loopy grin on my face.

There went the last of my dignity and grace.

"See you next week," he said to me and winked.

He winked. Winked.

My high school crush. The man I had thought about so many times, in many inappropriate ways, had just winked at me.

Why was it suddenly hard to get a full breath of air?

I blankly stared at him as he walked away, retreating back to his place on the other side of the room.

Then my view was blocked by my sister waving her hand in front of my face. "Yoo-hoo. Earth to Cora."

I turned to my sister and angrily whispered to her, "Why would you tell him I could show him around?"

"Because you had the biggest crush on him in high school, and as your sister, and pseudo wingman...or woman...I'm here to help you," Iris explained.

I turned to Christine, who was just watching us go back and forth. "Is murder illegal in *all* fifty states? Asking for a friend."

She snorted and chuckled at my question. "I think he's cute, and you should definitely meet up with him."

Ugh. Now they were ganging up on me.

"You don't want to murder me," Iris said. "In fact, you'll probably be thanking me later, so I will go ahead and just tell you you're welcome right now. However, if he hurts you or treats you bad, then I will personally help you bury the body."

I rolled my eyes at her just as my phone buzzed with an incoming text. I looked down to see a new message from a new number.

UNKNOWN NUMBER:

This is Jay. I'm looking forward to our date next week ;)

Date?

Jay—the sexiest man I had ever met, and the one I'd had the biggest crush on since I was fifteen years old—just wrote that he was looking forward to a date... with me.

Oh, God.

Expect the unexpected.

That was what I was learning from Jay Rainer. And I didn't like it one bit.

* * *

BUY HEAT ADVISORY NOW
at www.AllisonBettes.com

ACKNOWLEDGMENTS

Thanks to:

CrocoDesigns for formatting.

Katie Jaspersen @KJaspersenDesigns for the book covers.

My editors: Leah, Sara, Jenny, Monica, and Andie.

Haley my translator.

Sara Tonks for the author photo.

And all my beta readers, editors, street team, and friends.

ABOUT THE AUTHOR

Author photo by Sara Tonks.

Allison is a romantic suspense author who writes about soft-hearted badasses with brave, sassy women at their side—and she loves creating a good plot twist. She is a meteorologist/science writer by day, and a cupid-meets-crime-scene novel writer by night.

Her journey into the world of romance and suspense started when her grandma handed down her well-worn copies of Danielle Steel and Nora Roberts novels—she was hooked.

During Covid times, with time on her hands and a need for catharsis, she dove into writing her own romantic suspense novels. Her books are a thrilling blend of spicy romance, adventure, and suspense— think *Cupid Meets Crime Scene.*

www.AllisonBettes.com

facebook.com/AuthorAllisonBettes
instagram.com/authorallisonbettes
tiktok.com/@allison.bettes